Nightcap and Other Stories

The Fantasy Collection

Paul John Hausleben

The cover photographs are by Paul John Hausleben
Photographs of the author are by Ms. Cali Rose
Cover design and the cover concept by Paul John Hausleben
Rear cover model: Ms. Lydia A. LaGalla

Published by God Bless the Keg Publishing
Somewhere, U.S.A.

ISBN: 978-0-9906979-8-5

Dedication

To all the ghosts that I know.
To those whom I have yet to meet.

Nightcap and Other Stories

The Fantasy Collection

Paul John Hausleben

Contents

Acknowledgements

Thank you to my friends, and to my family for enduring my writing adventures and discussions. Thank you to Lydia for holding my Manhattan cocktail glass too many times while I fiddled with the shot. Thank you to the staff at the Oxhead Tavern in Sturbridge, Massachusetts for the hospitality, inspiration, the warm fireplace, and for allowing this eccentric author to tell stories and perform a few photo shoots.

"I do apologize in advance, for my abhorrent and eccentric behavior, while under the influence of the devil's brew."

Paul John Hausleben

04 November 2017

Preface from the Author

Here we go, with a venture into the world of, well, I am not exactly sure of what genre or type of stories that I have written here. The genre defies classification. One story is a kind-of-sort-of; fantasy story. The other stories might be ghost stories with a taste of science fiction and a dab of fantasy. Honestly, these stories might not fit comfortably within any specific genre and in retrospect, that works out quite well for me. I enjoy never fitting into specific notches in my work and in my life. It keeps me flexible and loose.

Occasionally, in the past, we have dipped our beer mug into the keg of fantasy brews, and taken a deep drink of such, primarily with the mysterious, quiet stranger in the black hat who decides to make guest appearances here and there. Then, of course, we dabble in the world of the unknown, when the brave and fearless, Walter P. Thrump, makes an appearance. The ever vigilant and never daunted Walter always seems to have ghosts, or famous icons of holidays that show up to chase him around the pages of his various adventures.

However, this collection is a bit different.

Everyone comments that my work is usually impossible to define. Why would I change it now?

This time, we run the course from the fantasy story, to ghosts, to time shifts, to blurred reality, to who knows what I am thinking about here? Slices of fantasy, topped by layers of romance and a side dish of a goodwill mission of saving all of humankind. I even pulled the versatile and rather annoying Pastor Paul John Henson out of the pages of Harry and Paul poppycock to assist in telling one of the stories.

Ah, who the hell knows?

I think we will just call them what we did and label them fantasy stories. It might be best if we do not over think this too much.

That works for me.

Regardless of the unclassifiable genre, I must say that it was a nice change of the pace and quite a bit of fun to conceive of these stories and write them.

The inspiration for these stories arrived in my eccentric mind from a number of different places. There is no clear-cut source of inspiration, but it seems to me that those types of moments are how the best sources of inspiration seem to arrive to me these days. Spontaneous and varied rather than boilerplates. This time, I cannot even blame it on a glass of cheap Scotch.

I must say that this unknown genre is fascinating to write in because there is no right or wrong. After all, I made all of these storylines up from nowhere. All of them popped out of my own mind. They are all the products of wonder and fantasy.

On the other hand, are they?

Perhaps we will follow these stories up with a few more ventures into the world of the unknown and unclassifiable.

We shall see what the future brings.

I can see it all now, PJH, leaning over his keyboard. A cold, late October evening, the spent leaves of autumn dancing in the wind outside on the sidewalk in front of the writing command center. The evil cackles of a witch flying on a broomstick in front of a full moon echoes throughout the night, a flickering Jack-O-Lantern sitting on the front steps of my porch. Shadows dancing between the trees from the moonlight. The imagined, gentle whisper of a gorgeous woman from my past floats into my ear, combined with a faint memory of her beauty and a whiff of her perfume, while a few random ghosts swirl above my head.

Ah, who the hell knows?

It is my hope and sincere wish that you enjoy this collection of fantasy stories, or whatever we decide they are, as much as I have enjoyed the experience of writing them.

Paul John Hausleben

04 November 2017

Prologue

Clifton Marlowe looked up from his pile of paperwork and he smiled at the sight of his manager, Mr. Jose Rodriguez, coming through the door of the store. Clifton looked at his watch and noted the time. Six O'clock. Six. Glorious. O'clock. Clifton was never so happy to welcome the daybreak as he was on this day. To say that it had been a long evening on his shift at the twenty-four-hour drugstore in the heart of downtown Boston, Massachusetts, would be a gross understatement. Akin to saying that the New York sports fans and the Boston sports fans argued a little over their teams.

It was a brutally long evening and morning and now; it was time to pack it all in and hand the reins over to Jose.

"Hey, good morning, Cliff! How was the shift?" Jose asked, as he looked over at his clerk. Jose could tell by the stacks of paperwork on the counter and the tasseled hair of Cliff that it was not a good shift for his clerk. Jose figured, what the hell, he might as well ask and give a happy greeting a try. The manager held a hot cup of coffee out in a cardboard container and smiled as he handed it to Cliff.

"Here. Coffee. Black. On me. Thanks for covering the double shift. I appreciate you. Alejandra was amazing," Jose said, with a lick in his eyes.

"You are welcome. I hope that the date was worth it. Thank you for the coffee. I have to say that after the night that I had—you owe me more than coffee."

Jose took a sip from his own container of coffee and

nodded while placing the coffee down on the counter. He pointed at the coffee container and said, "Okay. I owe you. I gotcha covered. Hey, watch the coffee. It is hot as hell." Clifton nodded and took a slow sip of the coffee while being wary of the warning.

Clifton explained, "It was a very long shift. Did you know that our cash register, or computer system, or whatever you call this son-o-bitch here on the counter, does not recognize, Leap Day? You know, the 29th of February?"

Jose picked up the coffee, took another sip and shook his head while saying, "No, I guess that I didn't know that. What the hell? Does this day even exist? Isn't it some man-made, bullshit day?"

Clifton shrugged his shoulders and said, "I dunno. When the clock struck midnight, then all hell broke loose. We were super busy and I could not ring up any sales. I had to find an old receipt book in the office, write out the receipts by hand and make change with the cash in the safe. Stupid-ass machine would not even open the cash drawer. Credit cards, get this, I processed them on this old, swipe thing that I found."

Jose nodded and suppressed a laugh. There was no doubt that Clifton's resourcefulness impressed him.

Jose picked up the paper receipts and thumbed through them as he asked, "I see you got it back on line. How did you get it worked out?"

Clifton laughed, smiled and said, "Some computer geek in the corporate headquarters finally called me back around one in the morning, and he walked me through the steps to make the cash register work. It still did not stamp the date or time on the receipt, but at least it worked."

Jose paused as he looked through the receipts and once more praised the work of his clerk as well as his extra effort, "Great. Thank you. Great work. It was busy, huh?"

"Busy, Hah! Unreal. Total it all up later. You will see the

dough. It seemed as if all of Boston came in here tonight. Police cars racing up and down the streets all night and all morning. Fire engines too. Crazy night. Like half the damn city was on fire."

Jose shrugged his shoulders and said, "Nuthin' on WBZ this morning. Just the usual bullshit. Basketball team won. Hockey team lost. Maybe frozen pipes, because of the cold?"

Clifton took another sip of his coffee and this time; it was his turn to shrug his shoulders.

"Could be? I dunno. Hey, Jose, get this!" The clerk was excited, and he set his coffee down on the counter and pointed at the receipts. "You will see it later, but just before two in the morning, this dude comes running in here. All out of breath. Wearing, no hat and no coat. He smelled like a ton of booze. If ya lit a match, this guy might have gone up in flames. Anyway, he asks me where the shoelaces are and the red birthday gift bows. He plunks down twenty bucks in cash for a five-dollar sale. I wrote him a receipt. Told me to keep the extra change as a tip. So, I did!"

Jose laughed and said, "Shoelaces and red bows. Okay. Very cool on the tip. Sounds as if you deserved it. Drunken shopping, huh?"

"Yup! The dumb-ass fool says that it was a birthday present for the most beautiful gal he had ever seen. He bought 'em too. I bet that friggin' gift went over like a lead balloon and she kicked his ass out."

Jose smiled again and said, "Yeah, man. I bet it did. That is what he gets for having too many nightcaps. Lead balloons, lost love, and empty promises."

Nightcap

A Story of Romance and the Unexplained

Paul John Hausleben

Nightcap

The Weary Life of Jacob McCabe

Jacob "Jake" McCabe trudged through each day in a mindless and bored stupor. Why not? All the days seemed to be the same. He viewed the world through an opaque window. He could see the motions and hear the muffled words, but it was so mundane and boring that he seldom really paid attention. He was present. He smiled, went through the motions, but after all of these years and all he had been through, he seldom took it very seriously.

Jake was a traveling salesman, and he often sat alone on the edge of a bed in a hotel room, flipping through channels on the television, never stopping to watch a show for very long, just flipping and thinking. Thinking about how he should consider himself lucky. That is lucky, in a roundabout way. He earned a very good salary, and most people would consider him a highly successful man in the business world. Jake held a lofty position within his company. Sure, he lived on the road, out of a suitcase, but he earned a nice salary. After all the years of selling whatever the hell it is that he sold, he could perform the sales pitch and work with his eyes closed. And therein was the trouble. It was mindless, and the glory of the road had worn thin. Very thin. In fact, after doing this for close to fifteen years, all the hotels appeared the same, and the restaurant food tasted the same. As of late, the gin joints all watered down his cocktails in the same manner, and they priced the drinks ten times more than they should cost.

Most of all, all the people whom he met along the way were all the same.

Same old, same old.

The company that employed Jake sold extremely high-quality surgical tools, medical supplies and precision medical instruments and equipment, everything from scalpels to microscopes to syringes to glassware. Products used in hospitals, laboratories, and universities, and Jake swore that after fifteen years, he had made a commission by peddling his wares to every hospital, university research center, and laboratory in the United States. There were not too many locations that he did not sell to, or call upon, or had visited. Now, with the internet, he did not even have to carry brochures of the product lines with him. Just a laptop, a smile, an order form, answer a few questions, take the customers to lunch or dinner, drop a few bucks on cocktails and hop a plane for the next stop. The commission money rolled in, and Jake banked it all.

However, commission dough did not buy happiness, nor did it always buy excitement. At least, not the type of excitement or happiness that Jake McCabe sought.

Yet, Jake knew in his heart that the end of the road was near . . . it was closer than anyone could ever imagine. Jake gave it a year to two more, and then it would be over.

The rumor mill within the company that Jake worked for was that the plans were to move all the manufacturing of their products overseas. Jake had seen it before within his industry. The lure of inexpensive labor was far too great for corporate accountants and executives not to succumb to these days. The bottom line was all too important and large profits and successes are never enough. They always want more and more.

The company had formed right after World War Two and it was the byproduct of retooling military production lines into goods for use in the civilian world. The company had now been in business and thriving for close to fifty years. Presently, the company manufactured premium products in the United States with skilled and dedicated workers. The products were the best of the best, and Jake had no trouble at all in peddling his products, because of their reputation for outstanding quality. When the inevitable move to overseas manufacturing occurred, Jake knew that the production would shift to some haphazard and poorly managed manufacturing plant with poorly skilled workers in some dump overseas.

Who cares?

And that would be the deathblow.

It was, in Jake's opinion, all very predictable. Perhaps Jake's mundane world and his now skewed view on life had tilted him toward cynicism. On the other hand, perhaps Jake was overly factual. In his mind, he could envision the press conferences with the announcements of the plans.

Despite assurances that quality would not suffer but the profits would increase, the result will be cheaper products at the same, or in fact, inflated prices. The company's reputation for making the finest products would be gone forever and they would fade away like so many other American businesses. Inferior products at top dollar are not a winning formula.

It seems as if in God, we trust and everyone else must pay cash.

Predictably, the deathblow would come in the words muttered by another clueless, high-level executive, "We have a duty to our shareholders to increase our profits. Our bottom-line is dramatically suffering due to the high wages and costs of medical benefits to the current line-up of employees and while we certainly appreciate all their hard work and dedication. . .."

Oh yes, indeed they do, but in their distorted view and mindless greed, they feel as if they have no duty to the factory workers or the employees who helped the company earn the reputation they now have, or the loyal customers who shelled out top dollar for a top-notch product for so many years. No, not in this modern world of business populated with countless clueless jackasses. Clueless, overly educated jackasses, posing as executives, all of them with spray tans, expensive overlays on their teeth and alcohol on their breath at ten in the morning. Executives, who are all, dishing out buckets of alimony dollars to their unceremoniously ditched high-school sweethearts, whom they married when they were still poor, still too young, but still somewhat honest and untainted by perceived fame and real money. Now with money in their bank accounts and stars in their eyes, they have lost all their wives and sweethearts as they thoughtlessly tossed them all aside in favor of the cute chicks sitting on the third floor with the tight backsides, loose lips and overly exposed chests.

None of these executives has a clue about the real world. They obliviously sit in their fancy offices and could give two shits less about anything but themselves. Now, there are some important things on clueless jackasses' agendas! Yes, golf dates are important, and the chick's tight ass is important, as are the covert or in some cases, advertised liaisons with the cute chicks, but not too much else matters in their worlds. After all, they just keep telling themselves that it is all about the duty to the shareholders and in making sure their bonus money ends up in their bank accounts. Because of these selfish decisions driven by business avarice, the now-unemployed schleps of the company would crawl away from their well-paying jobs, which are now overseas, and they would replace those jobs with lower-paying service jobs. Good honest jobs, which by their nature, paid lower wages. The executives do not care. They walk away with bonus money and move over to another corporation to wreak havoc upon others in much the same manner. How these jackasses continue to thrive and find jobs remained in Jake's mind, the real puzzle. Yet, they blame it on the economy and walk away filthy rich and unaccountable for their previous performances. Then the talking heads and the politicians will shake their heads and finger point as to the reasons of why the economy never really recovers.

Friggin' geniuses.

Yet, Jake had another year or two selling what it is that he sold, banking the money and waiting for the death spiral. Then, he might actually have something to brighten his days, a little excitement, or even a challenge. Maybe an end to the boredom.

Jake spent about three hundred days a year traveling, and honestly, he did not know what to do when he did return home. Home, for Jake McCabe, was a small five-room townhouse in south Jersey, in the same township where the corporate office for his company was located. On a clear day, from his deck, he could see downtown Philadelphia.

Whippy-doo.

It was not much, but it was carefree, maintenance free, cheap, had a few, cute young women for neighbors, who occasionally added to the view when they sunbathed topless on their decks in the summer, and for Jake, it was perfect. Not that he was home often enough to enjoy the view.

Of Philadelphia, that is.

He had an agreement with the property manager for monthly visits to check on his place, to knock the cobwebs down, oversee a housekeeping crew, adjust the heat and air conditioning and inspect the home for him. The electric bill and other utilities all were on auto-pay as were all the other fees. Jake paid the mortgage off years ago.

One month, his electric bill was seven bucks.

Jake threw the property manager a monthly management fee. When he returned home, he tossed him a few bucks on the side, and gave him a bottle of expensive booze for Christmas, and all was well.

It all wrapped up in a tidy bow for Jacob McCabe.

Sort of.

When he was home, other than gazing at the cute neighbors, Jake had one or two co-workers at the corporate office that he hung around with here and there. One of his coworkers, Mr. Wayne Hampstead, could be the closest person to a friend that Jake had. He always went out for a few drinks and shared dinner with Wayne whenever he returned home. They often went out shooting pool together or to a hockey game in Philadelphia if it was the hockey season. Jake liked Wayne. He was a good man, honest, a hard worker, he had been with the company for ten years or so, had two children and an attractive, pleasant and cordial wife. Wayne's wife worked hard at her own job and she seemed very loyal and did not seem to nag or harass Wayne. Amongst the female world, those types of women are difficult to find these days. His friend had a happy marriage, great kids and a good life.

Wayne was a very lucky guy.

Jake was so rarely in the corporate office that when he did appear, it was a major event. He was something of a celebrity. Not only was Jake McCabe the highest grossing salesperson in total sales, Jake was now the longest tenured sales employee within the company. Yet, for Jake, he could do this all with his eyes closed. He checked in with his direct boss via the telephone once a week, participated in conference and video calls and of course, the plague of modern business these days; he answered countless texts and endless email.

In his personal life, Jake had been alone now for about ten years or a little more. His wife grew bored with him, his lifestyle, and with Jake being away for so long. No doubt that she loved spending the money and the young guy, just out of prison, with all kinds of tattoos, who lived with his parents down the street from the McCabe's expensive home. Jake returned home without notice from a long road trip one day, and found them wrapped up tighter than tumbleweeds, making love like wild baboons, and decided that they deserved each other. Their two children were all grown, all long since off on their own, so he took off and let them have it all.

In the big picture, Jake couldn't care less. Let the loser have her. She was a pain-in-the-ass. He will find out quickly enough. It was a speedy divorce. Painless and uncontested. He gave his ex-wife half of everything, and the entire house. Half was all he required in this life, and he felt a sigh of relief at never having to pay the outrageous taxes and high maintenance on a house that he seldom even lived in or visited. It was a grand home, set in the finest neighborhood, and to Jake it meant nothing. It was just a big pain-in-the-ass and a money pit. He was happy to let them have it all. Jake sure as hell never had the chance to enjoy it. To hell with fancy subdivisions and status in society. In Jake's mind it all sucked big time.

Jake kept himself in good physical condition, nowadays, most of the hotels had fitness centers, he was not a bad-looking guy, still lean, still tall and dark and he caught the eye of more than just a few ladies along the way. Jake could have his pick of most of them. Young and old. The one-night stands were not the greatest, but what the hell.

Ah yes, a dubious lifestyle, not too much changed for Jacob McCabe. Yes, the money rolled in, but the boredom went on and on along with him. Then, on a February evening, in a hotel in Boston, Massachusetts, Jake's seemingly endless run of boredom came to an unusual and abrupt end. A remarkable end. An end that he could never have imagined, or even years later, figure out or describe. His greatest dreams and his wildest fantasies could not explain it, but then again, was it all a dream?

This world is full of great mysteries, unsolved, and perpetual and they remain mysteries that the greatest minds can neither solve, nor explain or understand. Perhaps, of all of these mysteries, the greatest of them all is love. Does love guide us, steer us, mold us and lead us? Does love do all of those things and even more? Can love conquer the greatest pain while simultaneously being the cause of it too?

Then, there is this little matter of this thing that we call time. What really is time? How do we define it? Where does it come from? Can we say that time is man-made, and that humankind created time as a tool to chart our lives and years with, in our human world?

Perhaps.

On the other hand, is time something deeper?

Much, much deeper.

Jacob McCabe Begins to Tell his Story

My best, and more accurately, perhaps, my only friend in the entire world, Wayne Hampstead fiddled with his beer mug, and while trying hard to attract the attention of the bartender he told me with some concern in his voice, "So you are looking a little shook up there, Jake. I have to say that in all the years that I have known you that I have never heard you quite so rattled as you were on the telephone when you called me. When you called me to meet you here after work, I could hear the quivering in your voice, and now that I see you, I can tell by the look on your face and the lick in your eyes that something is really bothering you. Usually, everything in your world is so controlled, sort of humdrum and commonplace."

I nodded my head and went to speak, when the bartender finally scooted over to us and waved his hands in an indication for us to order quickly, especially if they were just refilling of the brews. A lively Friday evening crowd packed our favorite gin joint this evening, and the bartender was running hard.

I saved the bartender a few steps by waving to him as I told him, "Yes, please, the same . . . for both of us. Keep the tab open."

Seemingly within seconds, Wayne and I had fresh brews in front of us. The bartender was efficient and very good at his job.

Over sips of the cold brews, I told my friend, "Wayne, my man, I have to tell you that, I am a bit rattled. I have no explanation for what happened to me on this last trip. A trip that started out just as ordinarily as all the thousands of others. A stop or two in lower Massachusetts and then off to my usual stop in Boston and that is where things became strange."

Wayne leaned back on the bar stool. He took a handful of some bar snacks from a small dish in front of us, and popped a few crunchy snacks in his mouth.

While he chewed and crunched them, he mumbled, "I see. Strange, huh? How so?"

"Well," I shook my head; it was going to feel good to get this story out of my head and off my chest. Maybe someone else could make some sense of it.

"Sit on back there Wayne, enjoy those beers, and let me tell you my incredible story."

Wayne nodded and smiled while sipping his brew, "I got all night, Jake. Wife and kiddies are off to her mom's house for the weekend, so go ahead. I am interested in what has a normally cool, calm and collected, Jake McCabe so damn worked up."

"Okay, it is a long story, but you said you have all night."

Jacob McCabe's Testimony

Here we go then.

It started out much the same, as all of these trips tend to do. The weather was a bit of a pain-in-the-ass. I had a delayed flight out of Atlanta, unusually cold for late February in Atlanta, had to wait for the stupid-ass deicing truck and then we made our way up to Connecticut.

I drove the rental car first to Worcester, there I made a quick sales call, filled out the usual order with a hospital that I have been calling on forever, and took the clients to lunch. Showed the customers a new product line, flirted a bit with a cute woman who just came on staff with them, and then drove the rest of the way into Boston. I checked into the hotel that I usually stay at, The Grand City Marquis Hotel. It has a fancy-ass name, but let me tell you that it is nothing special. It is just a typically overpriced bullshit hotel stuck in the middle of the old city, but I rather enjoy the parking arrangement. The parking is in a garage adjacent to the hotel, easy in and easy out, and the hospital that I call on is within walking distance of the hotel. No hassles at all, with traffic or parking.

It was cold and let me tell you for late February; the wind whistled through those buildings and I froze my ass off just walking from the parking garage to the hotel. There was no way that I was going to venture out into the city streets to eat. The hotel lounge would work just fine for me. Besides, despite the fact that the hotel is nothing special, the food there is very good. Exceptional in fact. They have a magnificent spinach and cheese ravioli dish and the chef has known me for years. He takes extra good care of me. Certainly, it was a better choice than freezing your ass off walking to some restaurant that charged you fifty bucks for a meager pile of spaghetti and meatballs that are more breadcrumbs than they are meat.

I checked into my room, set up the laptop, answered a few million emails, all of them the usual bullshit. I washed up, dressed for dinner, and wandered down into the hotel lounge and restaurant. The hotel had a high occupancy and I think that everyone in the entire hotel felt as I did, and no one else wanted to wander out into the cold city for a meal when you could eat here. After these many years of staying here, the night manager knows me quite well, and despite the evening dinner crowd, she managed to seat me at my usual table in a far corner near the kitchen door. I had gone out on a date here and there with her over the years, nothing serious. We never spent the night together or anything like that. We just tested each other to see if there might be a match. She wanted to date on a more serious level, and while I enjoyed her company, I always kept it friendly with her. We shared some general chit chat; she is a cutie, a very nice person, and while she still seemed to hope that I would take our relationship to the next level, she did not seem overly miffed at my desire to be only friends. After we caught up a bit, she brought me my usual Scotch on the rocks; I ordered the ravioli dish, and all was going rather well.

Honestly, when the hotel, bar, and restaurant are this crowded, I always scan the crowd for some women who I might want to meet or share some general chit chat with, you know, pass some time with. Not everything is always about sex. Often, you meet interesting people who are just fun to chat with and to discuss things with on evenings such as these. Tonight, however, despite the crowd, there did not seem to be any women around, at least none, who caught my eye. It might just have been *too* crowded, if that makes some type of sense, or I was just too tired and uninterested in anything, but having a few drinks, enjoying a good meal and hitting the sack early. Long travel days combined with business and long drives suck. No doubt that the trip had tired me out. I bid the manager good evening; the chef came out to check on me and the quality of the meal and with a tiny bit of a buzz on from three Scotches; I made my way to my room.

While I passed by the bar, I leaned in and said hello to the bartender. His name is Bradley. He is a very pleasant guy, a helluva bartender too, and he has worked at the bar for as long as I have been staying in the hotel.

"Too crowded to sit with me tonight, Jake? Missed yah."

"Hello, Bradley. Yes, I picked my corner table. Just a little quieter. Have you been doing, okay?"

"Yes. I've been okay, working, living the dream. You?"

"Same. Living the dream, earning the wage. Why, I do not know why, but I am earning the wage. Nuthin' to spend it on when you work all the time."

Bradley nodded, waved, and as he hustled off to the other end of the bar, he told me, "I know that you usually stay two or three nights. Occupancy goes way down tomorrow. Maybe, we can catch up tomorrow night."

I nodded and told him, "Yes, I am here for a few nights. That sounds like a plan." With that, I wobbled towards the lobby elevators.

This hotel is a high-rise, it towers endlessly into the sky and is stuck in the old section of the city. The view from the room was spectacular. After undressing and lounging around on the bed in my underwear, I grew bored stiff. My mind was uneasy, restless, and even though I was tired, sleep, for some reason, was not easy to find. After flipping through all the channels on the television, I checked my email once again and then officially gave in to the captivating view of the city. Restless, I sat in a chair and mindlessly stared out at the view through the window, and before I knew it, I fell asleep in the chair next to the window. When I woke, it was just a hairpin past midnight and as so often occurs when you are sleeping on the road, a catnap steals all the sleep from your mind and your body too. Now, I was not the least bit tired, and I grew even more restless. Why I was so restless, I could not quite place my finger on, but there was little doubt that sleep was going to be hard to come by now.

Looking back on all of this, it might have been for a reason. After pacing the floor, I finally conceded defeat and dressed. Casual dress, a pair of khakis, a long sleeve mock neck shirt and on the way out the door, I grabbed the room key and a few bucks in cash from a stash in my carry-on bag. I am not sure why I did that because I usually charge road expenses on a credit card or to my hotel room. I never carry much cash on my person when I wander on the road. It was strange, but something told me to have cash on hand. Anyway, I knew the bar was open until two in the morning. Walk-ins off the city streets often crowded the hotel bar when the nightlife of the city wound down. Bradley would be pissing and moaning at the action and between moans, he would pocket a ton of dough in tips. The guy made a killer of a living here.

Oh yes, a nightcap would do it. The Scotch was now a process in my worn-out liver and its influence was in the past. I needed a nightcap and I would sleep like a baby.

Yes, indeed. Like a baby.

Rode the elevator down from the nineteenth floor and when I walked into the bar area, I must say that I was amazed. Strange was a word that did not quite describe the scene that played out in front of me. There was not a single patron in the entire place. I glanced at my watch with the thought that perhaps I had made a mistake and lost track of time. My watch told me the time and the date. It was twelve-thirty-five in the morning on the 29th of February. I chuckled at the fact that it was Leap Day. A day that man created to fill a void in a calendar and a day that only comes around every four years.

I had to wonder, does this day even actually exist?

The bar remained lit with the back lights gently and gracefully illuminating the colors of the bottles and broadcasting their promise of a delectable, yet temporary, escape from your realities. The taps for the various brews sat happily in the dispensing handles; the bar was still open, but no one was home.

Except for the bartender.

I did a double take. No, honestly, that might not be correct; I did a triple take, or maybe even more. This bartender sure as hell was not Bradley.

No, it certainly was not Bradley in front of me. I settled into a bar stool on the far end of the bar and studied the glorious rear view of a woman, who was preoccupied with washing glassware in the glassware bath on the opposite end of the bar from where I decided to sit. She was a goddess, perfectly shaped, her tight black pants gripping her fantastic backside like a glove, her gentle hips swaying as she washed the glassware, oblivious to me studying and frankly, lusting after her. She had shoulder length black hair. Hair that was so clean, shiny, and jet-black that the lights from the back lights of the bar and various colors of the liquor bottles reflected off her hair. Her hair was gorgeous. It hung rather straight, and it moved and chased about her body as she moved. All I could do was to sit there and study her, while remaining mesmerized at her beauty, and now that I had admired her attractiveness from the rear, I immediately longed for her to turn around. I thought how if the front view was as amazing as the rear view, then I might just fall off this damn bar stool.

Finally, the impatience inside of me rose to a new level, so I leaned over the bar and waved in the air while saying, "Ah, hello there. Sorry to tear you away from such a riveting job, but . . . good evening. Or should, I say, good morning?"

When she turned around, I did almost fall off the barstool. Wish I had more of an ass, at least a big enough of an ass to have anchored me firmly in the bar stool. I am not kidding, nor am I exaggerating, when I tell you that her beauty was such that I held onto the edge of the bar to prevent myself from toppling over when she spun around and faced me. Yes, indeed! A goddess! Perfect facial features, a wide smile, and her perfect breasts, perfectly shaped and enhanced by a black pullover blouse that neatly tucked into the waistline of her black pants. Sorry, Bradley the bartender, but I ain't gonna miss you at all!

"Oh, I am so sorry!" She loudly spoke as she picked up a bar towel, wiped her hands and tossed it aside as she hustled over to where I sat. As she walked closer, her beauty surrounded her. Suddenly, this ordinary road trip had turned very extraordinary.

"Were you sitting there for a long time? I was washing the glassware, and to be honest, I was daydreaming and did not see or hear you there. It is so quiet in here right now, unusually so."

Her eyes displayed a shimmer of green in the light of the bar, a green color, which danced and twinkled at me. Her smile and beauty went through me and as she stood in front of me now, my eyes went from her smile to her breasts to her hips, and I am quite sure that she noticed me checking her out. Surely, a woman who looks as stunning as she does, might be used to such a gaze from a man. Yet, I did not want her to perceive me to be a typical lust-driven businessman asshole on a road trip. Even if, as of right now, after seeing this gorgeous woman, I was a typical lust-driven businessman asshole on a road trip. Despite my best efforts at trying not to gawk at her beauty; I failed rather miserably and I could not help myself. I answered her rather vaguely, with one of those stupid-ass dumb coy answers loaded with double meanings. Stupid flirting.

"Oh, no trouble. I did not mind at all . . . the view was

quite intriguing."

To my surprise, she did not frown or show any sign of disgust with my silly comment. Instead, she softly smiled and I caught her eyes carefully studying me. First, her eyes went to my face, and then her gaze lingered on my hands as they sat on the polished finish of the bar top. I displayed my hands neatly in front of me, my fingers purposely outstretched in front of me in an outward and unabashed display. Yes, no wedding ring, and no there, gorgeous; I do not take it off for road trips. I dumped her sorry ass years ago, and as far as I know, her tough-guy, mean-ass prison boy ended up back in prison on more felonies. Rumor had it that my ex-pain-in-the-ass was now married to her third husband and he, too, was finding out what I did so long ago. She was indeed a pain-in-the-ass.

My eyes studied her hands and no wedding ring existed there either.

My guess would be that she might have been a few years older than I was, but it was difficult to tell with a woman of this level of beauty. Age was not a factor in my attraction to her. Judging by her initial reactions to me, I think she felt as if I was not a bad-looking man, and that might have been dreaming or supposition on my part. Yet, I hoped it was true, and now, I felt some pangs of regret at not taking more time in front of the mirror before wandering down here. At least, I had a fresh shower; it was a close shave that I was lacking. Usually, women found me attractive, if not with overwhelming Hollywood good looks. Perhaps I landed just a cut above the average Joe. I dunno. It was not as if I had to beat the women off with a stick, but I attracted my share. But this woman was not the average woman.

No, no, no, I damn sure wish that I had shaved.

"Oh, I see. The view, huh? I must say that things have picked up considerably with your arrival. Suddenly, the atmosphere has improved around here. And yes, technically, it is morning. So, good morning."

Sparkly comments, followed by a wickedly sexy smile. A glorious pose, with a bent leg, a tilt of her head, a flip of her hair and a flash of her green eyes. I shivered at her golden voice and words.

"What will you have? A nightcap? A nightcap in the morning?"

"Yes, please. A nightcap. I dozed off for a few minutes in my room. Now, sleep is a lost cause. Dozed, while sitting in a chair, gazing like some idiot looking out at the city. I am on the nineteenth floor. The view there, as it is here, is quite spectacular."

She nodded with the smile still upon her face and offered, "Might I suggest a snifter of brandy. Warm, brandy. It always works for me. Manages to somehow, send a trickle of warmth and a touch of magic through your veins."

"Sounds perfect. Works for me. Pour it, please. Say, I was here tonight, or actually, last night, for dinner . . . what now seems as if it were a lifetime or so ago. I would have certainly noticed you, but I only saw Bradley working at the bar. Am I incorrect?"

I tried hard to read her nametag, you know, the little brass or plastic tags that the hotel staff wears on their lapels, but she had turned so quickly away from me to prepare the drink that I could not catch more than just a fleeting glimpse of it. Within a flash glimpse, I thought the first letter was an M . . . but I thought that I was wrong.

As she searched the multitude of bottles behind the bar, she explained, "No, you are correct. I relieved him at midnight. I will work until two and then close the bar down. I am just so amazed that you have been the only customer, it seemed as if I chased them away."

She found the bottle, took a brandy glass, unscrewed the top and poured the drink for me.

While she did so, she laughed a bit at her statement,

"Seems as if we are the last persons left on Earth. Even the lobby traffic has died down."

She walked over, placed the drink in front of me, and leaned in a bit. When she did so, it was difficult not to gaze at the hint of cleavage she revealed to me. I smiled, picked the drink up, and then placed it gently back on the surface of the bar. Now, I could clearly read her nametag, and I did so under the false pretense of also catching more of a glimpse of her amazing breasts.

"I doubt that you could have chased any person away, unless they are blind . . . ah, hello, Michelle. It is a pleasure to meet you this morning. I am Jacob McCabe. Most everyone just calls me, Jake."

I reached out my hand and Michelle stood up straighter and gently took it. While she was neither tall nor short for a woman, she had tiny hands. Yet, her touch was soft and her hands were warm, especially so on such a cold evening. We held each other's hands for an unusually long time. It was not a handshake. Instead, I rather describe it as a gentle grasp. I cannot describe the feeling when we touched; it was magical and the best that I can do to capture the moment was that her touch sent some type of wave of overwhelming joy throughout my body. I have never experienced a feeling or anything quite like it. There actually are no words to describe it.

"Please, surely the pleasure is mutual, yet, in some way, I feel very lucky to have you wander down here and keep me company. On second thought—the pleasure is all mine. Nice to meet you, Jake. Certainly, it is mine. What do you do for a living, or entertainment or both, to bring you in here for a nightcap on what has turned out to be such a strange evening?"

Now, I could feel that the conversation changed to a different level. I sipped the drink and it indeed immediately floated some warmth and additional magic in my veins. I leaned in and so did Michelle.

"By the way, you might be, Jake, rather than Jacob, but most everyone calls me, Shelly. Shelly McDermott."

Without hesitation, I took the opportunity to make the conversation more informal and more relaxed, "Shelly it is then. I am a salesman. I travel the entire country, on the road three hundred days a year, until tonight every stop looked the same, felt the same and smelled the same. I sell bullshit. What salesperson could tell you something different? Technically, I sell medical tools, surgical devices, instruments and laboratory equipment. Yet, I imagine that I am the same as every other salesperson is. I guess that I sell bullshit. No matter if you are selling furniture, magazines, appliances, or religion, you are selling bullshit."

She smiled widely at my statement. She leaned back in, put her one foot on the inside railing of the bar and gently grasped my hand. Our eyes locked, and her beauty overwhelmed me. Something connected between us and I cannot say if it was love at first sight or some other type of feeling, but it was a very powerful feeling and connection. Right now, as I try so damn hard to figure this out, I am not actually going to try to dwell upon corny nonsense and clichés.

"Damn, Mr. Jacob McCabe. I have seldom heard such true words or honesty from a man. I agree that when you stop and study it, I think you are correct and all that I sell are drinks and conversation, so I specialize in bullshit too."

"Sorry, I didn't mean to imply to you, that what you do here in any manner might relate to what I do."

"You didn't. Never say sorry to, Shelly. Truth is hard to find in an absurd world, Jake. And for sure, this bullshit world is absurd. Please, no one in management is around, in fact, no one at all, is around. Therefore, I might steal a brandy and join you. Meeting you will give me a good enough reason to break some rules."

"Please, do. Just pour it and put it on my tab. Room 1962. I sell bullshit to an absurd world, but damn sure make a ton of dough doing it. In a nutshell, Jake McCabe lives a boring and simple life. I have no wife and my children are all grown and on their own. I send them money here and there, but until grandchildren come along, I have no grand reason to spend too much money on them. My children all have good jobs and make a solid living, too. When the grand kiddies come along, then I can spoil them. I only have a small townhouse in New Jersey, and I am never there. Drive a company car, no fancy cars, shit, I will end up being dead and rich and so the kids will get it all, anyhow."

Michelle walked over to the bottle and poured a drink for herself.

As she poured the drink, she spoke, this time, with her back turned to me, her glorious rear view in full display, "Room 1962, huh? Very interesting number and coincidental too. Then, Jake, what the hell. Let's spend just a little of it today. I will join you for a sip or two and take you up on your tab offer too. We deserve it. Today is my birthday. I am a Leapling. Born on Leap Day in 1962. Is that screwed up or what? I only have my birthday every four years or so. Maybe, I never age or better yet, maybe, I do not even exist at all. Who the hell knows . . . right?"

She turned around, and with a brandy glass in her hand, Michelle returned to stand opposite to where I sat. Leapling? Never heard of that term, but I guess it makes sense. Wow, I must say that I now recalled that it was Leap Day and my previous thoughts on how strange this day was.

"Wow, interesting. I must tell you, Shelly, that until now . . . I never met anyone born on Leap Day or even thought about how unusual that is. That is what they call people born on this day, huh? Leaplings. Very cool. Well, I for one can testify that you do exist. I have some magic running in my veins now, mixing with some expired remnants of Scotch from dinner, so I will venture on the bold side and say, my goodness you do exist, and are one gorgeous woman."

I recalled thinking, what the hell, right now; I needed to be bold because this was a rare woman in front of me.

Now or never.

Therefore, I gave it my best try, lifted my glass and touched her glass while saying, "Cheers. Happy birthday. Seems as if I should give you something else, something special for your birthday. I think that you deserve something more than just buying you a drink or two."

She touched my glass and spoke in almost a whisper, "Thank you for the compliment and the well wishes. I must say that you are quite the handsome man. I love the sparkle in your eyes. Therefore, perhaps, you are correct and I do exist. For what reason, I am not sure, but perhaps, you are correct."

I thought how that was such a strange thing to say, but as she took a sip she smiled, so I dismissed the words as her teasing me a bit.

After our sips, she placed the glass back down upon the bar top and told me in quite a matter-of-fact manner, "I do want something for my birthday. I need new shoelaces."

With that statement, she lifted her leg and held her foot up to show me her shoes. I stood up from the stool, leaned over the bar top, and checked out what it was that Shelly was showing to me. Shelly's shoelaces were broken and too short to make the rounds of all the eyelets. The laces all were too short and tied off into a small loop on the tongues of her shoes. She started to laugh, a golden and hearty laugh and I burst out laughing, too.

Sometimes, you search the entire world for a soulmate and you think that you find them. You share sex, lust, kisses, life, pain, and conversation and they are all wonderful, but when you find someone that you can truly laugh with, then it lifts you to a higher place. I do not mean a few jokes or random silliness. I mean laughs and I mean to share heartfelt joy with in your life.

That is a true soulmate. A person who you can share and honor every range of emotion with during your lives together. It is a profound connection, when you share the mutual joy within your lives, when joyful emotions surround your love, and when your lover and you hold them close to your hearts. When you lock your minds, bodies and your hearts forever. When, no matter what happens, you believe in each other. That is the definition of a lover.

"Okay? Wow! Shoelaces. Really? You only have your birthday every four years and you ask for a pair of measly shoelaces. I am sure that someone special in your life will buy them and some other special presents for you."

The smile quickly faded from her face. She shook her head to indicate no.

She whispered just loud enough for me to hear, "Until tonight, there were no special persons in my life."

Her statement floored me. The look on her face and the lick in her eyes when Michelle spoke those words sent me into cold shivers.

I managed to squeak out some drivel, "Damn. You are not a woman with very high demands. I can tell that, to you, materialistic things do not matter very much. It seems as if you deserve a hell of a lot more for your birthday than shoelaces. I can write you a check and you can go and buy a sports car or a new wardrobe."

Once again, Shelley shook her head, and she spoke softly to me, "Why? What do they mean in this life? You just met me, and already you can see into my heart and see certain things such as those, which you just mentioned, are not important to me in this world. Now, life is long, or is it too short? Jake, honestly, I am not sure which it is. I do know whom it is that you love along the way, and how you treat them is all that really matters. Love is the most important thing and it will overcome the greatest sorrow and be the cause of it, too. Material things pass away. Even measly shoelaces. They all mean nothing. Yet I do need shoelaces, in order to help to hold me up and to propel me through this world. We live in a replaceable world where only love and respect mean anything. When we have the courage to peel off the layers of all the human emotions and press our face against the windows of our lives and force our eyes to view what we have done, we see that only love and respect are important."

She then shifted moods and returned once again to waves of humor and with a coy smile, she lifted her foot and pointed at her ragged shoelace, while telling me, "We all need to try to walk along rather proudly through our lives. As best we can, you know, as we make our way. Therefore, I have with some profound and wonderful insight, determined that shoes, Jake, they are important too."

When she said that, I looked at my watch, jumped off the bar stool and told Shelley, "Please, pour me another drink. The magic is amazing. I will be right back. I promise that I will be right back."

With that, I dashed out the side door of the bar, sprinted into the freezing cold air, and ran along the city streets. Hell no, I did not need a coat or hat. Something else was keeping me warm. I knew there happened to be a twenty-four-hour drugstore on a nearby corner, and I knew what I needed to buy. I do think the store clerk in the drug store thought that I was some type of lunatic. There I was, on a bitter cold night, a whiff of booze on me, no coat, and no hat, while bursting breathlessly into the store in the early morning hours of the day, asking between huffs and puffs where the shoelaces were and then asking where the stick-on birthday bows were.

Red bows.

I threw the cash at the clerk. I now understand the strange cash urge because all of this was fate. The clerk insisted on writing a receipt . . . something about his cash register not working because of Leap Day. I was in a hurry so I gave him a huge tip and ran out of the store. In a few short minutes, I returned to the bar. When I pulled the "present" of a pack of black shoelaces adorned with a red bow out of the bag and handed it to Shelley, it was then that I felt love. Therefore, to revisit the clichés and corny bullshit, yes, now, I do believe in love at first sight. In a few minutes, she had new laces in her shoes and I might have been incorrect or misjudging, but she had new shoelaces and perhaps a touch of love in her heart, too.

"Here, Jake. Please take the used shoelaces. Maybe someday, when you are desperate and down on your luck, you will find that they come in handy. You might need them to stand upright and propel Jake McCabe through this absurd world."

She handed me the used laces. I laughed and stuffed them in the pocket of my pants.

"I will keep them. You are correct. In this crazy life, you never know when used shoelaces will come in handy."

All too soon, two o'clock and closing time came. I signed the tab slip to charge the drinks to my room and mustered up some courage to ask for her contact information, and if I could see her again. Sitting there on the bar stool, sitting like some love-struck jackass, while holding my stupid-ass smart phone in my hand, I waited for her to take out a cellphone and we could exchange numbers.

It was more than just a grand disappointment when she told me, "Now, Jake. You just gave me shoelaces for my birthday. You have seen into my heart. I do not own a smartphone or a cellphone. Sometimes, I do think that I own nothing at all."

Michelle must have sensed my disappointment. She walked over to me, reached out her hands and told me, "You will see me again, I promise. Soon. I have to close out the bar. Good things come to those who are willing to wait.

Nightcaps are worth it. Will you wait?"

"I will."

She leaned over the bar, motioned for me to lean over too, and she kissed my cheek.

I heard her say, "Good."

With that one word, she pulled the drawer out of the cash register, closed off the lights of the bar, and she disappeared through a door behind the bar. I sat there in the darkness for a few minutes, not too sure what all of this meant, and when I finally realized that Michelle was not returning, I pulled my sorry ass off the stool and made my way to the elevator. Once again, it seemed so strange not to see another person in the hotel. Thinking about it now, I should have walked out to the front of the lobby to see if the nighttime security officer, bellhops, and desk clerks were on duty or not. I did not do that. Instead, I just pushed the elevator button, stood like a disappointed and lovesick teenager with my hands in my pockets and stared around me while waiting. Not a soul in sight. In fact, other than the store clerk and Michelle, I had not seen another person since dinnertime.

Here we are in a huge hotel, in the bustling city of Boston, and not another person in sight. Not a person on the streets when I dashed to the store. There were no cars, no taxicabs, any pedestrians, or police cars screaming down the main streets.

Friggin' bizarre.

I returned to my room. For some unknown and strange reason, I sat motionless on the edge of the bed for a long time. Did not move a single muscle. I can recall those moments very vividly. Even now, after all of this time. It was as if I froze in time and space. Unable to move. I could hear my own heartbeats. I swear to you that I could. After reflecting on all that happened to me, and trying as hard as I could possibly try in order to forget how gorgeous Michelle McDermott was, I took my shoes off and tossed them aside. I drew the curtains closed to prevent another gaze at the beauty of the city below and decided that since it was now close to three in the morning, I should sleep now.

After all, I had enjoyed a nightcap.

I was just about to undress for bed, went as far as pulling off my shirt, when to my shock, there was a gentle knock at the door of my hotel room. I would be a shitty liar if I told you that I hoped, wished, and dreamed it to be any other person on the face of this Earth other than Michelle McDermott at my door.

My heart told me that it was Michelle. Without a single hesitation, no apprehension, no viewing through the security viewfinder in the door in order to check who it was out there. I did not care if it was Jack, the friggin' ripper on the other side of the door. I flung the door open and there she stood. Glowing, seductive, her smile a mile wide, her green eyes flickering in the dim light of the hallway. She had changed from her work attire and now wore an amazingly tight-fitting black cocktail dress, a dress, which if she walked by them, any man on the face of this world would faint at the mere sight of her in.

I smiled.

She did the same.

In her hands, she held a bottle of brandy and with a seductive growl, she told me, "I told you that I would see you soon and that your nightcap would be worth it. Good things come to those who are willing to wait. I am so happy to see that you waited."

"I did."

"You bought me more than just shoelaces and a few drinks for my birthday. You bought me this bottle too."

"Good. Works for me. I love this stuff. Only just had it tonight. Never had a drop of it until tonight and already it is my favorite."

I grabbed her hand and gently pulled her into the hotel

room, took the bottle from her hands, and placed it on the top of the small shelf of the wardrobe. Her appearance and her dress mesmerized me in such a manner that I did not realize that I was bare-chested until she placed her hands on my bare chest. I turned and held her while kicking the door to the room shut.

It slammed with a positive latch.

Good.

I reached over, and with one hand, flipped the deadbolt and slid the door security lever tightly down upon the door.

A door closed on that absurd world, which lies out there on the other side. If it only was so simple to close it out forever. Goodbye, bullshit. Goodbye, deadlines, and numbers and sales quotas, and all the other things that in the end will not or never will have actually mattered. Yet, for just a few hours, we have this moment. I knew that the absurdities of the world no longer mattered. They were on the other side of that door. Now, it was just Michelle and a love-struck fool.

Alone. Uninhibited. New shoelaces and green eyes.

Her eyes gazed at my chest and she gently moved her hands up and down my chest while intently studying me.

"You are well built. No doubt, lots of hotel fitness rooms. A road warrior who takes care of his body. You are quite the man, Jake McCabe."

I did not answer her; instead, I had waited too long for this. In essence, I only just met her a few short hours ago, but it actually might have been a lifetime that I had waited for this. We kissed, long, deep, and wet. No doubt, I had waited for this kiss an entire lifetime and maybe a few more lifetimes.

No doubt.

In mere seconds, my hands explored her body, and she willingly allowed me to hike up her dress and slowly and gently remove her panties. She stepped out of them. She almost laughed as she bent over and undid her new shoelaces and forcibly kicked her shoes aside. With the same magical glow in her green eyes, she turned her attention to me. She worked with the belt of my pants and she fumbled a bit with the stupid-ass button that held the two sides of my pants together.

I helped her.

My excitement was rather obvious, and I gasped as she held me in her hands.

She whispered, "You feel glorious in my hands. Amazing manhood."

I answered, "And you are a goddess."

When I pulled the glorious dress over her head, and she undid and dropped her brassiere to the floor, she stood naked in front of me, and I stood naked in front of her. Nothing mattered any longer. Only love at first sight. Her breasts pressed against my chest, her glorious nipples were bursting with love, and they were hard. Yet somehow, if this makes any sense, they were soft too. Her body was more than glorious. It was a temple, and she was shaven clean. Not a whisker of hair lay upon her, no blemishes, no cracks in her heart, there were only openings to her soul, openings, which revealed her exposure. An exposure, without any regrets or worries, just an exposure of her endless search for love. She was soft, naked, and clean. Untouched and unfettered. Just the smell of her skin and the smooth touch of her hands upon my body sent shock waves of love into my heart. We made love uninhibited for hours. Explored every inch of each other's bodies, and nothing went untouched or unexplored. I am not ashamed to say and use the word, nothing.

When the first hints of the early morning light stole our precious darkness away, and it filtered and danced through the drawn curtains into the corners of the room, I knew that this glorious and magical time was ending. While exhaustion had long since overtaken our bodies, our love remained unfiltered and just as powerful as any force on Earth and perhaps in Heaven too.

In a haze of sleep, combined with ecstasy, I heard Michelle whisper to me, "Soon, I have to go. We need to make love one more time. I will need to climb on top of you and lock my eyes with yours while we make love. It is how I want to remember you. For now, for always, our love shared with locked eyes. We will make love one more time to last us until we can meet again. We might not understand all of this. You will be confused about our love. I will be too. Promise me, Jacob McCabe. Promise me that you will wait. Will you wait? No matter what, no matter the confusion or the doubts, or the mystery of this, please, promise me that you will wait. I have waited for you forever. Will you wait for me?"

I did not know what to make of her statement and when you considered that other than my catnap, I had been awake for thirty hours or thereabouts, consumed a lot of alcohol and made love for hours upon end, to the most gorgeous woman that I had ever seen or known, well, now that might be understandable.

"Yes, of course, I will wait. I promise, with all of my heart and soul. I, too, have waited a long time for love such as this."

She smiled and gently shook her head while saying, "Not as long as I have. You have no idea how long I have waited for you."

I was confused and asked, "Why? Where will you be? Where are you going?"

She did not answer me, instead, she smiled, placed both of her hands upon her glorious breasts to support them as she swung her legs over me and then she allowed her breasts to go free. While she climbed on top of me, we locked our eyes forever and for the last time, we made glorious and amazing love.

Never knew that I had such stamina and manly

fortitude. I lost count now as to exactly how many times we made love.

Afterwards, when we both had finished sharing our love and joy, I must confess that I rolled over, Shelley did too, and to my recollection, we both fell fast asleep. When I woke up, it was midmorning and Michelle was gone. My cellphone spit out angry texts and obnoxious voice mails at me. Luckily, for me, I only had an afternoon meeting and appointment to make. I still had time. I jumped out of bed. My head was clear, and another frank and honest testimony to the wildness of the evening, was that the male parts of my anatomy hung limp and withered.

I had worked them extra hard.

It seemed very strange that no sign of Michelle remained. There were no notes on the desk, no sign of her anywhere. There was a faint, yet a glorious odor of her perfume upon my chest, and in the room, and her scent remained very strong in the bed. I scampered over to the shelf in the entry area of the hotel room and the bottle of brandy sat upon the shelf of the wardrobe. No, it was not a dream, it might be Leap Day, her birthday, and a day that might not actually exist, but it was not a dream. Friggin' bottles of top-shelf brandy do not magically appear in hotel rooms. I had a bit of a chuckle at the fact that we never even touched it.

When I climbed in the shower, I had dull thoughts in my mind of struggling through another mindless day. In an attempt to boost my spirits, I then countered those thoughts with glorious hope and joy mired within the promise of seeing Michelle later tonight. I was not sure, but somehow, I remained confident that she would be working the late shift again. I had nothing to base that upon, except for my heart and our love.

Let me tell you how difficult it was to concentrate on selling medical instruments when you had experienced what I experienced. Looking back, I am sure the customers knew that I was a bit preoccupied. I had been calling on them for many years now, and they knew me quite well. Somehow, I successfully pulled off the sales call, and I wrote up a ton of orders. I managed to use some dumb excuse of a lingering headache and not feeling too well, in order to explain my inattentiveness and to beg out of dinner and cocktails. Besides, these were longtime customers, and they had milked me for many dinners and gallons of booze over the years. All that I wanted to do was to return to the hotel, to see and to hold Michelle. Tomorrow, I had to drive back to Connecticut and catch an airplane flight to the next horrible stop, which, as far as I knew, would be in Milwaukee, Wisconsin. I wanted to corral Michelle, tell her how much she meant to me, stop all of this traveling, and make plans for our future. It was time to stop the daily madness.

After the sales call, I quickly returned to my hotel room. I showered, dressed for dinner and made my way to the bar. Just as Bradley had explained last evening, the hotel occupancy dropped off considerably and the restaurant and bar were quite sparsely populated. I kept telling myself that was why no one was around early this morning. It seemed as if it was a valid explanation for why the hotel was so lonely for Michelle and me, but it did not explain the empty streets.

At this point, I tried hard not to dwell upon too many of the facts. Strange facts or otherwise.

I slid into a bar stool and Bradley spotted me right away; he waved and quickly grabbed a bottle of my usual Scotch off the shelf and a glass.

"Hey, how goes the day? Sell lots of very expensive widgets and fidgets to unsuspecting customers?"

I laughed and told him, "I did. It was a good day. Not as good as last evening, but it was a successful day. Last evening was the most magical and wonderful night in my entire life."

Bradley carried my drink over and he set it in front of me while saying, "Good, glad to hear it. I told you this place would clear out. Gonna be more manageable tonight. Say, why was last night so special? When you left last night, it seemed to be under control and quite ordinary."

I lifted my drink and smiled while taking a sip. Looking over the rim of the glass, I winked and continued with my long smile. A dopey ass, sly grin locked upon my stupid face.

After my sip, I placed the glass back down on the coaster and while Bradley stood in suspense, I decided to whisper a name to him. "Special . . . because of Michelle. Michelle, or actually, Shelly McDermott. Some credit has to go to catnaps, sleepless nights and enjoying a nightcap too."

Whispering her name provoked absolutely no reaction with Bradley. He stared at me and remained stoic, and actually, his face changed to a somewhat puzzled look.

Finally, he said, "Uh, okay, there Jake, if you say so. Catnaps? Who? Michelle, who? Shelly? Is that some chick that you met? Am I supposed to know her? I do not know Michelle McDermott. Never heard of her."

For a few seconds, I ran a number of different scenarios through my mind, but it was not as if I knew Bradley well enough to decide if he was joking with me or not. I mean I knew him for many years, but hell, in the big picture; he was a bartender on one of my regular stops. All he really did was to pour me drinks, and we made small talk. I played with a few different scenarios in my mind for a few seconds. Okay, you know, perhaps, Bradley spoke with Michelle and she told him about me and after hearing about our meeting, Bradley then decided to play dumb and catch me in a joke. On the other hand, perhaps, he was not actually paying attention to me and did not fully catch the drift of my conversation or hear her name correctly. While studying his face and reaction, either Bradley was one helluva damn good actor and he should be on the big screen, or something was really friggin' weird and strange here.

After the thoughts left my mind, I decided to pursue the idea that Bradley was messing with me here, "You know, geez, Bradley, she is kinda unforgettable. You know, the bartender, the gorgeous woman who relieved you at midnight last night and took over until closing. You know, c'mon man . . . Michelle McDermott."

After listening to me, Bradley smiled faintly and waved his hand at me while he laughed a bit.

At first, I thought, okay, he *was* joking with me here. When Bradley followed the wave with some additional comments, then the smile that appeared on my face quickly faded.

"Oh, shit, man. You musta had some good Scotch up in your room after you left here. You had me for a second or two. Did you have a bad hangover this morning or what? If you did, then I am happy to hear that you did not miss your appointment. Gotta, admit that it was weird closing up last night at midnight." Bradley then glanced at a regular patron settling into the bar to my right. He knew ahead of time what the order was that the patron wanted, and quickly grabbed a mug and started to pour a brew from one of the taps.

While he poured the brew from the tap, Bradley leaned in my way and he continued to speak, "Leap Day. What the hell is that, exactly? A friggin' day we make up time with, in a year where we elect a president. Anyway, technically, it is the only day other than Christmas that we close at midnight. Christmas is on purpose. This day is because of some local laws and bullshit about not having a valid liquor permit for the day until four in the afternoon. Ya know, we gotta close the bar at midnight on the twenty-eighth and we can't open until four in the afternoon today. Not sure that it makes much sense. Who knows? It only happens every four years, so no one knows, cares, or gives two shits less about it. It seems as if the day does not actually exist. . .."

Bradley smiled and carried the full mug over to the thirsty patron, and I sat there stunned. My mouth hung open, shivers went up and down my spine, and I began to tremble and shake. Bradley was sincere. There was no doubt that he was not messing around with me. Michelle's words echoed in my head, a head that I now hung over the bar top and held tightly in my hands.

In my now aching head, her sweet voice resounded, clearly and distinctly, "No matter what, no matter the confusion or the doubts, or the mystery of this, please, promise me that you will wait. I have waited for you forever. Will you wait for me?"

What the hell is going on here?

I thought for a second or two that the explanation was that I was nuts. I had gone raging mad and crazy out of my mind. The loneliness of the road had finally taken my sanity from me. In my loneliness, I invented a magical lover to spend time with and we escaped to a special place. Yes, that was the answer. This crazy situation was because I now was stark raving mad. On the other hand, was I, as Bradley suggested, drunk, and I dreamed all of this and blacked out? Was Michelle an invention of too much Scotch? No, no, I only had three drinks. I swear that I did! I then decided to try to take deep breaths and calm my nerves. I gave up right away, because it was not going to work; the deep breaths made my body tremble even more. I knew that earlier today, I held the most gorgeous woman that I ever made love to, ever saw, or fell in love with. There was no love like this love. It was once in a lifetime.

No way was I going crazy.

I took the Scotch and swigged it down. My hope was that the drink would stop my body from trembling. It did not.

That was a real love. Profound, powerful, deep love

from a different place, from a different world. Perhaps that is where the answer lies. In a different world.

Bradley looked over when the now empty Scotch glass hit the bar top with a loud thud. He bent his eyebrows at me and glanced at my face. After some small talk with the other patron and delivering his beer, he scurried over to me.

"You okay, there, Jake? You look like ya been seeing ghosts or are feeling sick. Not like you to toss drinks, ya usually a slow sipper. Were you hungover? Rough day recovering?"

I bent over the now empty glass and did my best act in order to hide the shock and horror that were rippling through my soul. It was an effort to conceal my struggle as I tried to put all of this madness together and decide if I were crazy, drunk, dreaming or if in fact, as Michelle and Bradley and even I mentioned, did the 29th of February actually even exist?

"Please another Scotch. Double. Neat. Screw the ice." Bradley still stood looking at me as if he, too, was now in shock.

"Okay, sure, sure, sure. Are you going to be, okay? You are not going to keel over on me, are you?"

"No, I am okay. Not sure, what the hell is going on right now, not hungover, but it is going to be all right. I think. Right now, things are mixed up."

Bradley nodded, still watched me carefully out of the corner of his eyes and prepared the drink for me.

He set it in front of me and gently told me, "Look, this is on the house. Maybe you should eat something. Alternatively, better yet, maybe go to your room for some room service and relax. This Michelle that you mentioned . . . she . . . is real?"

"Hell yeah, she is real. If any one person on the face of the Earth is real, then in my heart, I know it is, Michelle McDermott. Please, charge me for the rest of that bottle. I will head to my room, and yes, room service is a good idea. Please charge me out. Put it on the room tab. 1962 is the number."

Bradley looked at me very suspiciously; he nodded his head, turned to the cash register, filled out the paperwork and then turned back toward me.

"Jake, are you sure that you are, okay?"

"I am. Just a little change in plans, but I will be fine. Thank you."

The bartender pointed at the bottle in his hands and offered some worldly advice, "Okay, if you say so. Be careful with this amount of Scotch now. Ya leavin' out 'morrow, eh?"

"Yes, thank you for everything. See you in six months or so."

"Yeah. See you. Please take good care of yourself. Not sure, what this Michelle stuff is all about tonight. Sorry that I do not know her and shook you up a little. Here you go,"

Bradley handed me the tab and the bottle. I signed the tab, shook his hand, and picked up the bottle.

I was acting the entire time because I actually felt like passing out. I knew that I needed to head to my room and examine the proof, try to regain my thoughts and myself. No way could I entertain any thoughts of eating. My stomach was in such terrible knots that I would toss it right up. The Scotch ran around in my veins and dulled some of my senses. Yet, the pain of Bradley's words and his sincerity turned my life upside down. I hustled to the main lobby and while pushing the elevator button, I hashed out the events of last night, replayed the conversation, studied the entire scene, and tried desperately to figure out a sound and reasonable explanation for all of this.

The elevator door opened, and I walked in the car and I was relieved that there were no other riders. I could lean on the wall of the elevator car to prevent my collapse. Let me think. The 29th of February, Michelle's words when she asked if this day actually exists, her birthday on the same day, no one else around in the entire hotel, the entire weird and surreal scene. Her beauty, our endless lovemaking, her gorgeous body, her passion, the taste of her body, her lips, the smell of her perfume. She was, by far, the greatest lover I have ever known.

This shit was real. I was not crazy. Shelly was and is, real. The elevator stopped on the nineteenth floor and I stepped out. Let me tell you that it is difficult to walk when your knees are knocking and your legs can hardly support you, but I made it to my room.

It was not the Scotch making me wobbly.

When I went in the room, I headed straight to where I left the bottle of brandy on the shelf and yes, it was still there. The housekeeper had cleaned the room and changed out the bed linens, so there was little hope of detecting any remnants and whiffs of Michelle's perfume on the pillowcases or bed sheets, but I sure as hell knew where to find the other evidence that I required. As if the bottle was not enough evidence. That is how strange and unexplainable this entire encounter is and was! Bottles of brandy do not just friggin' show up and materialize. Or do they? Does the 29th of February even exist?

I headed straight to the casual khaki pants that I wore last evening. In a furious and frantic effort to find the last pieces of confirmation that I required, I found the pants in my luggage, grabbed them, and dug into the pockets. Sure enough, my hand pulled out used shoelaces and a deep dig into the other pocket, pulled out a receipt from the corner drug store for a pack of new laces and a red bow.

The receipt had neither time nor a date stamp on it.

Of course, I should have known that would be the case. Damn!

Once more, the question remains, does the 29th of February even exist? Perhaps it was all quite explainable with some very simple explanations, such as the cash machines or the store's computers were not set up for Leap Day.

On the other hand, could I even explain it at all?

I smiled and held the used shoelaces tightly in my hand. While still holding them, I reached for the bottle of Scotch, unscrewed the top and did not even bother pouring it into a glass.

Top-shelf Scotch straight out of the bottle.

Damn, not exactly a proper way of drinking fine whiskey and it might be a wretched waste of very expensive Scotch and years of aging efforts, but right now, it works for me. I took a long swig, sat on the edge of the bed, and thought. Shelley's words floated in the air all around me. I reached into the air and grabbed the words; they were as if they were the seeds of dandelions in an open field that blew away in a wind. I captured all of them and held them along with the shoelaces.

I heard her soft voice say to me, "Here, Jake. Please take the used shoelaces. Maybe someday, when you are desperate and down on your luck, you will find that they come in handy. You might need them to stand upright and propel Jake McCabe through this absurd world."

I smiled as Michelle's prediction came true. Right now, I required used shoelaces to keep me upright. I stopped shaking a little, my heartbeat no longer raced, and I knew it was all very real. I kept the smile still frozen on my face and at that special moment, our love impaled forever into my heart.

More of her words escaped my hands and once more echoed inside of my head, "Today is my birthday. I am a Leapling. Born on Leap Day. Is that screwed up or what? I only have my birthday every four years or so. Maybe, I never age or better yet, maybe, I do not even exist at all. Who the hell knows? Right? Promise me, Jake. Promise me that you will wait. Will you wait? No matter what, will you wait for me?"

I held the words in my heart. Not that I understood what she meant or what this was all about, but I trusted and, above all, respected her honor. A great deal of true love involved large amounts of respect and trust.

Even upon reflection of the words, I did not know what to make of her statement and when you considered all of what had transpired for me, for us, well, now that might be understandable.

"Yes, of course, I will wait. Why? Where will you be? Where are you going?"

No answer. Perhaps, in looking back, there was a very good reason that Michelle did not answer me; then again, she did, because after I asked her that question, with our eyes locked forever, she made love to me as no other woman ever had.

Therein was my answer.

I might add, when you find that one special person, you will wait a million years, a hundred lifetimes, or even more for them.

Therefore, the answer is simple.

Why dwell upon it?

In my mind, Michelle asks me again and I answer in less than a second.

Yes.

I will wait for you.

Yes, indeed.

Jacob McCabe Finishes his Testimony

"That is, it. Wayne, my friend, I have told you the entire story. Strange, bizarre, beyond weird, but I swear to you . . . my old friend, upon my honor, that this is real and is all the honest truth. Still, now, five weeks or so later, I have no explanations for this. An internet search for Michelle McDermott turns up a few, and I called the ones that I could find and even searched the social media sites and sent emails to various Michelle names that I found. Even tried just using Shelly McDermott. No luck, just some nasty replies and countless hang-ups on the telephone. Believe me when I tell you, Wayne, I have poured over the internet, crawled through old-fashioned white pages, exhausted every idea to try to find her. People that I call and inquire of her, they think I am nuts. Even ventured out on the limb and called the management of the hotel. They reported that they did not have an employee by that name and, in fact, never had one. They confirmed the fact that the bar closed on that evening after midnight. I say, no way. But, shit, let me tell you that I am not nuts. This does sound crazy, but Michelle was too real not to be real. Even hired a private detective. He exhausted every angle of the investigation, too. The investigation cost me a small fortune, but I would spend anything to find her. He even dusted the bottle of brandy for prints and only my fingerprints are on it."

While I rambled on and recanted this wild tale for what seemed as if it was half of the evening, the bartender had refilled our beers countless times, and he once more filled our empty mugs. As he grabbed the mugs for a refill, I leaned in and assured him that we both were going to call a cab. He nodded, with an obvious sign of agreement on his face, at my decision. Wayne and I both were wasted. Being wasted made this slightly easier to deal with.

I watched as the only person in my peculiar and strange world, who I could tell this crazy tale to, Mr. Wayne Hampstead, leaned back and shook his head.

Wayne, while still shaking his head, commented, "Shit. Wow. Beyond wild. You have evidence. The laces, the bottle of brandy. Geez, I do not know what to tell you or even suggest. Seems as if you have tried everything to find her and figure this all out. It is like some damn paranormal movie. A mind-bender. Yet, honestly, I believe you. Other than our friendship and having known you for many years, I do not know why or how I believe you—but I do. Please know that I believe you with all of my heart and soul. I can tell that you fell madly and deeply in love with her. It is all over your face and in your eyes. At this point, what do you think? Who is, Michelle?"

I answered Wayne as honestly, and factually, as I could, "To tell the truth, I have no friggin' clue as to who she is, where she went off to, or what happened to me . . . or to us. I only know that I am deeply in love with her and that the plan was for us to meet. Thank you for believing me and not thinking that I am a nutcase or a raging drunken fool. You are an honest friend and a good man."

"Of course, of course, Jake. There is no need to thank me. We are good friends and I care about you. So, once again, I ask. Who is Michelle McDermott?"

"I cannot say, for sure, I just do not know. I have been running around the country for years, lost my wife, my family seldom pays attention to me. Maybe, this was all meant to be. Maybe, Shelley is that one true love that you wait an entire lifetime or many lifetimes for to arrive. I just dunno. My life was a boring ass mess, a humdrum shell, an existence. Michelle gave me my life back, restored my soul, filled my heart with love, and gave me a purpose. Damn well, if I will allow this to pass by me or to lose her after finally finding joy in my existence."

Wayne nodded in agreement to my comments, and he spoke after a long sip of brew, "Let me tell you, of all the people in the world that needed to find a special person, well, my friend, you have my vote. The shit ya been through in your life. Living as if you were some damn vagabond traveling from city-to-city. Catchin' your wife in bed, rolling around with some punk-ass hoodlum. You gave the company everything, sure, you made lots of dough, but you gave it your all. I cannot suggest anything concrete or of value, but there has to be some reasonable explanation. There just has to be. Now, what are you going to do?"

Wayne leaned in and looked deeply into my eyes.

I answered without a second of hesitation, "I am going to do just what Michelle asked me to do. What I promised her that I would do. I will wait. She said that we would not understand all of this and it would be a mystery. That we both would be confused. While that might be one of the world's greatest understatements, I trust her. Above all, I love and respect her. In four years, if the good Lord grants me a few more years, then I know exactly where I will be. I will be back in her arms."

Four Years Later

Four years later, on the 28th day of February in a Leap Year, Jacob "Jake" McCabe checked into The Grand City Marquis Hotel in downtown Boston, Massachusetts. Jake waited day and night for four years for this event and for tomorrow to arrive. Finally, it was time.

It was all he could ever think about every single day. Four years of waiting is a long, long time. He endured countless sleepless nights and dreamt endless dreams.

He no longer had sales calls to make, nor did he have appointments to keep or boring sales meetings to conduct. He no longer had to buy cocktails, dinners, or lunches to sway customers into purchasing the products he sold. Most of all, Jake did not have to travel everywhere and laugh at stupid jokes and comments that stupid and obnoxious customers would speak. He did not have to flirt with washed-up prunes of female customers to lure them into making a purchase. It was now all over and Jake began a new era in his life. Jake's prediction of the demise of the company became a cold reality and when he saw the company begin the predicted spiraling down the proverbial drain, he took his pension, his 401K and his bank account full of money and retired. He now dabbled here and there with a small internet company that he began as a startup, selling widgets and some small items. The company provided some play money and allowed him to buy a new car every year without ever touching his savings. He also took good care of his grandchildren.

He was now a proud grandparent.

Jake had a Midas touch. He was a smart businessman and a salesman, with no equal. All the side business and money worked out well enough, but it did not settle his soul. Money was not an issue for Jake McCabe. He had more money than he could ever spend or ever want.

What he desired most of all was something that you could not purchase.

Jake did not find it even slightly unusual when the desk clerk handed him the card key for room 1962 and told him the directions to reach the nineteenth floor. Of course, it would be the same room. Jake smiled when the desk clerk proudly told him about the spectacular view from his room. He had no doubts at all of what was going to happen after midnight tonight. None whatsoever. Not a single one. True love was all about trust and respect. When Leap Day began, he knew that he would be at the bar in the hotel and there would not be another person in sight, all would be quiet; yet, he knew that he once more would stare into the lovely eyes of his true love. And her name is, Ms. Michelle McDermott. He had faith that their love would endure now and forever.

True love has no equal in this world. It has no measure, no rules and no doubts.

Things had changed around the hotel since his last visit. The cute restaurant manager had left her position, Bradley was no longer working the bar, the faces all changed, Jake was just another patron, he no longer was a celebrity around the establishment. Four years is a long time and all good things pass in this world.

Most good things.

Jake ate a pleasant dinner in the restaurant in the hotel, had his usual Scotch, the ravioli dish was no longer on the menu, therefore, he had a salad laced with some grilled chicken. It was a superb dinner. There was now a new chef, new staff, and a new direction here at the hotel.

Jake finished his dinner and the cocktails and headed off for his room. He had a few hours to kill. In his room, he listened to some music on his MP3 player; he showered, lounged around the room, and gazed out the window at the old city. The same room.

On purpose, he did not shave. Jake found it quite strange that he was not nervous, he was not uptight, and instead, he was confident. If he lingered too long on the thoughts, then yes, his heart raced a little at the thoughts of what this evening and in fact, the new day at midnight would bring to him, to his heart, to his life, and to his soul. Yet he tried his best to remain calm.

A few minutes before the hour of midnight, he changed into a casual pair of khaki pants and a long sleeve mock neck shirt, no use in changing the formula. Watching repeats of old movies is often more enjoyable than the original viewing.

It was now Leap Day.

It was time for a nightcap.

When the time came around and the new day arrived, the midnight hour found Jake riding alone down the elevator, entering into the hotel lobby and walking to the bar in the hotel lounge. He already could predict that no other soul was around. He passed no other person, no one in the lobby, no one in the hallways, no other riders on the elevator cars. Outside of the hotel, without even looking out the windows, Jake knew that there were no cars on the streets outside, no police sirens, and no pedestrians. Yet, this time, it did not cause him any thoughts of how strange it was that there were now only two people in this entire world.

He knew that right now, there was only going to be one person in the entire world that Jake would see. Now his heart ached and raced all at the same time.

It was time. In fact, it was way past the time. Only true love tested by separation could withstand the passage of time. It is the ultimate test.

Maybe true love will always remain a mystery, one of the strangest and most powerful of all the emotions, a feeling, which transcends time, space, and all other feelings. Once you find that special person, your one true love, then truly nothing else matters. Not time, not space, not the distance between you and your love, nothing. All that matters is what you both feel in your hearts. It is all that will ever matter, now until the end of all time.

Jake climbed onto the same bar stool at the end of the bar and he noticed how the back lights all looked the same, the glow, the feelings, and the atmosphere. Predictably, it all was the same. He knew it. He knew that nothing would change. Most of all, Michelle stood at the end of the bar, in the same location that he first saw her. Her back was facing him while she washed some glasses out. This time, despite how his heart raced at the mere sight of her, his body ached for her, and all he wanted to do was to run and hold her in his arms, he instead, resisted the urges and allowed the scene to play out all over again. He knew that nothing would change; he was . . . mostly correct.

Michelle reacted to Jake clearing his throat and when she turned around, she looked as radiant and as gorgeous as she did on that night and glorious day four years ago. She stopped in her steps, wiped her hands on the bar towel, tossed it aside, and smiled. Remarkably, there was no sign of shock on Michelle's face. Rather, she displayed peace and an outpouring of joy at the fact that Jake returned.

"You waited."

"Of course, I waited. Happy birthday, Shelley. This time, I will not bring you new shoelaces. I only bring you my heart and me. I love you with all my heart and soul. What did you expect? Time and the absurdity of this world could not come between us. Nothing can come between us ever again. Nothing."

"I guess that in my heart I expected you to wait, Jake McCabe. I really did." Sparkly comments followed by that wicked smile. A glorious pose, with a bent leg, a tilt of her head, a flip of her hair and a flash of her amazing green eyes.

With a coy smile, Michelle asked, "What will you have? A nightcap?"

"Yes, please. A nightcap . . . and you."

Michelle took a few more steps toward Jake and it almost seemed as if she would run into his arms, but she stopped and said, "Of course, a nightcap and I will join you. Join you now and forever. Now, in thinking about it, I must honestly admit that I am not sure what I expected. I know what I wanted, and it is as if a dream has finally come true. I dreamt of you day and night for four years."

"As did I too, Michelle. A lot of things changed in four years, but my love for you only grew deeper."

Michelle smiled and said, "Mine too. I love you too. With all of my heart and soul. It is just that in my long past, no one ever returned before . . . none of them ever waited. You are the one that I hoped, dreamed, and prayed that would come back, the one that I wanted to wait." She looked down, then back to Jake, wiped some tears from her eyes and spoke just above a quiet whisper, "Now I know for certain what I felt in my heart and body. You are the one. You are my one true love. We will now go together, off to live the rest of time, somewhere away from all of this absurdity. Somewhere forever. Do you want to know where we will go?"

Jake smiled, stood up from the bar stool, walked around behind the bar as Michelle rushed to greet him. The two lovers embraced, and they shared a remarkable kiss, a kiss that waited for four long years, or actually perhaps eons of immeasurable time to occur.

Jake whispered as they finished the long kiss, "No, I do not know or care, as long as you will be there with me."

"I will. Forever. You and I forever together. Jake, you have to understand that I too have waited a very long time for this day and for you to appear. Now that you are here, we will never be apart. We will have each other forever."

J.J. Duffy

Jeremiah James Duffy reported for his shift as the nighttime bartender at the main restaurant and lounge within The Grand City Marquis Hotel. He was in a bit of a rush, he scooted in a side door of the hotel, tried his best to avoid any of the wait staff or his coworkers, and especially, he wanted to fly under the radar of the night manager of the restaurant and lounge. He was a few minutes late, and he only had fifteen minutes to prepare the bar area for the opening.

He did not want to face any grief for a late opening.

"J.J.," as his close friends and associates affectionately called him, had assumed this shift and position when the longtime bartender, Mr. Bradley Laurent took a position as the Head Bartender over at a fancy, high-end hotel on the other side of the city. Bradley was here forever at the Grand City Marquis Hotel, and J.J. had big shoes to fill. So far, he did rather well. He was young, but experienced. Good-looking, smooth talking, efficient. He knew the buttons to push. J.J. was happy to have the position. It paid him handsomely. J.J. closed the bar at midnight of the previous evening. It was one of only two days of the entire year that the bar closed before 2 A.M. The bar closed early on Christmas and today, which was Leap Day. Christmas was on purpose, Leap Day was some nonsense about the liquor license not recognizing the date or some other bullshit that J.J. did not pay much attention to, or was of great concern to him. All he knew was that right now, he needed to shake his ass, get the bar in order, and open on time. As J.J. approached the bar and started to unlock cabinets and put items in order, his eyes focused upon two brandy glasses and a bottle of expensive brandy sitting on a stainless-steel counter next to the wash sink.

"Shit, damn! I hope no one else saw this. I must have blown it last night and missed this. How the hell did I miss this?"

J.J. spoke aloud to the walls as he quickly scooped up the evidence, dumped the glasses in the wash sink and tucked the brandy bottle away in the proper cabinet.

"Shit, I gotta stop sneakin' hits of hooch. Must have caught a buzz and missed that bottle and those glasses while locking that up for the night. The last thing that I need is to lose my job for not lockin' up stuff. I swear that I cleaned everything up. I swear that I did."

Wayne Hampstead's Testimony

"Yes, it is a little strange, but more power to him. He worked hard for a long, long time. Jake decided what he really wanted out of life, and he took it. Shit man, the guy never stopped working, traveling all over the place. It must have grown wearisome. When he packed it all in and retired, then I guess the townhouse no longer fit into his plans."

I was with the property manager and we were showing a realtor the townhouse property that my best friend, Mr. Jacob McCabe, left entrusted to me to take care of. The realtor looked all around, and within a few minutes of inspection, the realtor could easily see that the home was in pristine condition. I could tell in the realtor's mind that there was little doubt that the home would sell quickly.

I was not going to tell them the strange details of his wild story, nor mention the letter that Jake left for me before he went to Boston. A long letter detailing his wishes for me to sell the townhouse. This was after Jake, for the most part, and quite honestly, virtually gave the property to me for the meager sum of one thousand dollars, and for lack of any other description, Jake sold it to me. All that Jake asked in the letter was to give half of the proceeds of the sale to his two children and grandchildren, and I was free to keep the rest of the money. The only other condition that Jake requested of me was for me to run his internet company for a few years, and when his grandchildren were old enough, I was to sell it to them for a few dollars. In the meantime, I was free to take some profits from the company. Good thing I had this business, since the corporate jacklegs running the company where Jake and I had worked together had run the company into the ground. Yes, a grand business, gone. They had to move the production overseas. Some bullshit about, "Duty to the shareholders." Now, the shareholders have stocks they can wipe their asses with and that is about all. Jake was correct because it was all absurd. Now, I needed the money, so the internet gig was perfect. Jake McCabe was one helluva nice guy. Exactly as Jake had specified in his letter, I worked the details out with his attorney. Jake had made it legal and meticulously planned every detail of all of this ahead of time.

As the two men looked around, and I knocked a few cobwebs down with my hands, I thought to myself, that this was certainly one of the strangest and most unexplainable damn things that I had ever heard of, not to mention that I had actually experienced.

No doubt.

I was a happily married family man, so I needed to remind myself never to go for a damn nightcap in a hotel in Boston.

On the other hand, it might be interesting.

"I guess so, Wayne. Sure, I will miss him. Helluva nice guy. Not that we saw him that much anyhow. In my next life, I want to come back as Jake McCabe. He is a cool dude," the property manager said as he fiddled with the sliding door, which led to the deck. The property manager opened the door, and I stepped out on the deck, along with the anxious realtor.

"I can turn this over quickly, especially with that view of Philadelphia," the realtor drooled as he snapped a few photos from the deck.

He sensed an easy commission, a quick sale.

I heard the door to the deck open and turned my attention to the property manager.

While standing on the deck, with one foot remaining in the living room of the townhouse, the property manager asked me, "Do you know where Jake went off to, Wayne?"

I thought about it for a minute or two and then decided it was best to remain vague in my answer. Not that anyone would believe the story anyhow.

Why even try?

I shook my head and smiled, while I told them both, "Nah, not really. I just know that wherever he is, or whatever time of the day it is, that knowing, Jake McCabe, he is enjoying a well-deserved nightcap right about now."

THE END

The Kingdom of Aedan

A Fantasy Story for Children of All Ages

Paul John Hausleben

The Kingdom of Aedan

Chapter One

Tell Us a Story

I settled into my easy chair and with a long exhale; I leaned back. It had been a long day; in fact, it had been a long week. The duties of the office of the Bishop of the Northeastern Lutheran District were more demanding than I had originally thought they would be. My predecessor, Bishop Werner Clodhopper Beck Von Houten, seemed to have the position down pat. He was out on the golf course every day. I must be doing something wrong, because I was running hard, and could never seem to get out from underneath the cavalcade of paperwork, appointments, requests for writing of papers, and religious opinions and most of all, the endless telephone calls and silly emails.

Despite the demands, I rather enjoyed the position, and surprisingly, I did not miss being in the pulpit every Sunday. Perhaps, someday, I would return to a full-time pulpit assignment, but right for now, I enjoyed being an "executive" and having more time home with my family, rather than attending endless late-night meetings at the church, and playing referee to petty arguments that would spring up within the various church committees.

Although we were still members of Reunion Lutheran Church, which was the church where I originally served as Senior Pastor, we primarily attended a local Lutheran church here, close to our new home in Great Falls, New Jersey. My lovely wife, Binky and our two children, Paul William, and Heather Sarah, enjoyed the church and Sunday school too, and the church home fits our family, as well as our personalities. We missed Reunion Lutheran Church, it was the first church I served (and the only one to this point) and my family and I had fond memories of the parsonage, the grounds, the people, and the church, but geographically, Reunion Lutheran Church was quite a long drive away from our new home.

When we attended church services, we managed most of the time, to fly under the radar, so to speak, and while most of the folks knew that I was Bishop Paul John Henson, they were polite enough to leave my family and me in peace, to worship as a family and enjoy the services. Most people still called me Pastor Paul, or by my old hockey jersey number nickname of number twenty-seven, and that suited me just fine. I did preach on occasion at this new church, as well as at Reunion Lutheran and on the church circuit, when it was a special occasion, such as funerals or special holidays or events. I only preached upon invitation and I tried my best to keep a very low profile.

Now, the week was over and I was going to relax. My plans included not doing anything. It was time to goof off all weekend. In fact, I was fairly sure that we would sleep in on Sunday and skip worship service completely. After all, it was a day of rest.

I picked up the guide to the television stations and show schedule from the end table next to my faithful easy chair, and perused them for the time, channel and listing for the New York Rovers hockey game. It was a Friday evening, and Binky had prepared an awesome meal of beef stew and a wonderful dessert of homemade cherry pie. I ate way too much, but Binky was, in my opinion, the world's greatest cook. Now, I planned to settle in by watching the hockey game, and perhaps snoozing a bit in my easy chair.

I could hear Binky and the children finishing the cleanup of the dishes and the dinner, and I caught the chatter out of the kitchen. Ah hah! Here it is . . . continuous sports. Sports all the time, twenty-four seven, three-sixty-five. They broadcast all of this happiness on channel two hundred and something or other on the cable network box. Sports were big businesses these days. Now, I just needed to dial up channel two hundred or something. Therein was the challenge. My uneducated attempts at pushing of the buttons on the remote-control hand unit for the somewhat sadistic cable box ended in futility. The box did not cooperate, because I continually dialed in channel twenty, instead of being in the two hundred ranges of channels. Who has time to watch two hundred or more channels? Oh, geezzzz! I can never figure out these newfangled cable box thingys. I was going to need either Paul William or Heather Sarah to show me how it works. My children were both experts at operating this tricky device. I surely wished that we just had those ten or so channels as we used to have, with a plain, old antenna on the roof.

It was so much easier!

"Twenty-seven! How about a few lemon tarts that I made this afternoon for a snack? They are your favorites! I have my hands on them in the refrigerator!" Binky was yelling at me from far off in the confines of the kitchen.

Oh yeah. Binky made my favorite homemade snack. A full tum-tum, lemon tarts, and a hockey game. The Rovers versus the Philly Comets.

This is living.

"Please! Yes, I would love them!"

"Okay, dear husband. I will have one too. The children are having chocolate pudding. The children and I are finished in here and we will come join you in a second!"

"Okay, Binky. Do you want me to come to the kitchen and help you?"

"No, no, no, you relax, twenty-seven, I have it!"

I could have done without the yelling at the top of our lungs, back and forth, but it was all good. My wife was waiting on me hand and foot. A gorgeous woman such as my wife, Binky Hobnobber Henson was attending to my every need and desire, and my two wonderful children by her side.

I am a lucky man.

Oh yes, and homemade snacks, and a hockey game. In addition, Shambley is going to be the starting goalie in the net for the Rovers tonight. I rubbed my hands in glee and tried my best to turn the television onto the correct channel with the remote control. I still could not even figure that out, but I knew assistance from a ten-year-old was on the way.

Then, my happy balloon came down to the ground with a loud thud.

Binky called out, "We are going to have a nice, quiet family night together! I hope you are not trying to turn on the television and watch a hockey game! You cannot figure out the cable box or remote control, without Paul William or Heather Sarah's assistance anyway, my dear husband. Am I not, correct?"

I froze in time with the evil and perplexing remote control in my hand, as I pointed it towards the television, pushing every single button on the control in vain.

Oh no! A quiet family night together. What about the Rovers and the Comets? I heard a noise and realized that Binky and the children were on their way from the kitchen. I saw the light go out in the kitchen and heard footsteps and voices. In a vain effort to hide my true intentions, I put the remote control down and kicked it with my feet so it went under the chair's footrest. I grabbed the television listings and crammed them back into the stand next to my chair.

"Oh, wow! That sounds wonderful, Binky." I babbled like a fool, while trying to hide the listings, and turn the page to another day.

Binky entered the living room, leaned over, and pushed the "off" button on the television. The television screen darkened, along with the prospects of watching a hockey game. Our two children followed Binky. The children were obviously ecstatic to spend time with their father and Binky beamed proudly as she stood in front of me, proudly presenting the offering of her magical home-baked lemon tarts on a plate in one hand, and the children's snacks in the other. She placed the dishes down on a coaster on the end table, walked over, and handed me my dish of lemon tarts. My goodness, they smelled so wonderful! She smiled, posed, while fluffing her long, blonde hair and tugging at her form-fitting dress. My wife was a goddess. Even after giving birth to two children, her figure remained amazing and captivating. I loved Binky dearly and fully and she was indeed the perfect wife and companion. Our two children, Paul William and Heather Sarah, lined up in a row next to their mother and smiled while staring at me.

"Oh, Paul, we have been so fondly looking forward to spending a nice, family evening together! Please do not put your footrest down. I have to pick up the remote control that you just used, but despite your efforts, you could not figure out how to operate the complex device. Then in an effort to hide your true intentions of watching the hockey game from us, you tried in vain, to hide the device under your chair. Before it becomes broken, please, let me put it in the stand here next to your chair."

Binky smiled, reached down, and pulled the remote from the rather poor hiding spot that I had selected. She then placed it in the stand, while saying, "I will put it here next to the listings for the television channels so that we will know where it is. You know, the paper listings, which you just were checking, while trying to find out what channel the hockey game was going to be on."

Oh, oh! Busted and seized by the Binky Hobnobber

Henson radar once again. Binky could compete with anyone for the title of the world's greatest detective. I do not know why I even tried; you would think after fifteen years of marriage that I would know better.

"Oh, thank you for the snack, my dear Binky. I was not actually. . .."

"Oh, it is no trouble at all, dear Paul. Shambley is a bum anyway, so I do not know why you would even have any interest in watching the game tonight. The Comets will beat the Rovers to a pulp and, all you would do is rant and rave about how in your day that was an easy save, and how in your day, they used to play the game this way or that way. A nice, family night, with your loving children and loyal and sexy wife, is a much better pastime than another frustrating hockey game. There are at least forty more games remaining in the season to watch Shambley demonstrate his poor goaltending skills and for you to rant and rave about the old days. The children and I have been researching the leading goaltending statistics for the league this year. Our research indicated that Shambley's chances of finishing this season with less than a three-point five zero goals against average are very slim."

Binky stood next to Paul William and Heather Sarah and while standing at attention in a perfect line, they all nodded their patented, extended head nods in unison, while smiling at me. Shambley was toast when caught in a round of fire-breathing Binky research. Binky was correct because Shambley was a bum. I found myself following the rather dizzying head nods, and my own head was bobbing along in time with them. The Hobnobber head-nodding genes, as well as the research bug, were both strong ones and Binky passed them on rather effectively to our offspring.

Paul William was a huge hockey fan, as well as a New York Rovers fan, and he piped up, "Dear Mother is correct. Shambley is a bum. The Rovers will lose big time tonight."

Off all of them went again, nodding and agreeing. I sat back in my chair and sighed. I decided to wait until the head nodding was complete. I picked up one of my tarts and took a bite of it while watching the three of them finally run out of nodding propulsion.

Doom, doom, doom. The hockey game was fading rapidly from the evening's landscape. Yet, with a swallow of tart magic, I admitted that real men face up to their fate.

"So, gang. What did you have in mind for tonight? A board game, listening to music, or a special television program. Not a hockey game. No, no, no . . . we can watch hockey anytime. I do agree that Shambley is struggling, and I did not want to watch the Rovers get beat up tonight."

I fudged and flubbed my way through wave after wave of false enthusiasm.

"We want to hear a special story, dear Father. A good one!" Heather Sarah smiled at me. She was the spitting image of her mother now, except for her curly, red-haired locks tumbling down her shoulders in long and glorious waves, instead of her mother's blonde hair. She acted like Binky, stood like Binky, researched and checked into every detail as her mother did.

And she was just as gorgeous as her mother was. As well as a bit on the persistent side too.

Paul William was growing into quite the young man. He was around thirteen years of age or so now, and his sister was ten years old and a few months more. They still loved to all sit around and hear their father tell stories. I am not quite sure exactly why.

Paul was the older big brother, and he acted like it, too. He was tall. It appeared as if he was going to be as tall as I am or even taller than I am, and I was six feet five or thereabouts. He wore his blonde hair long, even just a bit longer than I wore my "hippie" length hair. Binky would never allow either of us to cut it shorter. He stood tall and strong, with an athletic build. It might have been my imagination, but he seemed as if he had started to look more like me every day. When he was younger, he was looking more like Binky, but now as he grew older, his face and appearance had started to change.

Heather Sarah climbed up into the chair next to me and forced me to scoot over, so she could sit as close to me as she possibly could. She was very much my little girl. She no longer carried her ever-present "Fritzie" the stuffed doggie with her everywhere she went, as she did when she was younger, but she still loved to hang around her father.

"A story, eh? Okay, how about a Bible story?" I stopped in mid-suggestion as a rapid and furious round of negative head nods began.

"You always tell a Bible story. We have heard so many of them already. Please not tonight, Father." Heather was rather forthright in her opinion, and certainly not afraid to share it either.

"Okay. How about I tell you about the time that Uncle Harry and I went to the. …

More "no" head nods mixed with soft groans to indicate that the gang had their fill of the seemingly endless adventures of their father and his best friend.

Paul William joined the chorus with his sister now, "We are sick of hearing those same old, Harry and Paul adventures. How many more can there be?"

I thought to myself. Ha! Little did he ever imagine how many more there were. Now, some would have to wait a few more years for the children to be a bit older for me to tell *those* stories!

"Something new and different, Father. Tell us a new, new, new, kind of story!"

"Okay, how about the time, Grandpa Henson. . ..

Nope, more head nods.

"All right now, Pussface the cat. . .."

Nope. More negative feedback. I was running out of

characters and I had many of them. Tonight, this was a tough crowd.

Binky sat on the edge of the sofa next to the chair, took a fork-full of her lemon tart, took a bite, and she smiled.

She chuckled a little at my current predicament and said, "Not so easy now, is it, Pastor Paul. The story well deepth in thy groundth doth not overfloweth tonight, eh?"

"Um, let's see, now. How about a story about the brave and fearless, Sergeant Walter P. Thrump and the time that he scaled the side of the. . .?"

Nope.

"I know!" I shouted enthusiastically. "The mysterious, quiet stranger in the black hat that I met. . .."

More negative indications. I picked up my dish and finished off the rest of the lemon tart in one gulp.

Binky laughed aloud.

She stood up and said, "While you dig deeper into the story vault, I will get you another lemon tart, dear Paul. I am sure after another one or two tarts, the stories will be rolling out of your mind like a runaway train."

"Thank you, Binky. I hope so." I handed her the empty dish and my fork and watched as she wiggled off to the kitchen to refill my glass. I thought, as I watched my wife walk away, what a gorgeous woman.

As I studied her glorious body from a rear view, I recalled the time that Binky and I drank a bit too much at a fancy shindig and we. . ..

Oh no. No, that story would never work.

After all, this was a family night and these are our children!

I sat back in the chair and Heather Sarah laughed at my stumbling for a story. The two children leaned into me rather intensely while studying my face for an idea of where I might be thinking to dig up a story from. My goodness, the pressure was on here. It was a full-on story assault.

Binky returned and handed me another tart. I was seeking some type of inspiration, be it food, mind, or otherwise.

"Thank you," I said, while taking a bite. My goodness that hit the spot. It was delicious. My wife was an awesome cook.

"Well, oh thou wisest of them all, twenty-seven. What haveth you decided?" Binky asked as she settled back into the sofa next to me.

I had been praying a little under my breath and suddenly, a faint whiff of inspiration and a glimmer of hope appeared on the stark, empty, bleak story horizon. Binky's Olde English phrasing while poking fun at me struck a chord within my mind.

I leaned in and smiled as I began to tell a story.

Chapter Two

A Wonderful Life in the Kingdom of Aedan

A long, long time ago in a time and place that history still has never recorded, or even known about, there was a wonderful place called the Kingdom of Aedan. It existed long before the birth of Jesus, in the land of Cymru, or what we now call Wales, or some people still call Cymru. The Kingdom of Aedan existed even before the Romans arrived in the British Islands, long before the legends of King Arthur. Long before them all.

It was a place full of peace, full of wonder, and full of joy.

The Kingdom of Aedan was near Caergybi, on the top of the Northern Dog. It sat upon the top of the flatlands of high, rocky cliffs, which overlooked the ocean, and the kingdom was full of beauty. Rolling green hills, gentle, idyllic, with breathtaking sunsets and stunning sunrises peeking over the top of the cliffs, of which towered over the vast ocean. The meadows of Aedan overflowed with colorful flowers in the springtime and summer, and wild strawberries and fabulous blueberries grew in and amongst the flowers in the fields and meadows. Fantastic and majestic trees dotted the landscape, and they all grew tall and strong and were filled with tasty fruits and berries to eat. The trees, filled with wonderful red, yellow, and golden leaves in the autumn.

Even the winters were gentle, with fresh, crisp snow that gently drifted over the landscape and covered the land in mirrors of white, glistening snow. In addition, cold, tumbling rivers emptied into deep, blue colored lakes, teeming full of fish, and rimmed with other wildlife.

The people, who lived in the Kingdom of Aedan, were peaceful people, who farmed the land, fished in the ocean and the rivers, and made tools and precious jewelry from the metals that they dug from the soils, and wove wonderful clothes from the wool of the flocks of sheep they kept in the fields and meadows.

The Kingdom of Aedan had no military to defend them, because there were no wars or other kingdoms around to attack them, and attempt to overtake their land. Only a small contingent of Castle Guard Knights guarded the castle and Kingdom of Aedan. The knights, endlessly and faithfully, guarded them from no actual or perceived threats.

The people of the Kingdom of Aedan worked hard to produce and grow their food, and to build their houses, and to market the fish they caught from the ocean, rivers, and lakes. They married and had children, and taught the generations of children, by telling stories of old heroes and legends, and of faraway places.

No one ever grew sick here in the Kingdom of Aedan. It was a place of enchantment where people simply grew old and died in their sleep, in peace, without pain or suffering. The Kingdom of Aedan knew no pain, it knew no wars, or sickness, or mean spirits, and it only knew peace, joy and hope.

Aedan was the land of plenty, and a wise king named Aneirin ruled Aedan. Aneirin now ruled the kingdom as the many generations of his family had ruled before him. The family had been the kings and queens of Aedan for longer than anyone ever knew or could even recall. King Aneirin's name meant "noble" in their native language and he was indeed a noble king, as his father was before him, and his grandfather was too. No one knew how they came to be the rulers of the Kingdom of Aedan and no one actually seemed to be concerned. The long succession of kings and queens treated the people fairly, they did not demand much in taxes, the royalty only received some trinkets, some precious metals, food from the field, and in turn, King Aneirin protected the people from nothing but their own people. The laws were fair, the rule breakers were rare, and when rules were broken, all the judgments from King Aneirin were fair and honest. Everything was wonderful in the Kingdom of Aedan.

There were some peculiar traditions in and amongst the rulers. Traditions of which had origins, long since lost in the past, yet, they persevered, for no actual reasons that any one person could explain. One persistent tradition was that the descendants of Aneirin for generations, and now Aneirin himself, always married from a noble family line. They married from families who were wealthier than the common workers were, families who worked in metal trading, or owned the farmlands, rather than the families who worked in them, or families who created fine wines from the fruits and berries of the land.

Only from a very select group of young women were the princes of the kingdom allowed to select a fair maiden to consider for marriage. These special groups of women, who were usually blonde-haired, were all born into these more elite families or if the royal line now fell upon a future queen, the princesses could only choose to marry from the noble families and they could only select blonde-haired men. The nobles arranged and determined the marriages, long before the children grew even to know each other, it was the way it had always been, and always would be.

Aneirin knew his future queen from the time that both of them were ten years old, and the marriage was set in stone between the two families from a very young age.

When he was just nineteen years of age, King Aneirin

married his beautiful Queen Anwen, who was a tall, blonde-haired woman with blue eyes and striking beauty. In fact, her name in their native language, translated to "very beautiful" and Queen Anwen's appearance fit her name perfectly. Together, they had three children; the firstborn son's name was Trahearn, which meant, "hard as iron." His father decided upon that name. From the first moment that he saw his son, he could tell he was going to be tall, strong, and fearless.

The second child born to King Aneirin and his lovely queen was another son. This son was now second in line to be the ruler of the Kingdom of Aedan, behind his older brother. The younger son received the name of Bran. His name meant "a raven or black bird" in their language, and King Aneirin chose that name from the bird, in which he saw sitting outside the window of the room, where his wife was giving birth to his second son. The bird remained on his perch, observing and chattering during the entire labor of his wife, and the bird flew away when their son arrived in the world, healthy and well.

The good king interpreted the arrival of the bird as if it was a sign from above, and he felt strongly that his son should receive the name from the remarkable appearance of the bird on that day.

The last child born to King Aneirin and Queen Anwen was a precious little girl. Her blonde hair and striking beauty, even as a little baby, let everyone know right away that she was Anwen's daughter. Her name was Eirian, which meant "bright and beautiful."

Together, the royal family lived a happy life in a large and fabulous castle, which the greatest of the tradesmen of the kingdom, constructed long ago of the finest wood and special quarried stone. It had majestic doors and windows, made from the precious metals taken from the earth and given by the workers in the Kingdom of Aedan to honor their king and queen. They had golden thrones made from gold found in the ground and they drank fine wine in silver goblets. The wines came from glorious vineyards of grapes that grew upon the wide and sunny hillsides of fertile soils perched upon the high cliffs of the kingdom. The royal family ate meals of only the best food, prepared by the finest chefs in the entire kingdom. The royal family all lived happily in the magnificent castle, and King Aneirin and his family ruled the land peacefully and faithfully.

For now, all was well in the fabulous Kingdom of Aedan.

Chapter Three

The Wise Sage of the River

Sir Faydearn, a loyal knight, was in charge of the guarding of King Aneirin's castle and of preserving peace throughout the land. He was tall, strong, brave, and fearless. The loyal knight was intensely loyal to the king and queen. He was the latest descendant of a line of knights that had traversed history and time. The history of the knights was so vague and so long ago that no one even knew how old the line of descendants was. Sir Faydearn's father served King Aneirin's father, and his grandfather served the king before him.

Presently, Sir Faydearn was the leader of a small group of knights, who were equipped for battle in case some far-off enemy invaded the Kingdom of Aedan in an attempt to overtake the land and overthrow the monarchy. The knights also trained to settle some type of rare uprising amongst the people of the kingdom. Yet, despite the faithful training, there were no threats to the peaceful Kingdom of Aedan. No one or any countries ever attacked or even arrived to visit the kingdom. On rare occasions, a stray ship would appear on the horizon of the ocean and drift into anchor in a safe haven amongst the cliffs, or a random visitor would wander into the kingdom. The team of knights would meet them to make sure the visitors meant no harm to anyone. Often, the visitors traded goods, jewelry, fish, fruits, or other food or products. The visitors told fabulous tales of far-off lands to the people in the Kingdom of Aedan, and inspired the local people to dream.

Then, the visitors were on their way once more.

Sir Faydearn did not particularly desire any visitors to stop and visit his beloved Kingdom of Aedan. He was wise beyond his years and he knew and had learned all too well from his father and grandfather the stories of old. They had taught and warned the wise knight that trouble and despair eventually would come to the kingdom, in which he swore to defend. Sir Faydearn knew from the intense teachings of his ancestors that despite their best efforts, trouble would eventually arrive, and that it would come from afar. Therefore, despite the peaceful atmosphere, the brave knight remained ever vigilant and always on duty.

One of the more important duties of the leader of the Castle Knights was to mentor, protect, and teach the young princes of the Royal Family to be men and to be leaders. Just as his father did before him when he taught King Aneirin, Sir Faydearn taught the two young princes, Prince Trahearn and Prince Bran, to defend their honor and themselves in a battle or in a dispute. He taught them how to fish and hunt, and how to tell the stories that told the history of the Kingdom of Aedan, and to speak, read, and write their language. The knight taught them how to observe and know the ways of the land, how to hike the forests and hills, how to treat the people with respect and, most of all, how to become skilled and strong leaders.

Sir Faydearn recognized immediately that Prince Trahearn was interested, and intensely loyal to the royal cause, and he deeply loved his father and his mother, and his brother and sister. As the years went on, Trahearn grew strong, tall, and brave. He was handsome and powerful; he could wrestle and fight with power and with no fear, as well as run fast and jump high. He carefully listened to the lessons that the knight taught them. He was growing into a great man. Sir Faydearn knew that someday, he would make a great king.

The younger prince, Prince Bran, was shorter in stature,

not as strong, slightly overweight from eating too much, and he was terribly lazy. He had very little interest in the things that captivated his brother, and Bran grew tired quickly and wanted to sleep and lounge around. Prince Bran was very different from his older brother; he was not as motivated, not as ambitious, and frankly, not as smart. Sir Faydearn also knew he was selfish and self-centered, and did not care or show affection for his father and mother, nor his brother and sister. Sadly, Prince Bran's self-centeredness made him cranky, unreasonable, and uninterested in the ways of the kingdom or in learning how to be a wise and powerful leader. Bran's main concern was for himself.

The queen herself, as well as the women servants for Queen Anwen, taught Princess Eirian. They taught her the finer points of being a lady and of being a royal princess.

One cool summer day, when Prince Trahearn was around thirteen years old or thereabouts, he went out on his own, exploring, as all young men do sometimes. He brought his fishing pole and gear with him, and despite the wishes and instructions of Sir Faydearn, he ventured into a forest in a different direction, alone. Prince Trahearn had heard magical stories and rumors of a river within the forest, a golden stream, in which was full of golden fish that simply jumped out of the river and into your creel. He was determined on setting out to discover the magical river full of the golden fish. He wandered off, and although he was wise beyond his years, the young prince soon realized that he was hopelessly lost. He followed the sun and watched it through the trees just as Sir Faydearn had been so keen to teach him, but it was to no avail. He spun in every direction, walking for miles, and when he checked his bearings, he found that the sun was now in the wrong direction.

Had the sun moved that much, and now the castle and his home were behind him, or was it in front of him? Prince

Trahearn was confused, upset, and now, despite his bravery, he was now concerned that he could not find his way to return to the castle. Above all, there was no magical river anywhere that he could see.

He set his fishing gear down and Trahearn sat upon some rocks, on what appeared to be the edge of the forest, and ate some fruit that he picked from a tree above his head. Luckily, the forests, and lands of the Kingdom of Aedan were full of wild fruits, berries and other food sources that were abundant and plentiful, and Sir Faydearn had taught him well as to which fruits were good to eat, and to avoid the few fruits that could make you ill, or even worse.

While Trahearn sat on the rock, eating his fruit, he began to ponder what his next move would be, and he realized that the afternoon was now rapidly waning. He only had a few hours of daylight remaining, and he had walked all day. Soon, it will be growing dark and spending the evening in the forest was obviously not what Trahearn had planned. The young prince also knew that his unexplained absence from the castle would cause quite a calamity.

Suddenly, Trahearn thought that he heard a noise emitting from the thickness of the forest, and he quickly jumped to his feet when he saw a man walking out of the forest toward him. The man had come out of the edge of the forest and he now stood before him, looking at Trahearn, and the man keenly studied the young prince.

His appearance was that of an old man. He was very tall, and he wore a brown robe that was long in length and that hung almost to his ankles. The robe had a fringe made of a golden fabric along the bottom edges and the fabric glistened and shone in the remaining sunlight. On his feet, he wore open-toed sandals with some type of symbol on the top of them near the two cross laces. The strange man had a long, white beard and long white hair that hung down to just below his shoulders in length. His hair and beard were both a pure white in appearance, even whiter than the crisp, white snow that fell upon the hills and meadows of the Kingdom of Aedan in the wintertime.

Around his neck, he wore a golden medallion, circular in design, in which was hung by a thin, golden chain to keep it steady upon the old man's chest. Trahearn noticed how striking the medallion was in appearance. Along the edges, it had a circle of small, red stones and the gold as well as the stones caught the dwindling sunlight, and they reflected an eerie glow around the old man. The medallion had a very strange writing engraved upon it, with letters of an alphabet in which Trahearn did not recognize. In his right hand, he held a long staff, in which he appeared to use to assist in keeping him upright and straight. After stopping to study the young prince, the old man shuffled his feet and began to walk closer to Trahearn, and as he did, the young prince observed how the stranger used his wooden staff to steady his legs as he walked along the path in the direction of Trahearn.

As he approached closer, Trahearn poised himself to run, just in case the man meant to bring harm upon the young prince. However, Trahearn felt he could easily escape the old man due to his age and slow pace. Somehow, for some unknown reason, he knew not to run, because the old man had a kind appearance, and Trahearn felt the glow of the strange medallion was enticing him to stay and find out exactly who this strange man was.

The old man shouted as he held his staff above his head at an angle, while he cried into the air, "Fear not! Do not run away, young Prince Trahearn! I have come to help you find your way! Not only to find your way home but also to provide wise guidance in your life!"

He brought the tip of his staff down hard upon the soil at his feet. When the end of the staff hit the ground, Trahearn saw the medallion around his neck illuminate brightly. It changed from the former soft glow; to as if it was on fire, and to Prince Trahearn's utter amazement, all the trees parted wide in the forest. The trees bowed down and bent over without breaking, cracking, or losing a single branch! The birds that were nestled in the bent and moving trees all flew off from their perches and nests and flew into the air, circling by the thousands, fluttering about above their heads, breaking into their secret languages as a joyful song filled the air. When the strange man's staff struck upon the ground, the ground trembled as if it were suffering from a quake and in order not to tumble to his feet; Trahearn held on tightly to the rock that he now stood next to. Because of the parting of the forest, the young prince could see clearly through the trees, and with the trees fully open and all bent over, he could see the castle and his home.

Trahearn was thrilled as well as amazed at the power and magic of the old man's staff. He felt his face break into a wide smile, and he knew that he was safe.

The prince shouted, and he pointed, "The castle! I now know which direction that I turned that caused me to become hopelessly lost. I have found my way! Thank you, for your kindness and assistance."

The old man smiled, held his staff once again high above his head and he waved it again in the air, and the trees returned to their normal position. The medallion no longer glowed with the overpowering light, but the brilliance, instead, returned to its previous lower level. Trahearn was amazed at the wonderful, magical demonstration!

"Who are you? How is it that your staff has such magical powers?"

"I am Afon, the Wise Sage of the River. My name means that I was born and have lived by the river. I have lived here in these forests for a very long time, and I knew your father when he was just a young prince, and his father before him, and his father too! Despite what you think and what you see, I have no magical powers, nor does my staff!

The only power, in which I possess, lies only in my experience and wisdom, which allows me to see things and teach things that others cannot see. You too, can see and do all the things, in which I can do too, since it is only time and experience that you require, my dear young and brave prince. I taught your father once, when he could not find his way, and many people before him too. When you return home to the castle, the brave and wise knight, Sir Faydearn, will tell you the wondrous stories of Afon and my life here next to the river of gold in the forest. It was the good knight who summoned me to find you. He knew of your unauthorized and foolish venture. The brave knight knows of my wisdom."

Trahearn was amazed at the words in which Afon was relating to him. The brave young prince sat upon the rock, gathered his fishing gear and supplies on the ground next to him and he carefully observed Afon and studied every detail about the wise sage.

Trahearn was smart and curious; he pointed at the medallion around his neck and asked, "Afon, with great respect for your words and teachings, I do not fully understand. You must somehow possess more than just wisdom and experience. I feel as if you must have some magic too. The strange medallion around your neck . . . it glowed with a light, in a brilliance and manner of which I have never seen before, and your staff, when struck upon the ground, opened the forest before my eyes. I saw it! It has special powers like nothing else that I have ever witnessed, or seen, or been taught about by Sir Faydearn."

Afon smiled again. He walked closer to Trahearn and sat on a rock next to the young prince. He reached inside of his robe, and he pulled out another gold medallion. This medallion was the same in details, stones and materials as the one around Afon's neck, only it was smaller and did not have a thin, golden chain. It was as if it was a golden coin. Afon reached out his hand with the smaller medallion inside of it and gently grabbed Trahearn's hand.

He placed the medallion inside of Trahearn's hand while explaining, "The medallions and the staff, will only be what you believe them to be. Despite what you witnessed, please, lose your stubborn ways. Try to understand that there is no magic in the world that we do not already have within our hearts, and neither the staff, nor the medallions, possess any special magical powers. In this world, there is only the wisdom and love that you alone learn and possess. Those, who possess the staff and the medallions, always use that love and wisdom for good and for kind ways. The medallion reminds you to trust in yourself, to trust in your heart and open your eyes to experience, love, and kindness. That is what the inscription engraved upon them teaches us. The staff is a reminder that when you are lost in the world, emotions such as love, and hope and trust will always guide you back to your home and to your loved ones."

Afon finished speaking and the wise sage looked up to the sky. He studied the sunset and then he scanned the details of the forest all around them. Trahearn noticed how the color of his eyes changed first from their normal bright blue to a striking gold, then a bright yellow, and then a deep red as he scanned the world around them. The revolving prisms in the colors of his eyes mirrored the colors of the two medallions. When Afon once again looked at the young prince, the color of his eyes had once again returned to their usual deep blue color.

Afon pointed to the strange words printed on the edges of the medallion.

While pointing to each individual word, Afon read the inscription, "We all have the power to believe and to see. Always trust the love and the true feelings within your heart to guide your path."

When he finished reading the inscription, the wise sage looked at the young prince and proclaimed, "That is why you became lost! Were you not taught by Sir Faydearn not to venture into the forest, without a map, or a sound and earnest plan?"

Trahearn nodded and softly said, "Yes, he warned me of the dangers, but I heard of a legend of a golden river that meanders here within the forest . . . a river that is filled with golden fish. I dreamed of catching a golden fish. A fish that would jump out of the river and into my creel."

Afon laughed and said, "You see, you were led astray by a false tale, by a hope of easy wealth, a prize earned without endeavor, and you did not trust the true feelings within your heart. You already knew what was right and what was wrong, yet, you became blind because of the thoughts of golden rivers and fish that would jump out of the stream and into your creel without effort. There is no golden river with golden fish that will magically jump into your creel without effort. Nothing, which is truly very beneficial, will come in this life without hard work and supreme effort, young prince. Nothing worthwhile is ever easy, and the person who tells you that, or believes it to be true, well, they are fools. They do not know the words of the medallion. Always trust the love and the true feelings within your heart to guide your path."

"Is that really what these words mean, Afon?" Trahearn asked while studying the strange inscription on the medallion.

"Yes! I just read them to you. Please believe. They say in an ancient language, a language that is even older than the language of Cymru, we all have the power to believe and to see. Wisdom and love will never fail you. Remember, your eyes will deceive you, but your heart never will. Always follow your heart, young prince. Trust only the eyes of your heart."

Trahearn smiled, because he now understood the lesson in which Afon had taught him.

"You will keep that medallion of which I just gave to

you, in order to remind you of the lesson, to guide you, and to provide comfort, in your time of desire or need. Remember. The medallion has no special powers, unless you empower it, young Trahearn. Now, listen carefully, young prince. Hear and heed my words and trust them. You will make a great king, and I can see waves of a great tumult coming! Waves, which will come crashing into the shores of the Kingdom of Aedan!"

Afon now stood up on his feet and he became animated and excited. He waved his staff violently in the air above his head. His eyes once again rotated through the color spectrum and the medallion around his neck glowed brightly once again.

As he stood, he proclaimed, "I have lived for a long time, and the Kingdom of Aedan has known only peace. Peace will become a hollowed out and a wretched dream! The world grows smaller as each day passes us, and peace will not last. Trouble will come to the Kingdom of Aedan from a faraway land. I can sense it and I can see it in my visions. Trouble that you cannot see at this moment, but surely will hear and realize. Nothing, except for wisdom and true love lasts forever and you will face many serious and difficult challenges."

Afon pointed his finger in the direction of Trahearn while he gently placed the tip of his staff upon the ground and his eyes returned to normal.

"Remember the medallion. You are strong and brave, as well as very smart and kind, but you are stubborn. You will break some rules, and the eyes of your heart will lead you in a different path than the traditions of the kingdom allow. Trahearn, please, never deny true love, for the fate of the kingdom will be built upon your love. When the tumult finally arrives, you must remember the lessons of the medallion. Prince Bran is weak and lazy. The future of Aedan will fall upon you! Trahearn, hear my words. Your sister is kind, and she is gentle, but I am afraid that she is very frail. Stand tall and brave. Stand for your people, guard your family and, above all, be true to your own heart. Now, enough talk. Sir Faydearn awaits your return. He will scold you in ways that I cannot. You must return home now. With the medallion in your pocket, and trust in your heart, you will find your way with ease."

Afon waved for Trahearn to stand up and the young prince obeyed the wise sage. He pointed his staff down the pathway through the forest and when he did, the medallion in Trahearn's hand glowed with the same brilliance as the medallion around Afon's neck.

"I see that you have learned your lessons well!"

Afon smiled, Trahearn looked at the pathway and then back in the direction of Afon. But the wise sage had disappeared in a flash of light and a roll of thunder.

Trahearn found his way back to the castle with ease, and upon his arrival home, he wandered into the knight's chambers. Sir Faydearn was very upset with the young prince. The knight strongly scolded him for his disregard of the knight's teachings and for Trahearn forgetting the lessons of how to find your way on a venture. However, Sir Faydearn did not scold him for his wayward journey without permission. When the young prince reached into his pocket, showed the knight the medallion, and as Trahearn told him the tale of meeting Afon, the Wise Sage of the River, Sir Faydearn smiled, and he too reached into his own pocket.

Trahearn was amazed when Sir Faydearn showed him a medallion identical to his own.

The brave knight gently explained, as he motioned for Trahearn to sit next to him, "It was I, who sent you on your way and allowed you to explore. I saw you sneak away through the secret door on the side of the castle, jump the moat, and cross the meadows to go and explore the world. Explore, as all young men your age will, and I knew you would go deep into the forest in search of golden fish and golden rivers. I knew Afon would find you, teach you and guide you, as he did with me, so many years ago. I watched with my heart and summoned Afon to find you with the eyes of my heart. Even though I feared for your safety, young prince, I knew that you had to learn the same lesson that I did when I searched for the same river. Only then, when you now see with your heart and trust what it tells you to do, will you be the man that the Kingdom of Aedan will require to wisely and honestly lead us all."

The knight put his arm around Trahearn and the two golden medallions glowed in the growing darkness of the sunset.

Chapter Four

A Stranger from a Faraway Land Arrives

The next years were wonderful, and young Prince Trahearn grew even taller, stronger and wiser while he grew older. His knowledge of the medallion went with him, and he was handsome and proud.

He was now a man.

Once a year, King Aneirin and Queen Anwen would open the castle for a gala event, right at the harvest time, before the winter set in. They called it the Holiday of the Harvest. There, they celebrated together the good fortune of another year of growing wholesome food and the fine fortunes that they all possessed for living in this fine land. The royal family allowed the people of the kingdom to come into the castle confines and wander the grounds. There together, they all would celebrate the Holiday of the Harvest. The people brought gifts for the royal family, and they served fine foods, the best wine, and featured music performed by only the finest musicians in the land. The people looked forward to the holiday every year; it was a wonderful time, and it showed how the people loved their king and queen and appreciated all they did for them.

When Prince Trahearn was around eighteen years of age, it was a wonderful, peaceful, and extra fruitful year in the Kingdom of Aedan. The weather had allowed the fields to be extra abundant, and the harvest overflowed the barns and storage bins. The Holiday of the Harvest was upon them now, and the growing season had been exceptionally bountiful to everyone living in the Kingdom of Aedan.

A grand celebration was underway, and this year was extra special to King Aneirin and Queen Anwen. This year, at the celebration, they would introduce their gallant Prince Trahearn to the young woman they had arranged to be his wife, and eventually the couple would become the future king and queen of the kingdom. She came from a noble family, a family of jewelry makers, who acquired land of value, and had worked to obtain prestige within the kingdom. They worked in the finest gold and produced trinkets and jewelry of high quality for the king in order to influence his decision. When the noble family presented their beautiful daughter, whose name was Blodeuyn, (which meant flower in their language) they did so with much pride. She was tall, and blonde-haired, with sparkling blue eyes, and wide hips suitable for bearing many children. King Aneirin was very pleased, as was the queen, and the families quickly agreed upon the union. Before Trahearn could even speak, his parents proposed the date of the marriage, agreed to all the terms, and finalized the plans. When a large crowd had gathered and the first feast dinner was well underway, King Aneirin summoned his firstborn son and the beautiful Blodeuyn to the throne above the grand hallway of the castle. There amongst many of the people of the kingdom, the king, the queen, and the mother and father of Blodeuyn, proudly toasted with the finest wine, the arrangement of the future union of Blodeuyn and Trahearn.

While Trahearn looked upon the young lady who was to be his future wife, he did see a beautiful woman standing next to him, she had stars in her eyes at her amazing good fortune at her betrothal to the prince, yet, for some reason, Prince Trahearn was uncomfortable with all of this. The young prince was indeed, as Afon had told him, rather stubborn, and while he had to acknowledge that Blodeuyn was very attractive and quite appealing, he had a powerful question. Why could he not choose his own wife? He found his mind wandering, and his eyes moved from the smiling and lovely face of Blodeuyn to the crowd gathered beneath them.

From his lofty post, high above the grand hallway, he saw in the applauding and wildly excited crowd, someone else. . ..

A young woman, whose beauty captivated Trahearn, she stood smiling at him, with green eyes shining through the distance, and her red hair tumbling down in waves upon her shoulders. Trahearn could hardly focus any longer. His mind spun around and around, and he could not even hear the words that his father was speaking as he announced his proposed engagement to Blodeuyn. He thought, how he had never, ever, seen such a lovely creature. Her amazing beauty was beyond comparison, beyond description, and it was more than love at first sight, it was a feeling in which Trahearn had never felt before. He then quickly glanced at Blodeuyn, then towards his father, and then at his mother, and his mind was even more confused. He was to marry Blodeuyn. It was the tradition of the royal family, yet this red-haired woman captivated Trahearn. His father would never approve of his meeting with the red-haired woman. After all, she could be, and was most likely, a simple commoner.

His own mind tried hard to convince him, "Erase such thoughts of the red-haired beauty from your mind Trahearn."

However, Trahearn could not stop staring at her. There in and amongst the crowd, his mind and his heart were aglow and then he remembered the medallion. He looked at Blodeuyn, a lovely, captivating woman. His eyes told him of her beauty, undeniable and deeply captivating beauty, but there was something missing, something was not there.

Maybe there was an empty heart inside of her.

He reached in his pocket, felt the medallion and gently pulled it out, while he thought of the words that Afon taught to him, "Remember your eyes will deceive you, but your heart never will. Always follow your heart, young prince."

Trahearn smiled as he saw, with his own eyes, the brilliant glow of the medallion, which he quickly slipped back inside his pocket. He had obtained the answer, of which he had sought. Trahearn thought how foolish it was to choose a wife and honor your love based upon a woman's hair color and her standing within society.

When the festivities ended, and the fanfare died down, Trahearn rushed down into the crowd with Sir Faydearn following him. The knight had followed the eyes of the young prince and he saw they had landed upon the red-haired beauty. While the rest of the royal family was enthralled with the celebration, the knight's keen senses and deep wisdom had alerted him to Trahearn's intentions. He knew all too well the power of true love for a young man's heart. After all, Afon had taught both of them that nothing lasts forever in this world except for wisdom and true love.

Sir Faydearn shouted as he followed the prince, "Prince Trahearn, you cannot, it is forbidden! She is a commoner. A worker in the fields!"

Trahearn turned around and faced the brave and loyal knight, his protector, and in many ways, his second father and a man whom he had great respect for, and he said, "I for one, as you always do too, will follow my heart!"

Sir Faydearn gave chase, but when he felt for his own medallion and pulled it out of his vest pocket to check it, he saw that it too glowed brightly with the answer that he required.

Within a world of turmoil, true love will always prevail.

Trahearn worked his way through the crowd and he eventually met the lovely young lady, who was at first, quite embarrassed and quiet in front of the Royal Prince, but despite the pleas and wishes of Sir Faydearn, they wandered off together, so that no one else could see them. The lovely young woman's name was Celyn, which is the name of the shrub that produces the bright, red berries, which even today we call Holly. She was indeed a commoner, the daughter of a farmer who worked in the fruit and berry fields. Celyn herself assisted in the harvest, and she was strong of body and of spirit. Her character was as perfect as her appearance was; she was pure in heart; she was pure in her soul, and quickly, Trahearn and Celyn fell deeply in love. They kept their love and their seeing one another in secret. Only the trusted knight Sir Faydearn knew of the romance, and they vowed to marry someday, when the prince felt it was the correct time to present to his parents his true intentions.

It was an early winter day shortly after the Holiday of the Harvest, when the forward watch guards of the castle alerted Sir Faydearn to the arrival of a stranger from a faraway land, entering the Kingdom of Aedan from the northern reaches. The Head Knight was ever vigilant and remained always suspicious of any strangers, because he knew the prediction of Afon, and he knew that trouble would come from afar when it finally arrived upon his beloved kingdom. The knights rode out on their horses to meet the stranger who came alone, riding on a horse, with saddlebags packed with supplies and precious metals. The metals that the stranger from a faraway land had in his possession were metals that were very different from the metals in which the Kingdom of Aedan produced from their ground. These metals were dull, not brilliant in appearance, such as the gold and silver that Sir Faydearn was used to seeing, but the stranger's metals were strong, very strong, and when Sir Faydearn struck the dull metal upon the ground, it did not bend, break, nor shatter.

The stranger was peaceful, and he explained in a

language that Sir Faydearn could not fully understand what his intention was for visiting the Kingdom of Aedan. Through gestures and drawings on tablets of stone, and in the soil, Sir Faydearn recognized that the stranger from a faraway land wanted to trade some of his goods for some gold and silver metals of the Kingdom of Aedan. He wanted to make jewelry out of the shiny metals. The brave leader of the royal knights recognized the usefulness of the dull metal to make tools, and if needed, even stronger weapons than the ones his knights currently possessed.

The stranger from a faraway land was tall and handsome, and he had dark hair and his eyes were wider than the eyes of the people of the land of Cymru and the kingdoms were. The stranger brought gifts of jewelry made of the strong, dull metal to give to King Aneirin and Queen Anwen. He did so, because he had heard of the legends of the beauty of the Kingdom of Aedan, and the legends of the wise and gentle king who ruled such a wonderful land. The stranger wanted to pay his respects and proper homage to the wise king. Since the stranger from a faraway land had gifts for the king and for the queen, Sir Faydearn arranged for the visit to occur the next day. He offered the stranger a place to sleep for the night, a place to feed and water his horse, and he bid him a goodnight.

The next morning, early in the day, the knight brought the stranger some food of fruits and berries as well as flattened bread made of flour from the fields. He found the stranger awake, complaining of fever and not feeling well. In addition to his high fever, the stranger had a hoarse cough. Between coughs, the stranger told Sir Faydearn that he felt his head spinning from the long journey. A long journey that brought him through the cold winter's days and nights and forced him to sleep on the cold ground in fields and amongst forests. Due to the stranger's cough and his illness, Sir Faydearn was hesitant to allow the visits with the king and queen. The loyal knight pondered whether to allow the stranger to visit, but in the end, he escorted the stranger to meet with the king and queen in their royal chambers. After a brief exchange of his gifts, some language interpretations, trading of the dull metals for some gold and silver, the stranger from a faraway land left.

He left, but behind him, he left something else; an unseen and unknown enemy. An enemy, which no one had previously experienced before in the wonderful Kingdom of Aedan. He left behind his cough, his dizziness, and his mysterious illness.

One by one, the horrible illness spread throughout the Kingdom of Aedan, and one by one, people died from the horrible disease. Sir Faydearn was ill with despair at not trusting in his feelings and trusting with his heart when he allowed the stranger to enter the castle. Why, oh why, had he not entrusted his medallion? It was a grave error on his part, or perhaps it was not, and because the future had to unfold as predicted, the medallion would have remained silent and dark. Despair and heartbreak overcame the brave knight and no amount of consolation from anyone, even Prince Trahearn, could change his mind. King Aneirin and his royal doctors were powerless to save his people from the fate of the terrible cough. No fruits of the vine worked to remedy the sickness, no wild berries, no special water or wine; everything was worthless in the face of this wretched disease.

When his beloved Queen Anwen and his beautiful daughter, Princess Eirian, both fell ill with the dreaded disease, the good and kind King Aneirin, summoned the leader of the knights of the castle to his quarters, and he pleaded with Sir Faydearn to go into the woods and find Afon. The king reached into his pocket and he pulled out his own golden medallion and held it in the air in front of his brave and loyal assistant.

You see, he too knew of the power of trusting in the eyes

of your heart.

Yet, the medallion remained dark and silent.

The king then instructed the brave knight to, "Go and seek Afon! Please find him, Sir Faydearn! Pick yourself up and help me save the people and the queen and my beloved daughter! Afon will know what to do!" The brave knight would never disobey a direct order from his king, so he saddled his horse and rode off to the forest by the river to find Afon. Prince Trahearn followed him, and when Sir Faydearn discovered that the young prince was in tow, he allowed him to come along on the mission.

When they reached the edge of the forest near the river where Afon lived, they called out his name, and they stood and called, and called.

It was all in vain because Afon would not appear. They called and called some more, but once more, he would not arrive. Puzzled and distraught, the two men sat on the same rock in which Trahearn had sat when he had first met Afon, and they waited. Their wait had no reward, for Afon would not appear. After hours of waiting and calling, the two men realized that summoning Afon was futile, because for some reason, he was silent. Trahearn reached into his pocket, held his medallion in his hand, and gripped it tightly. He looked at Sir Faydearn, who also reached for his medallion.

Both medallions remained dark and silent.

Trahearn spoke, and while he spoke, Sir Faydearn realized how wise the young prince now was, "Perhaps this was all meant to be. It might be the time in which Afon told us, the time to follow what our hearts feel and our eyes cannot see. I think Afon will not appear because he already predicted what was going to happen. You, my brave and trusted, Sir Faydearn, have feared this for years. You prepared your knights for a battle that you knew would arrive someday. Yet, this is a very different type of enemy, an unseen enemy. Defeating an enemy, in which you cannot see, is not easy. The world has become smaller, and maybe, there is nothing that Afon or anyone else can do. This was what was meant to be, it is all for some other purpose."

When Trahearn spoke the words, the medallions glowed in their hands, and the brilliance was brighter than their eyes could stand! They knew their supposition had been correct as to why Afon would not come to them. Their own wisdom had brought the answer to them; Afon could add nothing or help them in any way.

At the realization of the fact that the dreaded prediction of doom was now upon the kingdom, great sorrow overtook them both, and with great haste, they made their way back to the castle. When they finally arrived, Trahearn and Sir Faydearn found the castle life in turmoil; their efforts were in vain, and their arrival without a cure or some type of explanation was too late. Queen Anwen had died, as had the frail Princess Eirian. Within a few days of their deaths, Prince Bran took ill with the dreaded disease and he, too, passed away very quickly.

The terrible disease moved swiftly in its destruction of human life and few survived within the castle walls as well as beyond. King Aneirin was beside himself in sorrow and in grief, as were Trahearn and Sir Faydearn. No amount of consoling could ease the pain of the king! He wallowed away in misery, and passed severe blame upon Sir Faydearn, for allowing the sick stranger to enter the Kingdom of Aedan and to pass this terrible strife upon them all.

Turmoil and terror reigned in the castle and the entire kingdom. Prince Trahearn found refuge in the arms and love of the lovely Celyn. Thankfully, the illness had not befallen her, or her family, and their true love was their only consolation in such a terrible time.

Sir Faydearn was ill with grief; the brave knight filled his own soul with self-doubts as to his misguided judgment, and for not trusting his own feelings in his heart. While he sat alone in his chambers, in his body armor, he held the medallion in his hand and looked upon his own heart for answers. The predictions of these terrible times and events made it no easier for the brave knight to accept or understand.

In grief, the next morning, Sir Faydearn left in silence.

The king had exiled him from the Kingdom of Aedan forever more, for what King Aneirin believed to be a grave and unforgivable error. Despite the years of loyalty and unparalleled service of the brave knight, and the knight's many generations of service to the royals, the downtrodden and sorrow-filled king declared him, as well as his entire family, banished forever to wander the wastelands of Cymru.

The stranger from a faraway land had, perhaps even unbeknownst to him, brought great strife and tumult to the former glorious Kingdom of Aedan and it all transpired, just as Afon had predicted.

Trahearn now felt alone, his land in turmoil, his family lost, his father filled with grief and ill thoughts, and he now needed to decide his own fate along with his lover, Celyn, whilst holding in his mind, heart, and hands, the fate of his beloved land.

Chapter Five

Escape to the Land of the Southern Dog

The illness ran its course and eventually; it faded away, but not until it had enacted a terrible death toll upon the Kingdom of Aedan. The people buried their dead, and now they lived in fear of the return of the unseen enemy, of which they were powerless to defend themselves against in any manner.

Trahearn and Celyn snuck away whenever possible. When they were able to meet covertly, they spent as much time together as they possibly could, without detection or raising suspicion. Now that Sir Faydearn had left the castle, and was living in exile, Trahearn found that his role was to try to lead the small military force of muddled knights who remained in the castle. After the waves of sickness rolled through the kingdom, the battalion of knights grew feeble in spirit and demeanor and without their leader; their ranks were weak and disorganized. Trahearn did his best to boost morale, but he was an inexperienced substitute for such a brave and fine leader as Sir Faydearn was.

Trahearn deeply missed his confidant, mentor and friend, Sir Faydearn, as well as the knight's guidance and care. Trahearn deeply loved his father, but in many ways, Sir Faydearn was even more of a father to him, and Trahearn loved the brave knight with all of his heart. The persistent rumors were that Sir Faydearn had taken his family, and moved to live their lives in exile, to a village near Carmarthen, in the Land of the Southern Dog.

Since the illness befell the Kingdom of Aedan and the tragic deaths occurred within the royal family, King Aneirin had now radically changed in his demeanor. The king, who once was a kind, honest, and fair king, now grew cold, cruel, and iniquitous to Trahearn and the people of Aedan. He was violent with fits of rage and uneven thinking. He took to drinking large amounts of the fruit of the vines and often was drunk with wine, as well as wild thoughts of bitter revenge. He now had a mean spirit and ruled harshly, with cruel, heartless, and selfish intentions. He levied unfair taxes upon the people; minor infractions received heartless punishments and long prison sentences that were very often without fair judgment. The dungeons and prisons of the castle filled with subjects of the Kingdom of Aedan, who had committed minor offenses, or in some cases, no offenses at all!

Trahearn was powerless to speak to his father about his change in behavior, and he recognized that it was grief driven and without proper thinking. Trahearn also deeply and profoundly felt the loss of his mother, sister, and brother, but King Aneirin did not try to even speak with Trahearn or assist him with his own suffering. Rather than supporting his son, and working through their grief together, it now became solely about King Aneirin and his sorrow. His son's emotions were irrelevant, and all the king cared about or spoke about was how fate had dealt him such a tragic and terrible blow. He shut his son out, and all attempts by Trahearn to speak or console the king were futile. King Aneirin had grown bitter beyond description, bitter at life, bitter at fate, and in a strange and roundabout manner, bitter towards his remaining son. The bitterness was far reaching, and it consumed the king's entire soul, as well as mind and his heart.

One morning, in the spring of the next year after the death of some of the royal family, King Aneirin summoned Trahearn to his chambers.

King Aneirin sat upon his golden throne, drunk with the excesses of wine and filled with intense bitterness upon his tongue as he strongly told Trahearn, "Sufficient time has now passed since the tragic and wretched death of my queen, who was also your beloved mother, as well as the deaths of your brother and sister. I am too old to take a wife, or to father any further children. The staff of the rule must now pass to you, Trahearn. You will marry Blodeuyn tomorrow in a quiet celebration, a celebration that is respectful of the loss of those we have loved. A celebration, of which our dead loved ones, cannot attend. Regardless, you will marry, and immediately begin to repopulate the castle with our future heirs and eventually, the rule of the Kingdom of Aedan will fall upon you and your children."

Trahearn's heart leapt with joy because this was the opportunity that he had been waiting for. It was the chance to tell his father that he loved Celyn and his wish to marry her; instead of the unjustly arranged marriage to a woman he did not care about, or had not even seen since the Holiday of the Harvest so long ago.

Trahearn mustered the courage to tell his father his true intentions, "Dear Father. I have so wanted to speak with you about the marriage to Blodeuyn." Trahearn knew he needed to tread carefully here, for his father could easily become enraged. He fumbled and stumbled a bit in his words as he reached into his pocket and held the medallion tightly.

The king leaned forward in his throne and peered in at his son suspiciously; he had little patience for fumbling, and he sensed from his son's body language that this was not going to be a conversation in which he would be very pleased to hear.

"Yes, Trahearn, you have heard my commands. What is there for us to speak about, Trahearn?" King Aneirin said with some element of curiosity.

"Father, I am sure that Blodeuyn would make a fine

wife. She is quite lovely. However, I am in love with another. Her name is Celyn. She works in the fields for the family whose name is Alyce. They work in the fields of berries producing fine fruits for the wines. She is beautiful, with red hair and wonderful green eyes. Our children will be handsome and beautiful and we are deeply in love."

Trahearn stopped speaking as his father rose out of his throne and angrily pounded his fists upon the arms of gold.

King Aneirin shouted, "Enough of this! This is all nonsense. You have heard my command. This foolishness of disobedience will pass from your heart and from your mind. I will no longer listen to this talk. You bring great disrespect upon your mother, and your father. Blodeuyn is blonde in hair, and her features are like your own blessed mother and sister. Your children will be the same. It is the rule of our forefathers, and generations upon generations before both you and me. Have respect. You are Prince Trahearn and I am your father, but I am also your king. The wedding is tomorrow, and it will occur, just as I have ordered by my edict! Now, get out! Out! Out! You wretched son! Your heart is tainted by this evil red-haired witch who has cast a spell of disobedience and covetousness upon your heart, in an effort to blind you, so her inferior bloodline and family can capture our throne."

"That is not true, Father. I love you and honor you, but I am a man, too. My own man. Celyn is wonderful, and someday, the silly traditions and rules of our forefathers had to change. The world would force Aedan to change. It grows smaller. Afon predicted to me that this would happen, he told all of this to me," Trahearn tried in vain to calm his father, but it was to no avail.

"Afon! Wretched and useless, Afon. When we needed his wisdom, he abandoned us. He let my wife, son, and daughter die. Our calls and pleas for his guidance went unanswered."

In his rage and grief, King Aneirin pulled his own medallion out of his robe pocket and tossed it in anger, through an open window where it fell down and landed inside the water canal and moat outside the castle walls. Trahearn ran to the window ledge, and he watched helplessly while the medallion spun in its brilliance as it tumbled through the air and disappeared with a splash in the water.

"Enough of this wayward behavior! Our discussion is over," the enraged king cried out.

Without reason, the king now called for his Castle Guard Knights. He ordered them to escort Trahearn to his chambers and lock him away there until the wedding in the morning. As the knights led the prince away, he overheard his father instruct one of the Castle Guard Knights to bring him more wine, and to seek out this Celyn, bring her to the castle and imprison her in order to kill her!

The Castle Guard Knights were weak, and although Sir Faydearn had trained them, they did not have the skills or power to match the strength and cunning of the young prince. While he was being led down one of the castle hallways to his chamber, he easily overpowered the three escorts, subdued them, and he escaped the castle through a lower hallway window.

Trahearn was wise beyond his age and he knew that his father had grown old, bitter, and tainted. In anticipation of what Trahearn knew could be a similar fate that befell Sir Faydearn, Trahearn one day hid a bag of jewels, golden coins and other worthy and very expensive possessions in a secret hiding place within the castle walls. He did so; with the thought in his mind that someday, he might need to flee the kingdom, with his beloved Celyn, and those possessions would be valuable in their new life together.

That proved to be a very wise decision.

After gathering the hidden possessions from the secret

location, Trahearn's speed and training, allowed the young prince to move quickly from the castle grounds to the farm home of Celyn, and there he explained to her and her family, his father's evil plan. They professed their love for one another in front of her mother and father, and with her parent's blessing, they escaped into the darkness. Celyn's parents gave them their only horse, some supplies, extra clothes, and they were off in a tearful goodbye, but a necessary one.

"But where will you go, brave prince?" Celyn's father asked. He then added, "We are too old and weak now to travel very far. I did not die from the wretched disease, but it weakened me terribly."

"Yes, I understand. Celyn and I will travel far, to the land of the Southern Dog. There is a village near Carmarthen, where I hope to find my friend and mentor, the great knight, Sir Faydearn. There, Celyn and I will settle. It is where we will live, marry, and have many children. I will return. I vow to you, my dear father of my only love, that I will return with the brave knight, someday, to reclaim the former majesty of the Kingdom of Aedan. You have my solemn promise."

After he spoke the words, he reached into his pocket, pulled out the medallion. And they all marveled at the glorious glow that confirmed that Trahearn had spoken with the eyes of his heart.

"Now, here, take some of these golden coins. You will need them to sustain you because you must leave your home and you must hide here in the Kingdom of Aedan. My father and the Castle Guard Knights will be enraged that Celyn, and I have escaped, and they may mean to do you harm. Do you have trusted friends or family that will hide and protect you?"

Celyn's father nodded and reported, "We do. We'll be safe. I assure you. Our friends and family are brave and powerful and the Castle Guard Knights do not frighten us.

Besides, once they search our home and land and find no one here, the knights will assume that we all fled together. Please take our daughter and love her, be safe and we will wait for your glorious return someday."

Trahearn and Celyn escaped through the night, and her family hid from the Castle Guard Knights. The two young lovers journeyed far, and they traveled many miles, for many weeks, until they reached the Land of the Southern Dog.

There, in this new and strange land, no one would know them, and Trahearn could seek out Sir Faydearn. Along with Celyn, the three of them would plan his return. A plan for someday to return to his beloved Kingdom of Aedan.

Chapter Six

A Plan Evolves

In the Land of the Southern Dog, life was difficult. The land was not as fertile and the fishing waters were not as productive as the waters were in the northern land. Shortly upon settling there, Trahearn found a holy man, a friar of sorts, and Celyn and Trahearn were married in a simple and quaint ceremony. It was certainly a ceremony that no one would have expected to be suitable for a prince and his new princess! Then again, in the new land, no one knew them, and Trahearn was happy to remain unrecognized in his new home.

There, with the use of some of the bank of golden coins and other valuable possessions, Trahearn traded for some land, a large acreage, to farm and work to raise some fruit to produce wine and some fruits to sell and prosper with, in their new life. His wife was keen on the proper selection of the farmlands and she was used to such work. Trahearn was lean and his muscles were hard and strong. With hard work and dedication, the patch of land they selected proved to be fruitful. The young couple worked and planted the land. They produced fine fruit, and as a result, the wine they created was of good quality. Very shortly, it was in great demand. Their fame as fine winemakers spread quickly throughout the Land of the Southern Dog.

Soon, a strong son was born to Trahearn and Celyn and they named him after his grandfather, as Trahearn proudly proclaimed that his firstborn son would bear the name of

Aneirin the Second. Then a year or so later, another son was born, and he proudly received the name of Bran the Second, after Trahearn's deceased brother. The young family grew, and they were happy. The Land of the Southern Dog was not home, but for now, it was their adopted home.

One day, while checking his crops for quality and working the land with his tools, Trahearn was surprised to hear a familiar voice calling out his name. He turned and looked to the edge of the planting rows and even from a distance, he knew the voice, the way the man stood. He knew his mannerisms!

He dropped his gardening hoe and ran to greet the loyal knight, Sir Faydearn! Their excitement and emotions overtook the two men, and tears rolled down their faces as the two men embraced and reunited. Trahearn knew in his heart that he would eventually find the old knight, and his dream had come true.

Then again, with the medallion in his pocket, he knew that he could see so much more than just this day of reunion. He now could also see a plan for them and their families to return to their beloved Kingdom of Aedan.

A long day and night of reunion occurred. After a fine meal with great amounts of consumed wine and catching up on lost adventures and time, Sir Faydearn shared news of what he had heard from a traveler passing through as to the latest news from his recent journey through the Kingdom of Aedan.

The brave knight told Trahearn, "Your father, the dear King Aneirin, has grown meaner and meaner. He imprisons people and forces them into hard slavery for the slightest misgivings. It all has grown to be quite terrible to live within the kingdom. The king levies unfair taxes on the people of the kingdom while he also imposes impossible and unfair rules and laws upon the land. He drinks wine in excess, until he is unable to stand, and then he rants and raves as if he has gone mad! King Aneirin's spirit is consumed with intense bitterness, and kindness and forgiveness no longer exist within his heart."

Trahearn's eyes filled with tears and his own spirit crumbled while he listened to the tale of the fate of his father and the beloved Kingdom of Aedan.

Sir Faydearn stood up from his chair at the table and he walked over to Trahearn.

He placed his hand on the young prince's back and softly said, "The Kingdom of Aedan is falling into madness and ruin. You are still the great Prince Trahearn and the future ruler of that great land. You and I both know what it is that you must do, Prince Trahearn. I am still Sir Faydearn, the leader of the Castle Guard Knights, and I have sworn allegiance to the throne of the kingdom, and your father is the king. I have a small team of knights of whom I have trained here. My own son, the young, but brave Sir Fillamore, can be their leader. My son is tall, strong, and he has received the same training as what you have received, the same as all the generations before us and the same as I hope will be many generations after all of us. The Knights of the Southern Dog and my son are loyal to me; they will be loyal to you. I will allow you to lead them, but I cannot go. My heart is too strong to break my oath, even for the good of the kingdom."

Trahearn stood up from his chair and he knew what the implications were of what Sir Faydearn was suggesting. It amounted to treason to his father, and his heart grew sad to think that it had come to this. Sir Faydearn was the descendant of many generations of brave knights who had sworn the same oath, and even Sir Faydearn saw no other solution, but to suggest that his father needed removal from his golden throne and from his position as ruler of the Kingdom of Aedan.

Trahearn looked at the loyal and brave knight and he reached into his pocket and pulled out the medallion. Sir

Faydearn did the same, and the two men focused upon the medallions, while they desperately sought an answer.

No confirmation came. Strangely, the medallions did not glow with the answer to the dilemma.

Trahearn was young, but he was wise, and despite their differences, he deeply loved his father. His heart now broke to think of his loneliness and his bitterness.

He said to Sir Faydearn, "I do think that you are correct. There is no other way. First, I must speak to Afon. I need to make sure what I am going to do is the only way. Afon will guide me and he will know."

When Trahearn finished speaking the words, the medallions glowed brightly, and the colors of them spun in the sunlight and the glow warmed their hearts.

Trahearn smiled, and he proclaimed, "Send me your best knights and tell them to prepare for a battle, Sir Faydearn. I leave my home, my beloved wife, and my children under your brave guard. I will send for you when I have reclaimed the Kingdom of Aedan. First, I will seek Afon in the land of the river, and obtain his guidance and his wise advice. We will all leave in the morning."

After a tearful farewell, a long and passionate kiss for his beloved Celyn, warm hugs to both of his sons, and a handshake and a promise to Sir Faydearn, Trahearn left the Land of the Southern Dog. On the outskirts of the land, he met with Faydearn's son, the brave and honest Sir Fillamore and his team of about fifty knights. This was the small band of knights, which Sir Faydearn and his son had assembled on his behalf.

After a long journey of many weeks, they reached the outskirts of the Kingdom of Aedan. Trahearn left the band of knights and their leader on the edge of the forest as he traveled alone through the thick woods to seek the guidance of Afon, the Wise Sage of the River.

While Prince Trahearn moved through the overgrown paths, he followed the eyes of his heart and his own memories of so long ago, to find the spot where he first met the wise and powerful Afon. When he reached the spot, he held the medallion in his hand and called out to Afon to come, to provide guidance, to answer his calls this time.

After only two loud shouts, which echoed throughout the forest, Prince Trahearn turned around to see the Wise Sage of the River moving through the forest edges to greet him.

"Oh, Afon, you have finally appeared! I need your guidance, your wisdom, and your thoughts. The Kingdom of Aedan is in ruin, my father King Aneirin, no longer sees with the eyes of his heart and his spirit is broken."

Afon seemed surprised at the comments of Prince Trahearn, and he told him, "As I had predicted. Does this really come as a surprise to you? What guidance is it that you seek, young prince? Did I not tell you that I foresaw great tumults?"

The Wise Sage of the River shook his staff in the air, then he struck the ground with the end of the staff and the ground shook and great tremors occurred. Trahearn held onto a tree trunk to prevent himself from toppling over from the force of the ground quaking and shaking from the blow of the staff.

"Look upon your land, Prince Trahearn! Look upon what has become of your once proud and majestic kingdom!"

The trees of the forest opened and bent over once again, as they had done so long ago. Yet this time, no birds flew into the air with songs of praise. Instead of praise, this time there was only sorrow. Trahearn used the eyes of his heart, combined with his medallion and the power of the staff, and he could see the castle and the Kingdom of Aedan in detail before his eyes. Dark clouds hovered over the castle, and the formerly majestic stones of the walls were crumbling. The golden throne was gone, the gold traded in for sorrow. The farmlands were in ruins, with sparse crops grown. The people who wandered around the alleys and streets of the kingdom, all had sunken eyes and faces withered in despair. Their homes were mostly falling down and in disrepair, the streets were dirty, the land was full of darkness, and the kingdom now mired in misery. Prince Trahearn turned away from the pain of what the reality had shown him.

Afon spoke again in a loud voice, as he tugged at his beard, and the medallion around his neck glowed so brightly that Trahearn could no longer look upon it, "You have made a grievous error by running away from the truth, rather than face it, confront it, and accept it! The truth is much the same as is the true love of which you found in the arms of your beloved wife! You cannot hide from the truth any more than your heart can hide from true love. Come over here, here to gaze into this puddle of rain water gathered here on the path."

Afon signaled to Prince Trahearn for him to follow him to a puddle, which had collected water in a sunken hole in the old path in the woods. Trahearn followed the guidance of the wise sage. When Afon motioned for him to lean over and cast a reflection upon the water, Afon asked, "So gaze into the water and what is it that you see, Prince Trahearn?"

"Why, Afon, I see my own image."

"Yes! Of course, and that is the one person in this entire world whom you cannot hide your true feelings from. The truth in your heart will haunt you. You must face it, you need to accept it and never run from it again."

Trahearn nodded and acknowledged that he understood and accepted responsibility for how he did run away, how his beloved homeland now needed him, and it had fallen into ruin without his presence.

"Now, before I offer assistance, tell me why I came so quickly this time, but your calls when the horrible and dark sickness came over the land, fell upon deaf ears."

Trahearn looked at Afon.

He answered quickly, and wisely, "Because, in order for the Kingdom of Aedan to, in some manner, remain and survive, these terrible events must be allowed to occur. The world is closing in, it grows larger all the time, and it was only a matter of time until the Kingdom of Aedan faced ruin, unless we become part of the growing world too."

Afon smiled, and he slowly moved closer to Prince Trahearn.

The Wise Sage of the River loudly proclaimed, "Correct! The truth is in your heart now. I can see how wise you have become as you have grown into a man. You may have run away and made a grievous error, but you are wise and have now learned even more from your mistakes. The glow of your medallion answers your own doubts as to the validity of your answer. You once again, see with the eyes of your heart, as well as the eyes on your face. Now, you must go, and you must reclaim the throne to bring back honor and fairness to the Kingdom of Aedan. You must restore the glory and face the truth. However, most of all, you must teach your own father to once more see with the eyes of his own heart. He tossed his medallion away. And now, he can no longer see. His bitterness and his malice rule his soul. He will learn a painful, but necessary lesson in this way."

Afon reached inside his robe and he revealed pockets set inside the folds. The wise sage carefully showed Prince Trahearn three glass wine bottles tucked inside the folds of his robe.

He handed them one by one to Prince Trahearn and said, "Do not ask me too many questions, Prince Trahearn or you will fail. You must carefully listen, learn, and then follow my directions. Place these wine bottles in your travel bag and once again, listen carefully, Prince Trahearn. This bottle colored in red, is the Wine of Forgiveness."

Trahearn nodded. He took the bottle and carefully

placed it into his bag.

Afon's voice thundered across the forest as he instructed Prince Trahearn, "Next, this bottle colored in green, is the Wine of Kindness."

Trahearn did the same thing, with this bottle and after a quick study of the bottle; he carefully laid it in his bag while reaching out for the last bottle.

"This last one, in this black bottle, you need to be most wary of! In this bottle is the Wine of Bitterness. This wine is the wine, in which man drinks from too often. So often that they are drunk in bitterness. When you reach the edge of the Kingdom of Aedan, as you approach the outskirts of the castle, you must dismount from your horse, stand at attention and close your eyes. The eyes within your heart will guide you to the correct location to stop. Do you understand?"

Prince Trahearn spoke quietly, but with command within his voice, "Yes, wise sage, I understand."

"Good, now, you must follow the sun as it sets, and hold your medallion in your right hand. Your medallion and the eyes of your heart will lead you to dig into the ground next to a special tree. It is a tree that only the eyes of your heart will allow you to find. Out of all the trees in the land, the special tree will reveal itself only to your heart. Once you find the tree and you follow my instructions, you will see that it produces the Fruits of Love and of Hope. The red fruits are the Fruits of Love and the yellow fruits are the Fruits of Hope. Pick equal amounts of each of the fruits and preserve the seeds to grow more trees. For in order to offset the bitterness, deceit, malice, and evil that the future will bring to the entire world, the Fruits of Love and Hope will be required. They will be all that is needed in order to sustain all the people of the world forevermore."

The wise sage lowered his voice and bowed his head in a solemn pose. It was as if he felt the pain and suffering within the world to come.

With his voice, much lower in volume, he continued to speak, "Remember that we are nothing without love and hope! The entire world will need these fruits. Preserve the seeds and sow them with great care so that the trees take root throughout the world. There, in the ground at the width of the crown of the roots of the Tree of Love and Hope, in a location, which the sun will lead you to, you will dig and you will find a simple metal box. A metal box made of the same metal that the foreboding stranger brought with him, along with the diseases that he brought to wrought the land. Inside the box are goblets. There will be one golden goblet, one silver goblet, and one goblet made of stone. You use the golden goblet for the Wine of Forgiveness and the silver goblet for the Wine of Kindness. The golden goblet is the Goblet of Love. The silver goblet is the Goblet of Hope. The stone goblet is for drinking the Wine of Bitterness. That goblet is the Goblet of Despair."

Afon looked sternly at Prince Trahearn and he stared deeply in his eyes while waving the wooden staff in his hand over his head. He obviously wanted to emphasize the point he was about to make, because he shouted out, "Now, pay attention carefully, Prince Trahearn."

"I am listening to every word, Afon," Prince Trahearn acknowledged.

Afon dropped the staff to his side, and he allowed it to rest alongside his body. He kept his hand on the staff, but Afon did not use it to steady himself.

He seemed to be growing even stronger and more powerful as he continued to speak, "There will be little to no battle for control of the Kingdom of Aedan, yet, still arm the battalion to the mightiest level and remain vigilant. Never relax, prepare as if the battle will be fierce. It is as it is in all of life, complacency breeds laziness. The truth is that, since Sir Faydearn left in exile, the knights who remain have long since abandoned training and regimentation. They rule by intimidation and now are weak, disorganized, and poor fighters. You will easily win the battles. When you and your brave team defeat your father and his weak Castle Guard Knights, do not harm even a hair of your father's head in any manner."

After speaking those words and providing the instructions, Afon leaned in and carefully studied the prince's eyes as if to gauge his understanding and his courage.

He now placed his hand on Trahearn's shoulder as he spoke, "Carefully, disguise your appearance and your voice from him and lock him in his own cell, within his own dungeons. There, you will offer him two drinks from the bottles poured into the goblets of his choice. He can choose to drink the wine from only two goblets, and he must drink two of the wines, but he can never have all three. You also will warn him that the Wine of Kindness and the Wine of Forgiveness when drunk together, magically turns the Wine of Bitterness into water and bitterness will exist no more. However, a mere sip of the Wine of Bitterness overcomes the other wines, and reduces them to only water! If he drinks of the two goblets that make the king drunk on forgiveness and kindness, combined with love and hope, then you will free him, and he will once again be restored in his spirit and he will rule fairly and honestly for the rest of his days upon his rightful throne. If he is drunk on the Wine of Bitterness, poured into the Goblet of Despair, and the other wines turn into water, then he will lose his right to be king forever more. He will then live the rest of his days in bitterness and despair. It will be the king's own will to choose his path. This is fair and honest and the only way to the restoration of his spirit. All men someday must choose which wine it is that they will drink in their lives. It is a lesson for all of humankind."

Afon picked his staff up and he waved his mighty staff violently in the air, and pointed it in the direction of the

Kingdom of Aedan while Trahearn tucked the bottles into his bag. Trahearn knew better than to ask any questions since he had listened carefully and he understood the plan.

Afon smiled, and he bowed at the waist in front of Prince Trahearn while speaking, "Now, go first very bravely into battle, then go in peace and go in hope, and take the wisdom of the medallion's knowledge with you always."

Trahearn looked down to make sure the bottles were safe. And he was going to bid farewell to Afon, but when he looked up, Afon had disappeared.

Trahearn was alone in the forest once more, and he now followed only the eyes of his heart.

Chapter Seven

A Drink to Choose

Trahearn had his mission, he had his plan, and he and his small band of knights and Sir Fillamore set forth out of the forest and towards the land of the Northern Dog, and the outskirts of the Kingdom of Aedan. Prince Trahearn led the men on the last leg of their journey. He knew every inch of the land, the same land that he had wandered since he was a young boy.

When he reached the outskirts of the great castle, Trahearn looked up and he saw that the day was ending. The sun was setting in golden rays of bands of light over the hills behind the castle walls.

As Afon instructed him to do, he dismounted his horse, stood at attention, and closed his eyes. A vision appeared, and he saw golden rays of lights even with his eyes closed. When Trahearn opened his eyes, he took the medallion out of his pocket, and held it in his right hand, while his eyes scanned the many trees which dotted the landscape in front of him. The brave knights of his small battalion watched in awe and amazement when the medallion glowed brightly in his hand.

"Look! The medallion glows brighter than the sun! Yet, Prince Trahearn's hand remains unharmed," the brave knight, Sir Fillamore, shouted while pointing at the medallion. "Surely, brave Prince Trahearn, you are meant to be king of this great land!"

Trahearn spoke not a word, but he scanned the sunset

rays down to the ground, and out of all the trees in the area, his eyes settled upon one particular tree. It was a huge tree set low in a valley and it was a towering tree, whose branches seemed to reach into the clouds and touched the edges of the heavens. He smiled as the glow of the medallion confirmed what the eyes of his heart saw.

"Quickly, brave knights! Follow me, I will be king someday, but my hope is that tomorrow, and many days in the future, will not be the day of my coronation! Make haste! Bring me a sharp tool that we might dig with in the hard ground."

Trahearn ran to his horse, mounted, and struck his horse to provoke a gallop. Trahearn rode off quickly in the direction of the tree. The battalion called their horses into action, and they rode quickly while they followed Trahearn and his horse as they galloped across the open meadows and into the low valley of the outskirts of the Kingdom of Aedan. Trahearn stopped at the base of the tree; he dismounted and signaled Sir Fillamore for the digging tool. Sir Fillamore jumped off his horse, pulled the tool from his saddlebags, and handed it to Trahearn.

Trahearn's eyes followed the setting sun, the rays that the sun broadcasted, landed first upon the medallion that Prince Trahearn held in his hand, and then they landed upon the tree trunk. As the battalion of knights observed in amazement, they watched a single sunray hit the trunk of the tree, chase across the land and stop on a spot on the ground at the side of the tree. Trahearn took the tool, and he eagerly began to dig into the ground. Sir Fillamore signaled two of his other knights to help Prince Trahearn, and the three of them joined in the excavation.

After considerable digging, the tools struck upon a plain metal box. The men frantically dug around the box to pull the soil away from the box enough to lift it from the ground in order to open it. When they did, they pried the lid off and peered into the box. Trahearn reached in and pulled out of the box, three goblets, one goblet made of a dull stone, one silver goblet and one golden goblet . . . it was all just as Afon had foretold to him that it would be. When Prince Trahearn and Sir Fillamore held the three goblets in their hands, the earth under their feet shook and rumbled and thunder rolled in the air. The quaking was so powerful that the prince and the brave knights had to hold on to each other to prevent them from falling over. Their horses reared and danced in fear, and the men struggled to control them. When the terror passed away, they noticed that the great tree instantly grew and hung many colorful and magnificent yellow and red fruits upon its mighty limbs. Fruits of which none of them had ever seen before. Trahearn instructed his team to pick and to gather as many of the fruits of the tree as they were able to transport, and to carry. All of them carefully recorded the events in their minds and in their hearts. The battalion of knights followed the instructions, and they all looked upon the sequence of events in shock and in awe since they all realized that they were party to a magical scene.

Sir Faydearn had taught Prince Trahearn to be a powerful leader, and the prince barked out his orders, "Quickly, Sir Fillamore, please hold in your possession the goblets, and the three bottles of wine that are in my saddlebags. Give the fruits that we have gathered from the tree, the goblets, and the three bottles of wine, to two of your most trusted and bravest knights. Two knights, who will not partake in the ensuing battle. The sole duty of these knights will be to guard the goblets, the fruits, and the bottles with their lives. Split their forces, one to guard the possessions and the other to watch from afar. If one dies in battle and defense of these possessions, then the other must take his place and possession of the goods! They must not fail or allow the prized possessions to be gained by the enemies of this world."

"I understand the orders, Prince Trahearn," Sir

Fillamore said as he followed the orders, and he assigned two brave young knights to the mission. A knight named Sir Loudon, who was a command knight, to guard the bottles, fruits and goblets, and an honorable knight named Sir Fleur to provide the watch from afar.

Trahearn addressed his battle group while holding the glowing medallion in his hand. The glow of the medallion cast a bright glow in the near darkness of the twilight.

"We will attack the castle under the cover of darkness. I know the secret passages to enter the castle that no one else besides, Sir Faydearn and I know of their whereabouts. We will surprise the Castle Guard Knights, overtake them, and I alone, along with Sir Fillamore, will take King Aneirin into custody. We will conceal our faces under our armor. We never will allow them to see our faces or clearly hear our voices until we bring this to resolution. Fight hard brave knights, but reduce the bloodshed, for these knights are now old, bored and lazy. We will lock them all in the dungeons and take over the rule of the Kingdom of Aedan! We will follow the plan exactly as the Wise Sage of the River told it to me, so you must follow my lead and my command. Now, we attack!"

They all dressed in their full body armor and prepared their weapons for the conflict. Weapons that Sir Faydearn had made of the strange metal brought to this land by the dark stranger. Yet, in the darkness, there is always some light. These weapons were hard and strong, unlike the soft weapons possessed by the Castle Guard Knights of the Kingdom of Aedan. Horribly, the stranger had wrought power when he visited as well as bringing despair.

The Knights of the Southern Dog rode off into battle, led by Prince Trahearn, and Sir Fillamore. They tied off their horses on the outskirts of the castle and established a base camp on a knoll hidden by the cover of some dense trees. Sir Fillamore left the knight named Sir Loudon in charge of the base camp and the prized possessions. Sir Fleur took his clandestine post to watch from afar in the darkness.

Under the cover of the intense darkness, the battalion crept and Prince Trahearn snuck around dark corners and the edges of the castle, while leading the men. He led them all to a secret door hidden in the wall, just above the water moat that surrounded the castle. The same door, of which he snuck in and out of the castle when playing with his brother and sister as a young boy, now served him well to enter the castle undetected.

When they entered the castle, Prince Trahearn led them to the post where the first guards of the Castle Guard Knights would stand at nighttime watch, but to their shock, there were no guards. No guards were inside the hallways of the great hall, no knight stationed at the great balcony, none in front of the doors to the dungeons and even more shocking, there was only one guard on duty, a guard stationed in front of the door to King Aneirin's chambers!

Afon was indeed correct. The Castle Guard Knights had fallen into disarray without the leadership of the great knight, Sir Faydearn. Sir Fillamore ordered the battalion to hide in the Great Hall while Prince Trahearn and the leader of the knights entered the private chambers of the castle.

"Why, Prince Trahearn, there are no guards on watch, except this one and he appears to be sleeping. There will be no need for a battle. They have already surrendered," Sir Fillamore whispered to Trahearn, as the two men hid in the corner of a hallway, looking to the door to the king's chambers.

"Yes, it is just as Afon told me it would be. Without the leadership of your father, the once great Castle Guard Knights have become lazy and disorganized. We will return, assemble our troops, and find the knight's quarters. I am sure we will find the rest of the guard asleep in their beds or drunk with wine. This will be a quick and simple battle and I can see that there will be little or even no bloodshed at all. We will overtake the guards, then circle back, and arrest this knight. You and I will take my father and lock him in a dungeon too." The two men agreed to the plan, and they made their way into the darkness.

It was just as Prince Trahearn said it would be. The Castle Guard Knights were sound asleep, and the few remaining knights who were awake, were drunk with wine, and not prepared for battle. Caught completely by surprise, realizing the ambush, and the fact that their own complacency now allowed them no chance in defense, the makeshift leader of the Castle Guard Knights, a knight named Sir Ackra quickly surrendered.

The Knights of the Southern Dog led the defeated knights to the dungeons, locked them all away and stood guard, while Sir Fillamore and Prince Trahearn doubled back to the king's chambers. The sleeping knight at the door was stunned when Prince Trahearn and Sir Fillamore surprised him and he jumped to his feet and reached for his weapon, but it was hopeless. He too surrendered without a fight, and they bound him, gagged the knight, and left him in the hallway for arrest.

Opening the door to the king's chambers, the two men crept through the rooms, as Prince Trahearn recalled every twist and turn of the familiar surroundings. The emotions almost overtook Trahearn, but as Sir Fillamore comforted him and encouraged him, he found the strength to move along.

When they opened the door to the king's bedroom, they could see, even in the darkness, King Aneirin asleep in his golden, ornate bed. Prince Trahearn once more allowed his emotions to arise, and he staggered in his mission, until Sir Fillamore moved him along again. His emotions peaked at the sight of his beloved father once more, but also at his appearance. The once handsome King Aneirin had grown old, and sad, with a long, untamed beard and stringy, wild, long hair. He looked as if he was a madman and a destroyed shadow of his once-proud self.

Trahearn stood on the side of the bed and gently tapped the sleeping king with an edge of his weapon until the king finally awoke in horror. When the king awoke, and managed to shake off the sleeping stupor, he realized his fate.

Disguising his voice with his mouth guard and concealing himself with the heavy body armor, Prince Trahearn shouted, "Awake, mean and angry, King Aneirin! Awaken from your nightmares! Your rule has ended. The people of the Kingdom of Aedan have arisen. They have spoken, and since you have grown angry and your rule has grown corrupt and evil in determination, we are taking over the throne and you will rule no more!"

The king jumped to his feet and tried, even in his old age, to overpower the two young men, but it was to no avail.

King Aneirin shouted, "I am the great, King Aneirin! The ruler of the Kingdom of Aedan! My loyal Castle Guard Knights will come to rescue me, defeat you, and slay you for this intrusion of my private chambers. How do you dare to enter here, commit treason and try to dethrone a king?"

Trahearn spoke as Sir Fillamore tied the hands of the king together and he explained, "I am the knight whose name means like iron, (Trahearn actually gave his father a hint as to his actual identity) and this is Sir Fillamore, leader of the Knights of the Land of the Southern Dog. Your lazy Castle Guard Knights have already been defeated, they are imprisoned and the rule of the Kingdom is now mine. Your once great Castle Knights grew lazy and drunk with wine, since you sent their leader, the brave and great, Sir Faydearn into exile. Your own malice worked against you, King Aneirin, and now you too, will be imprisoned for your dishonor and evil ways."

"Sir Faydearn! Sir Faydearn, that dog. He allowed the disease to enter our land. He allowed the death and horror of a plague to spread terror across the kingdom. He caused my wife, my son, and my beautiful daughter to die of that dreaded disease. Now, my other son, my firstborn, the great, Prince Trahearn, is also wayward. He married an evil witch, a woman not of the blonde-haired contingent, and he too is gone. You will pay for this when my son, wherever he is, returns to save me. He will return when he learns of my imprisonment and save us all. He and I will torture you and slay you, and I will teach him to rule with an iron fist and to never allow the kingdom to fall again into ruin!"

Trahearn shuddered at the words of the twisted king, his own father, a king who once was so kind, so gentle, and ruled with fairness and kindness. And now, the king filled his heart and his soul with bitterness.

He understood now, more than ever, what the plan was that Afon had told him.

They led King Aneirin to a dungeon, and they locked the king into a dark, dank cell. The good Prince Trahearn sent for the knights guarding the prized possessions and instructed that the team of knights should bring the goblets and the bottles of wine to Trahearn. They would store and care for the special fruits in a safe place. There, they would dry the fruit and preserve the precious seeds. Prince Trahearn also instructed Sir Fillamore to interview all the imprisoned people, whom his father had locked away in the dungeons, determine whom King Aneirin treated fairly, or some who he treated unfairly, and release those that the knight felt were imprisoned unjustly due to King Aneirin's now twisted and corrupt rule.

Prince Trahearn's final request for the loyal leader of the Knights of the Land of the Southern Dog was for his men to drain the moat surrounding the castle. He asked them to search and find the precious medallion that his father had hurled into the water in anger, on the night in which Trahearn had fled the kingdom.

When Trahearn received the bottles and the goblets from Sir Loudon, he asked the young command knight to follow him to the cell of King Aneirin, so that the knight could assist Prince Trahearn and he could bear witness to the testimony of the king.

Trahearn stood next to Sir Loudon, and while still disguising his voice, and concealing his identity beneath the layers of his armor, he offered the solution to the king, "Formerly great, powerful and kind, King Aneirin, I come along with the young knight, Sir Loudon, to propose a way for you to return to the throne. A manner for me to prove to you that we mean only good for the Kingdom of Aedan. That we have only conquered you and the Castle Guard Knights, in order to show you the error of your ways."

Intrigued by the words, King Aneirin stood up from his bed in the cell, approached Prince Trahearn and he stood, listening from behind the iron bars.

"I hear you, evil knight of iron! What is it that you offer me?"

Sir Loudon handed the goblets of gold and silver to Trahearn, who held them in his hand, while nodding to Sir Loudon to show King Aneirin the bottles.

Trahearn told the imprisoned king, "I hold these special goblets in my hands. One is made of gold and it is the Goblet of Love. The other goblet is made of silver and it is the Goblet of Hope. These goblets come from the roots of the Tree of Love and Hope. The love and hope that all mankind shares and requires. The hope that kindness and forgiveness, rules the hearts and minds of the people of the world, and the love, which overpowers all bitterness and evil. Love, which sets lover's hearts aflame and causes mothers to hold and nurse their babies, and for old people to smile in joy at their own lives. The love, which in all of its power sustains us all forever. The love that conquers all!"

Trahearn carefully set aside the goblets. While repeating

the words of the teachings of Afon, Trahearn motioned his assistant to hand him the bottles as he explained the offering of peace to his father.

"This bottle, colored in red, contains the Wine of Forgiveness." Trahearn took the bottle from Sir Loudon, showed the king, and then handed the bottle back to the young knight. The two men repeated the sequence as the king watched the scene unfold.

"This bottle colored in green, contains the Wine of Kindness." Trahearn did the same with this bottle as he had with the previous one.

While Sir Loudon handed Trahearn the last bottle, the prince said, "This last one, in the black bottle . . . is the bottle, which contains the Wine of Bitterness. This wine is the wine, in which man drinks from too often. You are now, always drunk in bitterness! The two wines, Forgiveness and Kindness, are poured into and drunk from the Goblets of Love and Hope. Forgiveness into the Goblet of Love, and Kindness into the Goblet of Hope. The Wine of Bitterness is drunk only from this stone goblet, which Sir Loudon now shows you . . . that is the Goblet of Despair."

King Aneirin even from behind the iron bars of his dungeon cell, grew impatient, his arrogance, and malevolence were so firmly inside of his soul that he cut off Trahearn and spouted off his choice, "I will drink the Wine of Bitterness, poured into the Goblet of Despair and I will be happy to spit it back in your face!"

Trahearn shouted out, "Silence! You are so filled with hate that you choose not even to wait to hear my full offer! King Aneirin, look around, you are in no position to negotiate your situation. Here are your choices to make. Think carefully and choose wisely, King Aneirin and you will sit once again upon your throne."

Prince Trahearn moved in closely to his father, from the front of the iron bars. He lowered his voice because his intention was to explain the choices and restore his father's kind spirit.

"You may drink from the Wine of Forgiveness, and from the Wine of Kindness. These wines, we will pour into the gold and silver Goblets of Love and Hope. You may drink the Wine of Bitterness only from the goblet made of stone, which is full of despair. King Aneirin, please, choose wisely, because you may only select two wines from which to drink from, and you must drink two of the wines, but you cannot drink from all three. I must warn you that the Wine of Kindness and the Wine of Forgiveness when drunk together, magically turns the Wine of Bitterness into water and bitterness will exist no more. However, the Wine of Bitterness, overcomes the other wines, and reduces them to only water! If you drink of the Wine of Bitterness, even the smallest of sips, then all is lost forever. If you choose wisely, and become drunk on the Wine of Forgiveness and the Wine of Kindness from the Goblets of Love and Hope, then we will free you, and you may rule again from the throne of the Kingdom of Aedan."

The words from his son struck a nerve as the king looked up and stared at the iron mask from which the words were emitting. It seemed as if for just a moment, the words had a profound impact on the hardened heart of the king.

Prince Trahearn continued, "If you decide to become drunk of the Wine of Bitterness from the Goblet of Despair and the other wines turn into water, then you will remain forever in this prison and you will die here! You will lose your right to be king forever more!"

Trahearn stared at his father and sternly asked the old king, "What is your choice, King Aneirin?"

The brave prince was doing his best at holding back his emotions, holding back a display of love for his father, opening the cell door and hugging his father and showing his concern at his wellbeing.

The old king answered, "You have given me little

choice, evil knight, who is made of iron. If I choose the two drinks of forgiveness and kindness, then I will absolve every one of the pain that they have caused me. Someone has to pay for this pain. Someone has to be accountable. If I drink the wines that you wish for me to consume, then I will forgive them for the tearing away of my very soul at the loss of my family, the loss of my own life, and all that I have loved."

King Aneirin waved his hands in the air from behind the bars of the cell, and it was easy to see that kindness remained buried deeply within his heart. The pain of what had occurred to him, as the world closed in, had overtaken the good with evil. The king stumbled backwards and then he caught his balance and sat on the edge of his bed inside the cell.

He covered his face with his hands as he mumbled in despair, "If I choose the Wine of Bitterness, then I am lost forever. And my once glorious kingdom is no longer mine. Yet deep down within my heart, I want to drink the Wine of Bitterness, to hold close to me forever the anger that I feel. I want to mix the wines, to taste some of each, yet retain my bitterness, but sadly, your plan is careful and I cannot."

King Aneirin uncovered his face, and he looked at his two captors. Tears ran down his cheeks as they poured from his eyes.

The once great king, spoke again, very softly, his voice filled with emotion and pain, "Yet, I remember the golden times, when the kingdom thrived, when the fruits grew on trees amongst a backdrop of green, when the winters were mild and the snow glistened upon the hills in silent peace. I recall the celebrations of the Holiday of the Harvest when joy filled the hearts of the people of Aedan. Such wonderful times! Yes, I can vividly recall the laughter of my children. I see their smiles, their joy, and when my children played at my feet. I remember the kiss and love of my beloved wife, and I remember her beauty. I deeply recall her touch upon my hand and a glorious time when our love was so joyous. So joyous that it filled the entire world. When the hope and the love that you just spoke about were in abundance before the cruel world closed in and took our kingdom away forever."

King Aneirin bowed his head, and the tears rolled from his cheeks and fell upon the cold floor of the dungeon cell.

Sir Loudon and Prince Trahearn stood in silence, and they watched as King Aneirin struggled with his decision. A decision that they understood coming from a man's desire to blame others for their own fate, a wish and desire to always hold someone else accountable for the pain that they might be feeling.

A pain that results only in more pain.

After what seemed as if many lifetimes of anguish had passed between them, King Aneirin looked up and he spoke softly, "I choose the Goblets of Love and Hope, as well as, the Wine of Forgiveness, and the Wine of Kindness. I will drink them until the bottles are empty, and my head is swimming in the influence of their liquids!"

The fear in Trahearn's mind eased, and his heart filled with joy. Sir Loudon and Prince Trahearn quickly prepared the wines and poured them into the gold and silver goblets; they unlocked the cell and handed the goblets to King Aneirin. They watched as he drank the first two cups and then drank another and another. The wines washed away the years of bitterness, their magical powers turned the Wine of Bitterness into water and they washed away the years of hurt and pain of the past from King Aneirin's soul. Trahearn and Loudon were amazed as King Aneirin's appearance changed before their eyes! His face grew younger. The lines of pain and suffering disappeared as the love, hope, kindness, and forgiveness came over him.

Prince Trahearn could no longer stand to hide his identity from his father. When he saw that, the transformation of his father's spirit was complete; he tore his body armor off, removed his headgear, and revealed his identity to his father.

"Father, it is me! Your son, Trahearn! I have come with the wines and with love and hope, in order to relieve you of the pain, the suffering, and the guilt of our loss! I too loved my mother and my brother and sister with all of my heart, but we only have each other now. You have forgotten to see with the eyes of your heart, my father, my king. I love you, Father. My hope is that now, we are together forever!"

Trahearn collapsed in the arms of his beloved father and the two men embraced while tears of joy exploded from their eyes. They cried tears of joy from the eyes of their hearts, as well as the eyes upon their faces.

Upon seeing the grand reunion, the brave knight, Sir Loudon, dropped to one knee; he drew his sword from its sheath and held the sword across his chest in honor.

The young knight said, "I am quite sure that our leader, the great Sir Fillamore, will join his father, the brave and honorable Sir Faydearn and they will once again, lead the Castle Guard Knights. I, Sir Loudon, as a trusted command knight of the Knights of the Land of the Southern Dog, swear our loyal allegiance to King Aneirin, the great Prince Trahearn, and the Kingdom of Aedan. We will serve loyally and without fear, and if needed, we will die in the defense of such. The Knights of the Land of the Southern Dog will serve under the leadership of Sir Faydearn and his son. Their bravery and honor fill our souls and it is our honor to serve."

"Yes! We will summon Sir Faydearn and his family from his exile and he will once more lead our knights!" King Aneirin shouted in joy.

The king then nodded to his son, in order to have Prince Trahearn follow his lead. Father and son both placed their hands upon the helmet of Sir Loudon.

The king proclaimed, "We accept your allegiance, Sir Loudon, and the allegiance of your band of knights. Most of all we accept your honor!"

King Aneirin's soul filled with joy when he realized that once again he felt love, hope, kindness, and forgiveness. The king knew the goblets had given him the greatest gift of all, the gift of his soul restored and his son returned to his heart. The great King Aneirin smashed the stone Goblet of Despair against the stonewall of the prison cell, so the goblet's evil influence was lost forever and once he poured what was now water out of the black wine bottle, the bottle was broken too.

Father and son were reunited, and the Kingdom of Aedan restored to its former glory.

When Sir Fillamore returned the lost medallion to King Aneirin, father and son held their medallions together in their hands and watched as they glowed brightly to signal that the paths that both of them had chosen were correct. They knew that they would forever more, always follow their hearts and trust what their hearts could see.

Prince Trahearn sent for his family, and for Sir Faydearn and his family, and they traveled home from the Land of the Southern Dog. There in the Kingdom of Aedan, the castle once again had hallways that echoed with the cries and laughter of little ones, as the children of Celyn and Trahearn ran around the castle hallways and filled their grandfather with love, pride, and hope for the future.

King Aneirin ruled with kindness and fairness for many years. When he grew old and finally very peacefully passed away, Trahearn, the Castle Guard Knights, and the Knights of the Land of the Southern Dog buried him with full royal honors. They buried the good king at the base of the Tree of Love and Hope. King Trahearn assumed the throne upon the death of his beloved father, and King Trahearn too was a fair and honest ruler of the people of the Kingdom of Aedan.

In addition, the population of the Kingdom of Aedan grew larger and larger in numbers, and the outskirts of the kingdom moved farther, as the land prospered and the boundaries extended from the oceans to the mountains. The tree farmers carefully planted the preserved seeds from the Fruits of Love and Hope, and then they sowed more seeds when those trees grew the special fruits. Soon, the fruits spread their special emotions throughout the world, as more trees grew to overcome the bitterness, the hate and the evil. Still to this day, despite the pain of the world, there are more trees filled with the Fruits of Love and Hope in this world than there are any others.

While the population grew, the people of the Kingdom of Aedan continued to be happy and peaceful. They married and had children and taught the generations of children by telling stories of old heroes and legends of the brave Prince Trahearn and the loyalty of Sir Faydearn. They told stories of the wisdom and magic of the Wise Sage of the River named Afon and the hope and love of the good, King Aneirin.

And the stories and legends spread amongst many faraway places.

Chapter 8

A New Beginning and End

Sir Faydearn looked out the castle window of his chambers, high above the Kingdom of Aedan. He was old now, very old. He moved very slowly, and each step was painful. He smiled when he saw the secret door on the side of the castle open. Sir Faydearn watched as King Trahearn and Queen Celyn's son, Prince Aneirin the Second, walked out of the door. He jumped over the moat around the castle, and made his way, towards the forest on the outskirts of the Kingdom of Aedan.

Sir Faydearn carefully watched as the young prince made his way along the edges of the meadow, working very hard to conceal the fishing equipment that he carefully carried with him. Sir Faydearn turned away from the window and as his own son, the brave Sir Fillamore watched, the old knight carefully felt along a stonewall of the castle, pulled out a loose stone, and then carefully pulled a hidden lever down. The wall opened up and revealed a hidden chamber behind the wall.

Sir Fillamore did not say a word, but he loyally followed his father, when Sir Faydearn motioned for his son to follow him into the hidden chamber. There on the wall in front of the two men, on a golden hook mounted in the stone, hung a brown robe. A robe with golden fringes along the edges of it. Around the neck of the robe hung the sacred medallion. It was hanging upon a thin chain, and was suspended on the chest of the robe.

Sir Faydearn slowly shuffled along, and he pointed at the robe and said, "Your time has come now, my son. The world closes in now. I can see that in your lifetime, our great Kingdom of Aedan will absorb into the rest of the world. Now, my time on this ground grows short, very, very short, and you will carry on, just as all of our Castle Guard Knights have in the past, and they will, forever more into the future."

He opened a large wooden chest that sat upon the floor of the secret chamber, and he reached into a long drawer of gold hidden deep within the confines of the chest. Sir Faydearn put his hand inside, and he pulled out the wooden staff. The staff of magic that allowed people to see what they had never seen before.

Sir Faydearn again reached down inside the chest, and this time, he pulled out a small brass jar with a bronze lid. He unscrewed the lid to the jar, tipped it over, and some seeds tumbled out and fell into his hands.

"Here, my loyal and brave son, is the love and hope that the world requires. As you travel, sow some more seeds here and there. The grand wishes and guidance of mankind will now fall upon the eyes of your heart. My son, take the wooden staff. You are now the new holder of the power. First dress in the robe, then take the staff and strike it firmly upon the ground and you will become, Afon. Please, sow the seeds, take my medallion, and transform as you must, in order to teach the young man to see with his heart, and not only with his eyes. It is that profound lesson and that essential task, which is ours, now and forever. Never cease. Guard the medallion, robe, the staff, and the seeds. When you someday grow too old, as I have now, then your descendants will take up our cause, because we need to spread the message, far and wide, one person at a time, making sure that humanity has the wisdom to never forget about the power of love and hope, from now, until the end of all time."

Chapter Nine

Here is Where the Story Ends, or Does it?

I took a big bite of the last of my lemon tart and placed the now empty dish and my fork down upon the end table next to me. Paul William and Heather Sarah looked at me and they both smiled.

I realized that I had been babbling for a very long time. Even though I was babbling this wild fantasy story in front of my loved ones, I was slightly embarrassed at all of it.

"Why, Paul! That story was absolutely amazing! That might be the best story that I have ever heard you tell. It was remarkable. You must write that one down and turn it into one of your books as soon as you can my, dear husband. You mean to tell me that you just came up with that story off the top of your head?" Binky stood up from her chair and she walked towards me, while shaking her head and smiling at me.

I nodded my head and said sheepishly, "I guess so, Binky. The tarts might have helped inspire me, but it just came to me while I told it. Who knows sometimes, where all of these weird thoughts come from, my dear Binky? Sometimes, I just do not know, or understand it, or even try to figure it all out."

Heather Sarah looked up at me, while her brother and her mother both squeezed in next to me on the sofa to join in a group hug.

Heather Sarah said, "I know where it comes from, dear Father. It comes to you because you are the same as the characters in the story. You are one of the people who can see with the eyes of your heart. You can see that way because God allows you to see with the eyes of your heart as well as the eyes in your head. Now, dear Mother, Paul William, and I can all see the same way. If only everyone would see it that way, too . . . can you think how fantastic everything would be, dear Father? Besides, it is so wonderful that the Trees of Love and Hope now fill the whole, wide, world."

Our daughter's words amazed all of us. For such a young girl, her thoughts were deeply profound. Her intelligence was remarkable.

I leaned over and gave her a hug and a kiss.

Yes, Heather Sarah was indeed quite correct. We could only hope that somewhere in some faraway place, or maybe, right around the corner from our own home, the leader of the Castle Guard Knights was still teaching his lessons and spreading his precious and glorious seeds.

THE END

The Lamp upon the Table

A Fantasy Story of Ghosts, Romance, and the Unexplained

Paul John Hausleben

Prologue

They say that true love never dies. True love transcends all of time, all of space and all distances to prevail. Nothing can stand in the way of two lovers who find one another and hold on to each other, despite the trials and many tribulations that life can throw in their path.

It is a gift from God, a way to perpetuate his creation.

It is pure magic.

When you have that strange feeling that you have been in a location before, or spoken the same words to the same person before, it can be a spine-tingling experience.

Who knows where it comes from? Is it all a blurred reality or is it an experience from the past revisited?

The line between true reality and the past is blurred. However, can you and your love transcend it?

The greatest power of all is love. It bridges lifetimes and breaks hearts, tests and fortifies emotions. It inspires the greatest of melodies, which are the melodies contained within a person's heart. Love knows or cares very little about what is right or what is wrong. Love does not play fair or by any sets of rules.

Love is all-powerful.

It inspires the greatest and most touching actions, emotions and motivations of humans. Love stimulates the most poignant words of poets, songwriters and authors, as well as the words, whispered by lovers in the heat of passion.

Love will endure forever. Perhaps, if anything can span

reality and the past, then love can.

After all, without love, there would be no hope, no joy, and no reason to go on in this rather dreary world.

When two lovers reunite after being lost, or when they find one another for the first time, and know in their collective hearts that this is the one person whom they have searched for all of their lives, or even longer, perhaps, over all of time, then their joy, fills Heaven and Earth.

It is the greatest of all joy.

We all want in our hearts to believe and to feel that true love can never die or ever be lost. All of us love to hear of, believe in, and wish for the proverbial "happy ending" when it comes to romance.

It just has to be.

Yet, in actuality, it often seems as if the pursuit of the happy, romantic ending results in heartbreak, despair and love lost.

Or, does it?

Is true love ever actually lost?

On the other hand, does reality instead blur our vision of the actual past?

True love endures forever, it overcomes all, and rises beyond what we can see, comprehend, or even try to begin to understand.

It just has to be.

It cannot be any other way and it will always be that way until the end of all time.

The Lamp upon the Table

Chapter 1

O'Reilly's Safe Haven

Mr. Liam Murphy was the man whom everyone in the company loved. He was easy going, wonderful to work with, dedicated and polite. All of his coworkers were quite fond of him and yet, everyone for some reason, felt sorry for him because it seemed as if he was so lonely. It seemed as if he had no life outside of his job as a sales and marketing executive with a large corporation. A corporation, which he worked for over ten years or thereabouts. He never spoke of friends, hobbies, or even going out to the movies, or sharing a beer with some people with whom he worked.

It seemed as if he harbored and hid, rather well, some type of inner sadness. Everyone felt that way, except for Mr. Liam Murphy.

He was perfectly content.

He did not feel any pain any longer or hide any sadness.

On the other hand, did he, and was he only telling himself that was the case?

He kept telling himself that he was over the loneliness, over the emotions, and that he had accepted life as it had come his way. Liam loved his job at the corporation. Liam found the job easy; his management chain was fair, honest and pleasant and the salary and benefits to be fair and competitive. He made a decent living, he enjoyed his coworkers, he was outgoing at work, friendly, and likeable.

When the end of the day came along, Liam was perfectly satisfied to leave it all behind him, go home to his small apartment, and be alone.

The solitude and quiet were not loneliness to him, it was actually a friend. No one yelled at him any longer, no one criticized his every move, his decisions, or told him what he should eat, harped on him if he had too many beers, or continually asked what his plans were for fixing this or that around the house. He had played those games, obeyed her rules. He lost the battles, but in his heart, he felt as if he ultimately won the war.

His now ex-wife, after a long marriage, big houses, fine-trimmed lawns, raising two wonderful children, and paying an awful lot of bills, decided that a younger man in their neighborhood much better suited her fancy. She grew bored with Liam and apparently, the younger man was far more exciting than Liam Murphy was. Liam came home from work one day. He found his belongings out on the driveway, his clothes neatly packed in containers, and a letter pinned to the boxes.

A letter, with an explanation, in which contained the often spoken, but always-dreaded, opening line of, "I still care about you, but you are boring and I am not in love with you as much as. . .."

His formerly loving or depending upon if you believed the words of the note or not, a somewhat loving wife had predictably changed all the locks in the house too. Oh well, he did not fight it. After all, what was the sense? She made her decision; it was time to accept the change and move on in life. Liam moved on, rented a small apartment, and started his life over again. He handed over the house, the headaches, and his wife to the younger man. Let him decide if he wanted to win the war or just a few battles here and there.

Once he was an available man, he became a bit of a hot commodity at his employment, as well as the small Irish pub in which he frequented around the corner from his apartment. The ladies all worked very hard to catch the eye of the single and very handsome Mr. Liam Murphy. Liam Murphy attracted quite a bit of attention from the single ladies and even some married ones, too. Ah, how the ills of this world can easily befall us all!

However, Liam mostly kept to himself, he was polite, easy-going, made a few casual friends with certain women, but he was not willing to become involved in another disastrous relationship so soon after he just cleaned up the train wreck of which had become his life.

Tall, lean, trim and strong, Liam was handsome, with thick black hair, a finely trimmed beard, captivating green eyes with a distinctive sparkle, and his face framed in dark features with his Irish heritage shining through in his appearance. Attracting ladies of all ages, and from all lifestyles, was not, or never was, Liam Murphy's trouble.

Friends he was willing to have, but as far as some romance goes; Liam felt as if he was not ready for a relationship yet. Besides, once he was involved in a steady relationship, that was usually when things fell apart. Even though he could have his pick of available and not so available women, in his heart, Liam Murphy felt as if in the end, guys like him always lose. Liam felt as if it was always the way it was always going to be. The gorgeous woman, his true love, if she even existed, would always inevitably reject him and in the end, cause him nothing but heartache and pain.

Therefore, he now was very reserved; he smiled, thanked the various ladies for their kind comments, exchanged general comments, shared some friendly conversations and time and went quickly off in the other direction.

Once Liam returned to his apartment, he puttered around, put on some quiet background music, watched a little television, read books, and dabbled in his new hobby of photography.

It was a hobby, in which he had long desired to become involved in, and now that he did not have to cut grass, trim hedges, fix cars, clean gutters, and make repairs every weekend, Liam had plenty of spare time on his hands. With this extra time on his hands, Liam took up his new hobby with enthusiasm.

The purchase of the camera was actually a rather spur-of-the-moment decision for him. One weekend, while killing some time out in a local shopping mall, Liam wandered aimlessly when he spotted the camera on display in the window of a camera shop. Before Liam even realized it, he had spent a considerable amount of money on a top of the line, newfangled, auto-focus, 35 mm film camera. Even though Liam knew very little about the camera, Liam was not disappointed. The camera took amazing photographs, and he did not even understand what half of the buttons actually did!

His new hobby became a welcome diversion from the everyday activities or the lack thereof.

In reality, the new hobby was a temporary escape, merely a pastime, because nothing ever really went Liam Murphy's way. He did nothing outstanding, and every day was the same, nothing spectacular, nothing earth shattering. He seldom, if ever, heard from his children. They had their own lives, their own interests. He spent birthdays, holidays and all other days alone.

Loneliness comes in many varieties. Sometimes, it is hard to separate bad luck from boredom, or just plain fate.

On occasion, he walked the few short blocks from his apartment through the streets of Haledon, New Jersey and tipped a few mugs of stout or ale at a local watering hole. Liam frequented an Irish pub owned by a man named O'Reilly, who had apparently owned it forever and just a little more.

"O'Reilly's Safe Haven Irish Pub" was the name of the

pub, and it sat on an angle on the corner of the main street through Haledon, and a side street. Haledon was a little borough tucked into the north corner of the big city of Paterson, New Jersey. A borough famous for nothing, except that the local folks were proud to say that Haledon had more gin joints, taverns, bars, and pubs per square mile than any other place in all of America.

Liam never researched that fact to confirm it, but indeed, he felt as if it was at least close to the truth because there were quite a few around!

One early spring, or late winter, depending upon your preference or level of optimism, a cold Saturday afternoon found Liam Murphy wandering into the doorway of the corner bar known as, "O'Reilly's Safe Haven Irish Pub."

It had been a difficult winter, and dirty corn snow, still lay in anguished piles along the sidewalks and along the edges of the roadways. The last snowfall had been during the first week of March, but the weather had remained cold enough for the snow to remain frozen there as sad reminders of when winter long since wore out its welcome. With the beloved holiday of the Irish and folks who pretended to be Irish, right around the corner, spring was now right around the corner, too.

The proprietor of this fine establishment, Mr. Thomas O'Reilly was behind the bar, his left foot resting on a stool, his bar towel draped along his other leg and his attention fixated upon a television hanging above the corner of the bar. A smoky haze enveloped the television screen, a haze lifting from the multitude of smoking patrons puffing away on cigars, cigarettes, and pipes within the confines of the pub. O'Reilly spotted Liam walk in, his eyes lifted and his attention turned away from the football match on the television, and he waved to Liam to take his usual seat at the bar. A seat in which was presently open.

It was now later into a Saturday afternoon, the pub was quiet, there were a few regular patrons drowning some sorrows, creating smoker's haze and watching the football match, but Liam only generally nodded in their directions.

Liam Murphy very much kept to himself these days.

"Eh there Liam, how rya?" Thomas O'Reilly greeted Liam Murphy in his typical loud, happy greeting, laced with his heavy Irish brogue. Fifty-plus years of living in New Jersey had contributed very little towards fading the Irish accent of the owner of O'Reilly's Safe Haven Irish Pub.

"Decided to come by here today instead of my competition over there at the Widow's Pub, eh? How are ye keepin' laddie?"

"Hello, Thomas. Well, I guess there might be too many Welshmen, Scotsmen, and Englishmen over at the Widow's Pub these days. To be honest, I never considered a visit there. How are you?" Liam commented with a sly chuckle while he settled into his usual seat at the bar.

The Widow's Pub was a small tavern a block or two over, a tavern frequented by many in the small enclave of English, Welsh, Scotch, and Irish folks who had settled in this area so long ago. The silk and lace trade of Paterson brought many people of these common heritages across the big pond, all of them seeking work in Paterson's mills and factories after the big wars ravaged their native lands.

"Having the same as usual this afternoon, Liam?" Thomas looked over to Liam for confirmation as he held an empty glass poised and ready to fill under the spout of stout. A nod was all Thomas needed to fill the glass, and Liam nodded and waved his hands to indicate the pour was on.

"Is the match worth anything today, Thomas?"

"Oh, bloody well, no! 'Tis a terrible match. Nottingham Forest versus some other team that I never heard of with poor goalkeeping, an easy goal from much too far out on the pitch. All in all, a very lousy game. I dare say, drunk, I could stop a few better than this goalkeeper can."

Liam did not answer the comment about the match, but instead, he watched while Thomas brought the glass of stout over to him.

He handed Liam the glass, while commenting, "Still bloody cold out, eh? The sun will not be splittin' any stones anytime soon I do imagine, Liam."

"No, summer is some ways away, Thomas. Oh well. Cheers and to your good health," Liam spoke a toast while he lifted the glass to take a first sip of the frosty delight.

"Why thank ye, Liam and I will add to you a bit of luck, while I toast ye back."

Thomas reached for the glassware storage shelf behind the bar; he selected a small shot glass, filled it with a taste of Irish whiskey and downed it. Thomas O'Reilly was a large man, with big hands, a big head, and a huge personality. His hair was thick, pure white, and neatly combed over to the side. Thomas possessed a solid face with a strong chin, red cheeks, and pure blue eyes. His charisma, as much as the location of his establishment, had ensured the longevity of the business for all of these years. His wife worked the kitchen in the rear of the pub, cooking up typical Irish pub fare of fish and chips, bangers and mash, shepherd's pie, and she intertwined it with American delights of some burgers and other dishes to bring it all close to home.

On occasion, you would see the couple's son-in-law and daughter working the floor or behind the bar, but for the most part, it was usually Thomas and his wife. Thomas set the shot glass down, leaned in close to Liam and placed his one leg on his customary stool hidden behind the bar. As he leaned in, he spoke in a lower whisper, with his usual booming voice lowered a bit in volume.

"If you do not mind me sayin' so, dear Liam, you look as if you need a bit o' luck of the Irish today. I think that I might have just the remedy for ya."

"Oh, is that so, Thomas? Do I look that bad?"

"Not so bad, just as if you are in need of an adventure. You look a bit on the downside. Perhaps, it is a wee bit of boredom, eh? Are you still snapping away with that new camera? Did ye figure the bloomin' thing out yet?"

Liam sipped his drink while gently nodding his head to affirm the question that Thomas asked.

He spoke between sips, "I am slowly figuring it out. At least I think that I am. Thomas, I must say that despite how complicated it is that I am rather enjoying the hell out of it, too. Not too sure what I am doing yet, too many bloody buttons, but I sure am having a bit of a good time learning."

Thomas smiled and said, "C'mere, 'till I tell ye."

Although Liam himself was born right here in Paterson, New Jersey, his parents came from Ireland early in their marriage, and he understood the phrasing and nuances of Irish spoken English, mixed with the occasional New Jersey twang. O'Reilly was simply telling Liam to pay attention to what he was going to tell him.

The big man reached under the counter of the bar top, pulled out a colorful brochure, and gently slid it in the direction of Liam. The brochure slid across the bar top and came to rest against the glass of stout. It gently tapped the side of the glass and the foamy delight inside lapped at the edges of the glass, lacing a trace of foam along the sides.

Liam was puzzled, he looked at the brochure sitting on the bar top and then glanced at O'Reilly.

Thomas O'Reilly said not a word. His face glowed and a wide smile sat upon his red-cheeked face.

"What's this, O'Reilly?" Liam asked the jovial barkeeper.

"The cure for your boredom, laddie. Check it out, then I will tell ye the best part." Thomas O'Reilly waved with his hand to encourage Liam to pick up the brochure and see what it was advertising. Thomas stood behind the bar with the wide smile still welded upon his face, his clear eyes flickering in excitement at the prospect of what he just proposed to Liam.

Liam reached for the brochure, picked it up, and in the dim light of the pub, he glanced at the full color cover. On the cover was a fabulous picture of a sprawling facility, framed with a backdrop of breathtaking trees, landscapes full of colorful flowers, shrubs and other plant materials. However, the most striking feature of the photo on the brochure's cover was a scenic lake, shining as if it was a mirror, which adjoined the backdrop of the rest of the landscape.

Liam whistled gently, O'Reilly still smiled, and Liam read the title on the cover aloud, "The Centrebridge Resort and Inn on White Pine Lake. Centrebridge, Massachusetts. Nice, but I am not sure why you gave this to me, O'Reilly."

"Let me tell ya why, laddie. A good friend of mine, a dear old friend, just wrote to me and told me that he had a stroke of good fortune and recently secured the rather prestigious position of the general manager of this fine establishment."

Liam nodded his head at the news, but he did not say a word. He picked up the glass of stout and took a sip, leaned back on the stool and listened to the rest of the explanation.

Thomas O'Reilly continued, "I am not surprised that he secured such a marvelous position. He has been managing resorts and hotels ever since he came across the pond. He moved on the position quickly, moving from his home and previous employment in Boston, to Centrebridge, which is near the Connecticut state line. He extended a generous offer for my wife and me to visit with him and stay at the resort at a fifty percent discount!"

"Well now, that should be a nice holiday, and I might add there, Thomas, a rather thrifty one, too. When do you leave?" Liam asked, picked up the sales brochure and handed it to Thomas. Thomas folded his arms defiantly across his chest and indicated that he refused to take the brochure back from his friend.

With a loud laugh and a wave of his hands, Thomas O'Reilly bellowed, "Ya are thick as a bloody brick, dear Liam! We are not going. It is Saint Patty's Day in a few short days, man. However, I did ask my friend if the discount would apply for you. I told him about you, and your new hobby of photography and how the scenic beauty of the resort and the area would be perfect for you to dabble in."

The jovial and rollicking barkeeper came closer to Liam. He looked around to see if any other patrons were listening to their interaction.

When he became convinced that the rest of the pub gatherers were watching football, he leaned in and said, "I fibbed on the truth a wee bit, Liam. I told my friend, ye were a professional photographer and the resort could pick up some free publicity if you come up and shoot around a bit. Sorry, old boy."

"Oh boy, I am sure that was a bad idea, Thomas. I cannot even figure out the buttons on the camera yet. Besides, I do not actually take any holidays. Rather enjoy being a bit of a homebody."

"And that, my friend, is exactly why you should go! Look at you, stuck in the mud ya are. The same routine day after day. How do you think you will meet some new pretty lassies if you stay around here, Liam? You already made up your mind that ye aren't interested in any of the lassies around here. Maybe, ye will find a pretty lassie there and push a few buttons on her, rather than just on a camera."

Thomas chuckled at his own comment; he took his rag, picked up the glass of stout, wiped the counter furiously, and went to replace the glass.

Seeing that it was almost empty anyway, he handed it back to Liam and instructed him, "Here. Swig it right on down. Refill is on me. Ye need the inspiration to come out of that hole ye are livin' in."

Liam took the glass, swigged the remainder of the stout, and handed Thomas the now empty glass. He watched as Thomas carried it over to the spout and refilled it, and while he watched, Liam pondered the bartender's words and observations of his lifestyle.

As he refilled the glass, Thomas O'Reilly tried his best sales pitch to convince Liam Murphy to make the trip, "Come on, Liam. When did you take your last holiday? Knowing ye, it must have been over ten years ago! Life is short. Pack the camera, some warm clothes, take a few days off and go on an adventure. Who knows what could happen? It will renew the spirit. The telephone number is on the back of that brochure. Timothy MacQuaid is my friend's name. County Monaghan he and his family are . . . ye should just give in and ring him up."

O'Reilly grabbed a small bar napkin and pulled his pen out of his pocket and scrawled a telephone number on the napkin.

"Better yet, here, use this number to call him. This is a direct line. Do not call the resort number. I am sure the discount thing could be something that Timothy does not want to advertise."

Liam leaned back on the bar stool and he deeply pondered the rather enticing offer. Thomas carried the glass of stout over and set it in front of Liam. His clear, green eyes were sparkling; he now sensed that Liam was softening a bit to the offer.

O'Reilly offered a few last words.

"I ask ye laddie, right now, how rya, now, eh? Life is short, my dear, laddie. Very, very short. . .."

Chapter 2

Will O' the Wisp

A week or so later, Liam found the ride to Massachusetts turning out to be surprisingly pleasant. While he drove along the highways and byways, Liam Murphy could not help but think how good this felt. The day had broken clear and bright. The traffic, once he broke free of the greater New York City metropolitan area, was light and Liam Murphy actually felt relaxed, a bit spry and if he examined his heart closely, rather carefree. Thomas O'Reilly had been correct. Life is too short, and it had been a long time since Liam took some time off to enjoy something of his own choosing. Even his longtime manager at his place of employment, when he recovered from the shock and awe of seeing the vacation request form presented by Liam sitting upon his desk, was happy and enthusiastic at the prospect of Liam taking a few days off to enjoy life.

To say that this was long overdue would not come close to giving the statement of, "to enjoy life" proper justice.

Liam had risen early in the day, packed his precious camera gear, some warm clothes, and his luggage and thrown it all in the trunk of his car. He set off; map in hand, the sales brochure for the resort sitting next to him on the passenger's car seat. He was off on an adventure, to take pictures, relax, and to enjoy a few days in the beauty of New England in a late winter setting.

A little adventure and perhaps just a little more. While he passed the many miles, Liam thought about the rather comical telephone conversation he had when he made his reservations at The Centrebridge Resort and Inn on White Pine Lake. There on the telephone, Liam had to make a careful and rather roundabout confession to Mr. Timothy MacQuaid, carefully doing his very best to preserve the reputation of Thomas O'Reilly, while he vigilantly explained that while he was, indeed, a photography buff, to call him a professional that would constitute a rather dubious stretch of the truth.

"Ah yes, Thomas was always a bit prone to the telling of tall tales. His tendency to exaggerate is even worse when he has dabbled in a wee bit of strong drink. Oh yes, the tales that man can tell. Liam, I do understand and we still are quite fond of O'Reilly despite his bullshit ways. It is part of his magic you know," Mr. MacQuaid seemed undaunted on the telephone, as he replied with what appeared to be a very accurate assessment of O'Reilly's tendencies to exaggerate everything, including the bogus claims of Liam Murphy's photography skills.

"Any friend of Thomas O'Reilly, whether a professional photographer or not, is a friend of mine. Come, enjoy! We will be looking forward to meeting you in person," Mr. MacQuaid told Liam with a heavy Irish brogue and as much enthusiasm in his voice as his jovial friend possessed.

Centrebridge, Massachusetts, was a small town in a picturesque setting, and it did in fact straddle the border between the states of Massachusetts and Connecticut. Liam was actually caught off guard when he spotted the exit on the highway appear so quickly. For some reason, he had resigned in his mind that the drive would be so much longer than what it turned out to be. A short drive off the exit ramp, down a main road, a turn or two, and Liam soon found himself turning next to the entrance sign for the resort and inn, and parking his car on the outskirts of a large parking lot.

He pulled his luggage and camera gear out of the trunk

of the car; he turned and made his way between piles of snow stacked neatly here and there in the parking lot. As Liam walked towards the front entrance, he could not help but be in awe of the natural beauty of the setting of the facility and the adjoining grounds. For once, a sales brochure with the typically retouched photographs did not present a false depiction of the actual setting.

It was even better in person than the photographs depicted.

The facility was large, much larger than Liam thought that it would be. It was primarily one level, with a tall peak rising above what appeared to be the main entrance and lobby, and a stone chimney which rose even higher above the roof peak. The rooms for the inn extended along one side, and what appeared to be meeting rooms, perhaps a conference center or other amenities, sat opposite the side where the rooms were located on the other wing of the building. The facility had a rustic appearance to it, and it seemed as though it was stuck in time for just a few years, as if the last twenty years or so had not actually passed.

It was obvious that there were no renovations or updates performed on the facility and property in a long time; it was not rundown by any means, just weathered. Liam thought how it was as if he had taken a step back in time, maybe to twenty or so years ago.

He, at one time, had considered a career as an architect, and when money for a prestigious college dried up, and his life took some different turns, Liam settled for a career in sales and marketing. Deep down, he felt he still had an eye and interest in architecture as well as landscape and various objects. Perhaps that is why capturing images with his camera was now of some interest to him.

His discerning eye now had a mission to stay occupied.

Liam stood there for a long time, standing in the roadway leading to the main entrance; he set his luggage down on the ground, stacked his camera gear on top of the luggage and adjusted his camera bag over his shoulder. He was studying the beauty of the trees, as well as all the grounds.

Small piles of snow remained, telling the tale that even in southern New England; most of the long winter was now over. There remained a covering or two of snow on various grassy areas of the property, but only in the shadier locations where the sun could not work so easily upon them. Judging by the size of the snow amounts remaining, Liam thought how the area must have not have had any significant snowfall in the last few weeks or so.

Liam's eye for photo opportunities was keen, and he admired a long, wooden split-rail fence, the grounds, the lake, the entire setting. He thought how if the owners and management of this facility and property decided someday to update and modernize the property and building to a more modern appearance or architecture, then the facility would lose some of its pastoral and retrospective appeal. The facility sat in a bowl of landscape, surrounded by tall maple trees and rows and rows of white pines. The rustic wood rail fence ran the entire length of the side of the facility along the roadway leading to the entrance of the resort. The lake was close, just off to the side of the property and it sat calmly, still frozen in large locations, but the open water was shining just like a mirror on this cold, but clear, March day.

Liam stood there for a bit more of time, staring at the property and admiring the view of White Pine Lake. The shores of the lake comprised, at least along the resort frontage, of narrow sandy beach areas, now cold and stark, with dried leaves scattered about on the sand, while all awaiting the warmer days ahead. Along the lake frontage, just past the beach, were vast lawns, still sleeping while they remained brown and drab, or under snow cover. Sitting upon the lawn were a few park benches lined up in rows all to provide a spectacular view of the lake.

He almost reached into his bag and pulled out the camera, but he thought about how he would have plenty of time for snapping photos. First things first, he should check into the resort and then wander the property and grounds. He had ample time left to this day; it was just past noon, and he would have enough light left in the day to wander about and see what type of photographs he could take.

Keeping with the spirit and tone of the rest of the architecture of the sprawling facility, the front entrance to the resort and inn was rustic, with a high portico overhang, framed in cedar planking leading to a set of double doors.

On each side of the entrance there were stacks and stacks of firewood. There were equal piles of hardwoods, and birch wood piles loosely stacked, with a few stray pieces of wood that tumbled into the walkway in front of the entrance. The strong and captivating odor of a wood-burning fireplace floated in the air, and Liam looked up at the stone chimney to see gentle puffs of smoke rising out of the top of the structure. Liam surmised that these woodpiles were where the staff must keep the firewood close and handy; to keep what was obviously, a grand entrance fireplace lit and the lobby warm and inviting.

Passing through the double doors and walking into the grand entrance, he was not disappointed. A large, floor-to-ceiling fireplace, set smack in the middle of a wide-open lobby, flickered and danced with roaring flames. Liam's eyes confirmed his prior suppositions while he admired the inviting source of the smoke and the marvelous odor. It was late winter, teetering upon early spring, and even though it was a bright clear day with abundant sunshine, the day was cold. The fireplace took the chill off the lobby while many guests and staff opened and closed the lobby's front doors.

Around the center fireplace, set upon a deep pile throw rug, were some plush chairs and seats with long wooden arms. The lobby floor was a gray flagstone; rustic, uneven in the matching grout lines and a perfect floor for wear and tear suffered during the harsh and long winters of this climate. The ceiling in the lobby was high, with an open beam, bare wood construction with the beams set in an intriguing crisscross type of pattern. A long counter lined the right side of the lobby and once Liam established his bearings; he made his way over to the front counter. A few people walked briskly about the lobby, some folks were chatting in a corner, and a housekeeper dusted the furniture in the lobby with a feather duster.

A tall, very attractive young woman, wearing a suit jacket with her nametag emblazoned upon the front lapel, smiled and greeted Mr. Liam Murphy.

"Welcome sir, to The Centrebridge Resort and Inn on White Pine Lake. It is my pleasure to serve you. If you are checking in, then your name please?"

Liam approached the counter, smiled, set his luggage down, and said, "Yes, hello, thank you. I am checking in. Liam . . . Mr. Liam Murphy is the name."

"Oh, Mr. Murphy, yes, it is so nice to meet you. I hear that you are quite the photographer! I think you will find our scenery quite suitable for landscape photos if that is your goal. Our general manager extends his personal welcome. Here is a note from him, with some discount coupons for our bar in the resort to enjoy a drink or two. He also asked me to convey to you his heartfelt apology, but he had a meeting off the site this afternoon, and he could not be here to welcome you in person."

Before Liam could interject his actual skills and qualifications, and attempt to refute the tall tales that O'Reilly, as well as what he surmised to be Mr. MacQuaid had woven, the young woman rambled on once again.

She had an abundance of energy.

"Now, if landscape shots are not your sole interest, I could certainly make myself available for some portrait shots . . . especially for a handsome man such as you are!"

She winked, and she smiled widely at Liam, who shifted uncomfortably on his feet at the forward proposition. A fleeting, yet strong thought crossed Liam's mind, as he did have to think that perhaps O'Reilly was correct and he had holed himself up as a loner for too long. After all, this was an attractive young woman.

"Please wait, Mr. Murphy. Let me step away here and obtain your paperwork. I will be right back." The young woman returned shortly. She asked Liam to fill in some questions on the form, and then present his credit card. She handed him his room key, as well as a detailed explanation as to how to find his room.

She left him with a wink and a smile as she offered, "He could come by and chat with her at any time, if she could be of any further assistance."

"Thank you . . . and yes, indeed, say, ah. . .." In order to address her by her name, Liam leaned in awkwardly and he struggled to read the young woman's nametag, without staring too much at her large and very attractive chest. He felt it was the least he could do to address her rather forward approach to him. She filled in the missing blanks with another wink and a wide smile, "Charlotte. Charlotte Walker."

"Yes, thank you. Charlotte, could you please recommend a nice place to have dinner this evening? I stopped and had some lunch on the road, but I am looking for a place that might, you know, fit in with the entire mystique of a New England experience. I think you know what I mean."

"Why, of course, Mr. Murphy. Right here inside the resort is a cocktail lounge that serves fine drinks and typical snacks and bar food, and I might add, you have two coupons for. I get off my shift around midnight and it is open until two in the morning. Wink. Wink. However; if it is fine dining that you desire, there is a fine restaurant, right here on our property. Perhaps, you just missed it.

Once the sun sets, you will see it. The flames from all the oil lamps along the front walkway and in the windows, burn brightly and they illuminate throughout the night. Almost like the Will O' the Wisp does across the lake."

"Excuse me? Will of the what, Charlotte?"

"Yes, maybe you will be lucky enough to snap a photo of it. The Will O' the Wisp, are mysterious lights that appear here and there in the woods on the other side of White Pine Lake. You know, Stingy Jack, Will the Smith . . . it might even be the old sea captain trying to find his way to return to the tavern. We have lots of ghosts and other strange things around here. After all, this is New England, Mr. Murphy. We have our stubborn legends and folklore."

Liam waved his hands in the air and laughed as he explained, "I am sorry. I am a city guy from New Jersey. Anyway, I will take your recommendation. I will follow the oil lamps, try to avoid the ghosts and look for the spooky lights, too. Ah, the restaurant Charlotte?"

She smiled and spoke a little softer, "Oh yes, sorry, I got caught up in the folklore, besides you have such remarkable green eyes. They are quite captivating. You are obviously of Irish heritage with your name, but you speak as if you are indeed from New Jersey. Were you born in America or in Ireland and grew up in New Jersey?"

"I was born in Paterson, New Jersey. My parents were born in Ireland."

Charlotte nodded, while all the time locking her eyes rather dreamily upon Liam's eyes.

She caught up with her dreamy emotions and explained, "The restaurant is, The Oil Lamp Tavern. It is right next to us here. Highly recommended. Rated by the critics with five stars too! I would say it qualifies as a genuine New England experience, food, fireplaces, wooden floors and the tavern is haunted too! Originally, the tavern actually was a Quaker meetinghouse. It was built in and around 1750 or thereabouts and with meticulous care and the assistance of expert trade workers, the building was removed from its original setting and moved it to this location about ten years ago."

Charlotte leaned over the counter and pointed out the front door in the direction of where Liam would find the restaurant. Liam tried hard to focus on the directions, rather than Charlotte's slightly exposed cleavage, which was now bulging out the top of her uniform blouse.

"You must go! The décor is incredible, and they never let the oil lamps on the table or along the walkways ever extinguish. Day or night. You can always see the soft glow of the oil lamps on the tables, even through the windows in the middle of the night. It is some type of long-standing tradition or legend that all the oil lamps on the tables and on the outside walkways will glow and remain lit until the owner of the tavern finds her long-lost love or something like that. She married a sea captain who was lost at sea in a terrible storm and she became a widow."

Charlotte now leaned back from the front counter and placed her back on the wall behind her. It was obvious that she enjoyed relating this tall tale and history of the restaurant to visitors. With her good looks and an attractive figure, Liam surmised that she garnered a large bit of attention from admirers.

"It is quite spooky there, too. Some workers in the tavern tell me that the ghosts of the sea captain and others still frequent the tavern. They have all heard and seen many strange and unexplained things there. The legend says that when his widow finally finds her long-lost love, the sea captain's ghost will then extinguish one oil lamp on one special table where her lover always sits, drinks and enjoys dinner. It is all so spooky, but romantic, too. Ah, oh well. Someday, a brave and handsome man will rescue me and carry me away from all of this!"

Charlotte Walker waved in the air with both of her arms to encompass the lobby. She leaned over the counter; she batted her eyes and sighed deeply as she appeared to be lost in the silly romance of the local legend. Liam thought how Charlotte had a very engaging personality, but perhaps she was a bit lost in her dreams too. He also thought how that was not such a bad way to be.

She recovered, reached over to a nearby shelf and picked up a pamphlet, as she said, "Here is a pamphlet, with the menu and the history of the tavern on it. Follow the lights of the oil lamps. May I call you, Liam?"

Liam smiled; Charlotte was very cute, nice eyes, a wonderful smile, with short brown hair, very neatly kept. Even wearing her assigned jacket and uniform for the position of working the front counter, Liam could tell that she had an appealing, and whom is he kidding because he stared a good bit at her blouse that was open and revealing a good bit of her cleavage; she had a gorgeous female figure.

He felt some pangs that he had not experienced in quite a long time, and he felt enthralled that such a beautiful young lady actually seemed attracted to him. She was at least ten years younger than he was, but who really cares.

Age is just a measuring stick.

Liam felt his confidence building.

"Ghosts and legends, eh? Bloody well, sounds as if it has a bit more than just some romance. Sure, sure, absolutely. Please call me, Liam. Thank you, Charlotte. Thank you for sharing the legend and the ghosts and all that folklore, but also for being so engaging and extending such a nice welcome. I am actually not much of a photo. . .."

He was going to finish off the conversation by proclaiming his actual qualification as a photographer and at the last minute, he changed his mind. What the hell, he might as well play it up just as O'Reilly and MacQuaid did. Time to change his ways as a loner. Perhaps, he would even ask Charlotte over to the tavern for a drink when she is finished with her shift. It was time to change his ways!

Loneliness lingered way too long in his life now, and he did not want someone to write the word loneliness upon his epitaph.

Life is short.

"I will keep you in mind for a few photos." He almost offered up a drink and dinner invitation, too, but he faltered.

"Oh, please do so, Liam!"

With that somewhat open conversation and invitation, Liam grabbed his luggage, his camera gear, and made sure that his camera bag securely hung over his shoulder. Off with his room key in hand, he went. He followed the map of the interior of the inn that Charlotte had given to him and upon reaching the center of the resort and inn; he could see why she did. It was a bit of a maze, and it was easy to determine that the inn and resort developed in stages over the course of many years and added on with a number of additions from the original facility. The interior was a mirror image of the exterior. The exterior was outdated, but somehow it was so inviting.

A step back into time.

He walked through an open interior with a grand atrium, equipped with dusty and opaque skylights and sparse indoor plant material, in random planting beds scattered amongst open pavilions and walkways. A hot tub and an indoor swimming pool were set in the center of the space, surrounded by rooms on three sides, along with a bar, and a small restaurant on the remaining end. The rooms all had sliding glass doors and windows as well as decks, which opened to the center atrium. The atrium had a warm feel to it, and Liam felt that the architect had designed a very inviting and unique space here.

In fact, it was unique.

Liam found his room and, after fumbling with luggage, key, and other gear, he opened the door. It was exactly what he needed. A large suite, two televisions, of which he knew he would not watch because Liam seldom, if ever, watched television. There was a smaller suite of rooms attached to the master suite, which also led to the wooden deck overlooking the lake.

Perfect.

He could set his camera up on a tripod and snap the sunsets and the sunrises over the lake to his heart's content. After checking out the room, unpacking his luggage, double-checking his camera and then washing up, Liam settled into a chair at a small desk in the room. His eyes caught the pamphlet that Charlotte had provided with information all about The Oil Lamp Tavern. The front cover photograph was awe-inspiring; with a remarkable nighttime photo of the tavern captured with perfect light. He could only wish to be able to take such a photograph someday. Liam's curiosity peaked, and he picked the pamphlet up and started to read it.

"The Oil Lamp Tavern was built in 1766 and was originally constructed and utilized as a Quaker meetinghouse. It was then converted to use as a tavern. After many years of falling into disrepair, the new owner of The Centrebridge Resort and Inn on White Pine Lake, purchased the historic structure, and moved it to the present location within the resort's grounds. After a careful restoration, the new owner opened the tavern as a five-star rated restaurant serving superbly prepared, traditional New England dinners and other traditional fare, as well as, top-shelf wine and spirits and locally brewed craft beers. Glancing at the menu, Liam was more than intrigued. The menu was extensive, with offerings such as Yankee pot roast, a traditional New England roast turkey dinner, fish and chips, and a host of other mouth-watering entrees.

Liam spoke aloud, "Wow. How interesting. A five-star restaurant within walking distance of the front door of the hotel. Mix in a little history and a few spooky legends and you have a gold mine. However silly it is to leverage ghosts and legends and such, it is a very cool business model."

Printed on the back of the pamphlet were additional histories and more of the legends and folklore of The Oil Lamp Tavern.

Thoroughly intrigued, Liam continued to read some more.

The Legend of the Oil Lamp Tavern

"Here in New England, we are proud of our past and our local legends and folklore is steeped in ghosts, mysteries and the unexplained. Our beloved Oil Lamp Tavern is a part of history here in Centrebridge, Massachusetts and it too, has its share of ghostly legends and mysteries.

In keeping with local folklore, the oil lamps on the exterior of the tavern and the lamps on all the tables of the tavern always remain lit. This is a tribute to the original owner of the tavern after its conversion to a tavern in 1805. When her parents both died rather suddenly, a beautiful young woman took up the family business of operating the tavern. There, she met a handsome, but adventurous man of the sea, a dashing swashbuckler who was passing through Centrebridge. He was a wandering and wayward chap with the name of Captain James O'Leary. He was a sea captain of his own vessel, which sailed out of the north of Boston. The legend tells us that the first words he told the beautiful woman were, "I do apologize in advance, for my abhorrent and eccentric behavior, while under the influence of the devil's brew."

They fell in love, and the captain swore off his previous evil ways, his excessive drinking and wanderlust upon the high seas. However, when hard times fell upon the tavern and money was short, the captain returned to the sea to earn a living. There, in a terrible storm at sea, the vessel sank, and the captain went down with his ship.

His shipmates testified that as the vessel slipped under the waves of the sea, they could hear the captain cry out, "For the love of the finest woman of all women, it was all worth it!"

Upon hearing of the loss of her beloved, the widow refused to accept that her husband had been lost at sea. The widow vowed to keep the lamps continually lit along the front walkway until he returned home. She also promised to keep the lamps upon the dining tables lit until his return. The legend tells us that the ghost of the old sea captain did return to the Oil Lamp Tavern and he continually searches the building and grounds for his lost love and his ghost chases away any prospective lovers and spurned lovers of his beloved wife. If an oil lamp accidentally extinguishes, the captain's ghost quickly relights the lamp to prevent any false loves from stealing his beloved's heart. The legend says that when his widow finally finds her long lost love and they reunite, the captain's ghost will then extinguish one oil lamp on one special table where the two lovers now sit and reunite in love. The lamps upon the front walkway will no longer burn during the day at all. There will no longer be any need for them continually to light the way to the tavern's front door.

Fact or fiction or just a spooky legend, our proud tradition of the lighting of the oil lamps continues today at, The Oil Lamp Tavern."

"Geez. It all seems awfully stereotypical, and a little stupid and quaint, but I must admit that it is a rather good story. As a marketing and salesperson, myself, I have to admit that it is outstanding marketing." Liam whispered aloud to the four walls after he finished reading of the legend. After all, he might not be a professional photographer, but he did know something about sales.

He spent the rest of the afternoon, (while he chuckled a

bit, due to his supposed reputation) reading the instruction manual for his new camera, as well as a book he recently purchased, which promised to make him a photography expert. Liam thought . . . good luck with that. He then spent some time exploring the grounds, snapping pictures of the lake from his deck, and experimenting with his new camera. He was rather enjoying himself until he realized that the daylight had faded and his belly reminded him that it was well past the time for him to eat.

Even through the dim light from his deck, Liam could now see the glow of the many oil lamps at the tavern glowing in the cold March air. He washed up again, changed into a casual pair of pants, a freshly pressed button-up shirt and he made his way out of his room and out a side door of the inn. He had thought for just a brief moment of passing by the front desk and chatting with Charlotte, but he was not yet willing to test his newfound self-confidence to any great extent. For some reason, Liam felt it was too soon to do so. He thought about how he needed to work on that confidence factor just a bit more. Out the door, into the cold night air, Liam Murphy went, and he walked hastily in the direction of The Oil Lamp Tavern. The captivating lure of the flickering of the oil lamps in the cold evening air pulled Liam in their direction and set an air of mystery upon the night.

Tomorrow, perhaps, he would encounter the Will O' the Wisp, across the lake. Tonight, his mind was set upon that Yankee pot roast and a pint or two, or three of stout. He admitted with a smile that the vision of Charlotte and her smile and shapely figure would cross his mind a bit, too.

Chapter 3

The Finest Woman of all Women

Karen LeClaire sat at her desk in her office, which was located on the top floor of The Oil Lamp Tavern. She was reviewing some book work, speaking on the telephone to contractors, architects and her financial advisers and doing her best to make sound decisions, while answering a few of their questions. Planning construction projects for a property of this magnitude required planning and quite a bit of capital outlay too!

She did some double-checking of food orders placed in preparation for the Saint Patrick's Day festivities, which now loomed closer and closer as winter waned.

The tavern supported a small enclave of residents in Centrebridge, who were of Irish heritage, and the tavern always did a brisk business on the holiday. Even though Karen herself was of French descent, spoke fluent French, and was well aware of what her actual heritage was, she happily joined in and was an active participant in the holiday. Karen universally subscribed to the belief that on Saint Patrick's Day, everyone was Irish. Besides, the holiday was an exceptional day for business, too.

Karen was single, gorgeous, wealthy, successful and always in control. She had long black hair, flawless facial features, a long neck, and a perfect figure. She dressed immaculately, and she prided herself on her extraordinary self-confidence, her appearance, and keeping herself in good shape. She jogged around the lake, worked out daily in a local gym in a brutal and demanding exercise program, but she felt as if the benefits paid off, not only in her attractive figure and appearance but also in her emotional well-being. Karen felt that if you look good, it was certainly going to make you feel good, too. Despite the demands of the past year or so with the challenges the resort, the inn, and to a certain extent, even the tavern faced, Karen kept her frame of mind and positive attitude.

She was the envy of every single man in the community, and most of the married ones too! Karen had once been married. Unfortunately, the marriage did not turn out too well because her husband proved to be prone to be lazy, unmotivated and while he was indeed charming and handsome, his lack of ambition, and his penchant for riding Karen's coattails and earnings, while he lounged about and wasted money, finally, drove them apart.

Good riddance, Karen often felt. She tried hard to convince herself that she did not need any man interfering in her life right now.

After working a long career as a key executive in a worldwide corporation headquartered out of Boston, she returned to her childhood home of Centrebridge. When the famous resort, tavern, and the inn came up for sale, then Karen knew this was the chance that she had been waiting for. She had invested parts of her large salary in some very wise investments over the years, and wealth was not an issue for Karen. Finding something to keep her driven personality and active mind busy was the immediate challenge. She felt as if she found what she needed!

She bought the entire operation, the entire parcel and all the buildings too, and she was the proud owner of it all!

Karen noticed the time, closed her books, and shut the light out over her desk. She always tried to mingle with some tavern patrons, and tonight would be no exception. Karen would check on the staff, say hello to some new faces, smile her attractive smile, wiggle her amazing figure around the dining floor, and say hello to some of her regular guests too. It was all part of her business plan and when you looked as good as Karen LeClaire did; you were sure to arouse a bit of attention and ensure the return of many of the patrons.

After working the floor of the tavern for a bit of time, she would return to her office and finish up some more paperwork. Owning an establishment such as this was not for the faint at heart. It required hard work, long hours, and dedication.

Especially now.

Karen loved every minute of it, especially the hard work part. It kept her mind busy and occupied.

She had to admit, though, she would often work late in her office, but only while she knew that the nighttime labor was still in the back of the house of the tavern, cleaning, doing dishes and other closing tasks. Once they finished, Karen would leave too because the noises, creaks and groans that the old tavern produced late at night, when it was quiet, sometimes, unnerved her.

She tried to tell herself that it was because the building was well over two hundred years old.

She did not subscribe to the haunting theories of some of her staff, and while she had never actually seen the ghost of the old sea captain, or of his widow, or any other ghost, Karen had heard and encountered some very strange things in her year or two of owning the tavern and resort.

One wild evening, about six months earlier, the sounds of someone walking downstairs in the tavern, and the distinct noise of the opening and closing of the very thick and heavy, main entrance door, rattled Karen's nerves so badly, she ended the night by locking up early, running to her car, and exiting the driveway rather quickly. The next night, when she returned to work and spent some late hours in her office, the noises did not occur and Karen decided to keep the entire incident to herself, never mentioning a word to anyone.

She knew that some staff had their own strange experiences and encounters, with noises, and unexplained occurrences in the old tavern, with one kitchen dishwasher quitting his position, when a late-night incident unnerved him so badly.

In fact, Karen tried hard either to dismiss the memory of the adventure with the front door and strange footsteps, or better yet, not to work late when she was alone.

But, why take any chances? Besides, it gave her an excuse to return home early.

Liam Murphy approached the entrance to the tavern. He stopped and admired the glow of the oil lamps through the windows of the tavern, as well as the lamps at the base of the walkway leading to the front entrance and the lamps hanging upon the corners of the building.

He thought, "Ah, so there is the, Will O' the Wisp. It is most likely just an illusion. Could be just the flicker of the lamp's broadcasting on the lake."

From the outside, the tavern looked as if it was simply a typical, two-story New England, colonial type of residential house, boxy, framed, tall and straight. Large, double-hung windows allowed a clear view of the inside of the first floor of the tavern, and Liam could see a roaring fire in a stone fireplace at the far end of the dining floor. He looked up and noticed a chimney gallantly puffing out dark smoke into the cold night air. He not only could now smell the odor of wood from the large fireplace in the lobby of the inn next door, he could also smell the burning of the fireplace within The Oil Lamp Tavern.

Liam made his way up the walkway, turned the knob, and entered the lobby. The lobby area was small and narrow, with oak wood floors and rustic décor. A framed five-star review of the tavern from a prestigious Boston newspaper and other tidbits decorated the walls. He eyed an interesting portrait on the wall of the ship captain who was lost at sea, in the legendary story, and Liam thought how if it was not a fictitious story, then the dark haired, and green-eyed captain with the last name of O'Leary, portrayed here, was a handsome chap.

An immediate right turn brought him face-to-face with a smiling hostess. Looking over her shoulder, he could see the open dining room, the fireplace on one end, the ceiling open with wooden exposed beams, an oak floor with oak tables and chairs. It was rustic, but by the same token, it was quaint. A bar, also framed and covered in rustic solid oak and finished to a mirror-like shine, was on his left side, staffed by a large, rotund, smiling older chap with red cheeks and a full head of white hair.

As Liam scanned the dining room interior, he noticed that upon every table, an antique oil lamp sat, enhancing the atmosphere with a warm glow of invite, the wicks of each oil lamp flickering in unison within their individual glass chimneys.

"Good evening, Mr. Murphy. We have a special table set aside for you right next to the fireplace. After all, it is not very often that we have the pleasure of a guest of your importance. A world-famous photographer and an extremely handsome one at that!" The gregarious hostess was greeting Liam with a smile and some rather overblown exaggerations. She smiled widely, a smile revealing bright white teeth that glowed, even in the dim light of the interior of the tavern. The happy hostess was short, attractive, yet just a bit round and plump, but Liam could not help but immediately admire her mannerisms.

He usually did not trust any person who smiled a lot, however, for this collection of very attractive young women around here; he might just make an exception.

"Oh, yes, good evening. I am here for dinner, perhaps, a

few drinks too. Yes. Thank you, but to set the record straight, I am not exactly a very good. . .."

"Right this way, Mr. Murphy," the hostess picked up a menu and waved her hand, indicating that Liam should follow her.

As he waded through the early dinner crowd, a few women here and there looked up at him and they smiled while they obviously studied him as he passed by. Liam smiled back. Since his encounter with the enchanting Charlotte at the front desk, his confidence was building and his ego boosted. Liam finally decided to play into the whole charade. Perhaps even work it to his advantage. Come out of his shell.

Well, maybe.

Pretty, young lassies all around, all paying extraordinary attention to him, in fact, more attention than he had received from any young females in many years! Usually, he attracted the old battle axes.

So, what the hell, why not?

Since no one seemed to want to listen to the actual truth anyway, and he was, even with the discount provided by O'Reilly and Mr. MacQuaid, spending a bit of money to stay here, he figured that he might as well go along with the entire charade. It was not as if anyone was going to believe the truth now, anyway! After all, in his defense, he had tried.

The hostess led him to a table right next to the fireplace; she smiled, pulled a chair out from the table and waved for Liam to sit.

"Here you are, Mr. Murphy. A private seat that is far away from any autograph seekers and I will make sure you are not bothered while you are here to enjoy your meal.

Liam took the chair and started to sit, he smiled, sat and he thought, autograph seekers? Okay? That is certainly a novel idea.

Once over that thought, Liam managed to sputter,

"Thank you, ah, sorry but, I did not catch your name."

"Joanna," the hostess answered quickly.

"Yes, okay, thank you, Joanna. This is perfect. Say, if you do not mind me asking. How did you know who I was when I came in?"

Joanna smiled, and she stood with her hands on her hips as if to exaggerate the fact that this was an overtly easy question for her to answer.

"Why, Mr. Murphy. Please now, don't be silly. Of course, you must know how we know all about you. My good friend at the front desk over at the inn, you know who . . . Charlotte! She clued me in on whom you were. She mentioned how distinguished, tall and handsome you are and that you would be joining us this evening. She described you perfectly, and I have to say, that the color of your green eyes as they reflect in the oil lamp upon the table are rather amazing. Did anyone ever tell you that your eyes sparkle?"

Joanna turned away, and she did not wait for an answer. It was not as if Liam was planning to answer her anyhow. While she drifted back seductively to her post, Liam could hear her say, "Your server this evening is, Michael."

Liam watched her walk away; she turned on a maximum wiggle, hip sway, and bounce. She, too, was quite cute. He swallowed hard; he pushed back a hint of lust and thought about how glorious it was to be around such pretty women. My goodness, he thought, all this extra attention was apt to go to his head.

The interior of the tavern was amazing, a perfect setting, and his New England experiences were now complete. The warmth of the fire at his back provided a soothing feeling, and from his table, he could see outside the window and view the late winter evening settling in on the little town.

In addition, the lamp upon the table broadcasted just the right amount of light; the flames flickering and dancing in front of him. The colors from the glass chimney reflected a prism of light and colors upon the polished finish of the oak table.

It was all extremely enjoyable. Liam found himself immersed in the experience and hungry, too. He picked up the menu and found it to be identical to the smaller version he already perused in the pamphlet that Charlotte had provided to him. Besides, why was he even bothering to look at the menu? Liam knew exactly what he was going to order, anyway.

Michael came by, dressed impeccably in a striking black suit, and the efficient server promptly took his drink order. In a bit of a twist on his plans, Liam ditched his usual stout and instead ordered a double top-shelf Scotch with a single, large ice cube. Liam then ordered his food, deciding upon the pot roast dinner. As far as his drink order went, at the last moment, Liam shifted gears on his drink order because at this moment, he was feeling too classy tonight to stick with a plain, old glass of his usual stout. After all, Liam needed to play the part. He was a world-famous professional photographer.

Michael proved to be an excellent server. He paced the meal correctly, seemed to know exactly when Liam required attention and when he wanted to be left alone.

First, the drink, then another drink, followed by a crisp, fresh salad, and then the main dish, the coveted Yankee pot roast, smothered in unforgettable gravy with just a touch of mushrooms. It was all tantalizing and amazing, perhaps the best meal that Liam had ever experienced.

He sat there thinking how five stars did not exactly summarize, how enchanting this meal actually was in both content and atmosphere. Not a single morsel of the food disappointed him. The pot roast melted in his mouth, it was fork tender, and the side dishes that accompanied the meal, which were some ground turnips, green beans and a baked potato, soon had Liam stuffed and happy.

Liam Murphy leaned back in his chair, wondering why

it had taken him so long to take a holiday such as this one, and when Michael came to clear the table of the spent dishes, Liam could not pay enough compliments to the chef for the meal he had just devoured. He had to turn down an alluring array of desserts, which Michael presented to him. He simply had no room left in his stomach of which to even entertain eating another thing.

However, Liam did have another drink, and when Michael set the drink down upon the table, and he left Liam alone . . . it was then that he saw her.

She was standing next to the bar at the far end of the dining hall.

Lean and tall, with a perfect face and long black hair. The woman was speaking to two patrons; a couple who were sitting at the bar, and because of her relaxed mannerisms, Liam imagined that she must know them. She was laughing, and she seemed so confident. In fact, she was radiant. She was wearing a tight black dress, which flattered and enhanced her amazing figure. The dress was professional, yet dynamic, and she wore some type of necklace around her neck, it was too far and too dim for Liam to make out the details or type, but occasionally, the random light in the dining hall reflected off the stones mounted upon the necklace.

The first thing, which came into Liam's mind while he sat there captivated at the beauty and charm of this woman, was the sentence from the legend in the pamphlet, "For the love of the finest woman of all women, it was all worth it!"

The romantic sentence of the legend resonated through his mind. The proclamation of the legendary captain eerily facing his demise seemed so fitting for a woman such as she was. The story seemed so powerful now, whereas previously, he felt it was part of a silly and rather quaint story, a stereotypical and hopelessly romantic story of old. A cagey marketing attempt at cashing in on folklore and legends.

Gazing at and admiring this woman over the top of his drink, through a slightly drunken haze, he could see how a man could fall so deeply in love with a woman that such a statement would, in fact, be true.

Liam sat back in his chair, studying her from afar, while the woman made her way through the crowd, meeting and greeting some patrons, speaking with the staff and pointing here and there. Just the way in which she walked, the way in which she moved, amazed Liam Murphy. This was a woman of rare and intoxicating style and beauty.

Liam surmised that she was the night manager, or perhaps the general manager of the tavern. In reality, his wandering and supposition fell just short of the truth in that she was actually the owner and proprietor of not only the tavern, but of the entire resort.

My goodness, what a woman.

Liam's thoughts danced, and his heart raced at the sight and thoughts of this captivating woman. He felt a pang or two of disappointment when he lost sight of her as she went through some doors, most likely doors to a hallway, which led to the back of the house or the kitchen. While pondering the thoughts of admiration racing through his head, he returned to sipping his drink, enjoying the fireplace, and staring out the window.

Liam raised his hand to wave Michael over and ask for his tab when a soft voice from behind him caused him to jump in his seat.

"How was your meal tonight, Mr. Murphy? Oh, my goodness! I am so sorry to have startled you."

Liam quickly recovered from his nervousness and he felt a gentle hand on his right shoulder. To his utter shock and with his heart fluttering, he looked up to see *the woman* standing next to him smiling with her hand on his shoulder.

"Oh, I am sorry . . . my goodness, I did not hear you

coming, until you spoke. I am sorry for my reaction," Liam stumbled over his words and his startled reaction.

"No, please, my apologies. I should have approached you from the other side of the table. I can see now that you were lost in dreaming out the window there. I am the owner of the tavern and of the resort and inn. I just wanted to thank you and make sure that you enjoyed your meal."

She posed at his table, smiled and said, "Hello, my name is, Karen LeClaire."

Karen extended her hand and Liam stood up, smiled, and reached for it. He gently grasped her hand, and he immediately felt her warmth and the softness of her touch.

"Hello, Karen. It is my pleasure to meet you. I am Liam Murphy. However, apparently, for some reason, you already knew my last name."

Liam Murphy melted away . . . right then and there; her remarkable beauty melted him away.

Karen ignored Liam's remarks as to knowing his identity and instead, stuck to a business angle for the visit, "Please let me ask you? How was your overall dining experience? We strive for excellence here. I hope you enjoyed the dinner, service, and drinks. Is there anything else that I might be able to obtain for you?"

Liam was stumbling, thick-tongued, and just a bit tipsy. To some embarrassment on his part, Liam was still rather awkwardly grasping her hand while he tried hard to focus past her beauty, but despite his best efforts, he could not.

After what seemed as if four lifetimes passed by him, and making a note of his slightly altered state, he finally managed to say, "I do apologize in advance, for my abhorrent and eccentric behavior, while under the influence of the devil's brew."

Karen let go of his hand and burst out laughing, waving her now free hands in the air while explaining to him, "I am afraid that is copyrighted material, Mr. Murphy. However, please, no apologies are required in advance, for whatever you might decide to do. I assure you that over our many years here, we have seen much worse behavior than yours is right now."

Liam felt like an ass. His skills amongst the ladies these days were less than perfected; he had been out of the circle for too long. Deep within a slightly drunken haze of scattered brain cells, he realized that he was blowing an excellent opportunity, and he finally regained composure and focus. Focus, Murphy, focus, his brain kept telling him. Okay, now, check her out. No wedding band and he swore that she, too, had glanced at his hand when she first had introduced herself.

Recovering, Liam said, "Sorry, I assure you that I will remain under control and not infringe upon any copyrights. I had read the story of the tavern legend in my room a little while ago. It seemed to me that the story fit my presently slightly altered state from consuming your amazing Scotch that you do pour here. Okay . . . well, never mind."

He felt awkward standing, and embarrassed at his rambling drivel. Therefore, Liam went to sit back down into his chair.

Karen sensed that he was uncomfortable. She nodded her head, pointed towards the table and said, "Please, you are our guest. Please, sit and be comfortable. May I join you?" She pointed at the empty chair at the table to ask if she could sit there. Only an imbecile of a man would refuse her! Any man would find it difficult to stand after gazing upon her, hearing that glorious, soft voice and smelling the intoxicating scent of the delectable perfume that Liam just enjoyed when she moved by him.

"Please do join me, it will be my pleasure."

Liam watched her glide over to the chair, gracefully pull it away from the table and slip into it. He could now see the fabulous necklace hanging around her neck, dangling from a chain. It was a sapphire framed in gold and silver, with some diamonds running around the perimeter of the gemstone. A stunning display and a fitting enhancement to her astonishing beauty. In the glow of the lamp upon the table, she astounded him.

"I must say, Mr. Murphy. . .."

"Liam. Please, just call me, Liam, and if I may call you, Karen? Anyway, please call me, Liam." Liam cut Karen off and his assertiveness struck a chord with her. Liam suddenly regained some of that lost confidence.

She smiled and said, "Then, Liam, it is, and yes, Karen is fine, too. Please do call me, Karen. Honestly, I must tell you that you have caused quite a stir amongst my staff here at the tavern, as well as, a certain front desk clerk here at the resort. A stir amongst specifically, the female staff. Something about a world-famous photographer, your appearance, and I do not mean to embarrass you, but, your deep, green eyes seem to have been a topic of conversation."

Liam did not know how to respond. The world-famous photographer charade had to end, he did not want the fallacy to perpetuate, but he sensed by her delivery, the sparkle in her eyes and her body posture, that Karen seemed to be in some roundabout way, agreeing with the other female members of her staff.

The less than assertive portions of Liam's personality overtook his confidence. He decided to avoid the attraction angle of the conversation and finally put an end to the false reputation.

To do so, Liam decided that was where he would start the conversation, "Well, honestly, about the world-famous photographer. . .."

"Mr. Murphy . . . wait, I apologize . . . Liam, please tell me. Did you enjoy the meal? I am so sorry, but I did not allow you to answer my previous inquiry about the meal."

Liam thought, my goodness, damn, how he would *never* be able to tell the truth. No matter how hard he tried to dispel the bullshit, no one would allow it!

While he pondered his next move, they both noticed the flame in the oil lamp upon the table, suddenly flicker, it sputtered, struggled, and for a second or two, it seemed as if the flame would extinguish.

"Oh my, the flame cannot go out. We keep them burning all the time and just switch them out with standby lamps when they require service. It is our tradition," Karen said as she prepared to jump into action, positioning herself to either relight the lamp or replace it with extra ones that lined the windowsill behind her.

While Karen spoke, the flame suddenly recovered, it sputtered a little more, but then it burned bright and strong.

Karen commented, "Strange. It must have been a draft across the flue of the fireplace. I think the wind is picking up quite a bit outside."

When Karen carefully studied Liam's face in the recovered flame, his amazing green eyes, his dark features, and his handsome appearance suddenly captivated her. For a fleeting moment, she thought she recognized a resemblance to the portrait of the captain hanging in the entrance lobby, but she dismissed it for being just a trick of the flame and a wandering imagination.

However, she thought, there was no doubt; flickering flames, wandering imaginations, or whatever, this is an extremely handsome man. She could see why the female members of her staff had become so enthusiastic about his presence.

Liam turned and observed the fire burning in the fireplace and he shook his head a bit as he noticed that the flame in the pit had not altered due to a draft. He turned back, and finally answered the question that Karen had asked, before the flickering interlude of the oil lamp intervened in their conversation.

"Strange, yes. I know the lamps must never go out. Part

of the shtick, and rather effective marketing. In my opinion, your amazing food, impeccable service, and drink are all that you need for marketing, Karen. Finally, to answer your question about how my dining experience was, I have to say, this was the finest meal that I have ever enjoyed. Remarkable. I thoroughly enjoyed the meal. Michael is an impeccable server and I extend my extreme compliments to the chef, your staff, and to you, the owner."

Karen smiled widely. Her face lit up, and she clearly enjoyed the praise from Liam.

"Thank you. I am very glad that you enjoyed it so much. I am sure a world traveler such as you are has dined in some of the finest restaurants in the world. Therefore, the compliment means even more when coming from you. I will have my maintenance crew trim the wicks up on these lamps. No doubt, the flames are all going to start to sputter now. It has been my great pleasure to meet you."

With those words, Karen stood up and smiled at Liam while explaining, "I have to greet some more of our guests. Please have an after-dinner cordial, on the house. I will let Michael know."

When he saw Karen stand up, Liam quickly stood up, he extended his hand, and quietly said, just above a whisper, "Thank you. I will enjoy one last drink, and I assure you that I will be back tomorrow night."

"Thank you, Liam. We look forward to serving you," she said, and off she glided across the dining room floor to greet some more patrons. Liam sank back down in his chair, slightly wavering in a drunken stupor, slightly hazy, but as he watched this incredibly beautiful woman move across the floor, he knew what the flutter in his heart and in his mind meant.

Liam felt as if the connection between them was immediate and it was magnetic. Admittedly, it was slightly primal in nature, yet undeniable, and it resonated throughout both of their hearts and souls.

Liam now knew that a certain young woman, working the front counter, nearing the end of her shift, as a front desk clerk at The Centrebridge Resort and Inn on White Pine Lake, was about to be severely disappointed. Until just a few minutes ago. Entertaining Charlotte tonight after her shift ended had been a fleeting thought in the back of his mind. However, right now, he dismissed the thought entirely because all he could focus on, if he was able to focus upon anything right now, was a certain Karen LeClaire. Liam also knew that gorgeous young ladies such as Charlotte Walker did not often fail in obtaining her wishes and motives when it came to handsome men pursuing her.

Oh well. Sorry there, Charlotte!

Liam enjoyed the on-the-house cordial, paid his tab, left a handsome tip for Michael, and while teetering and wobbling just a bit, he bid Joanna a good evening and made his way back to the hotel. It was a clear, bright and cold evening, and the short walk and fresh air were very refreshing to Liam.

It helped to sober him up a bit.

A little.

When he returned to the hotel, instead of walking past Charlotte, and having to deal with a rather unpleasant conversation, Liam covertly ducked in a side entrance, and wandered the hallways back to his room. He was a bit tipsy for sure, a bit confused, but one thing was clear in his mind, he had never before seen a woman like Karen LeClaire was. Ever.

In a different time, or place, in the altered state that he was presently in, Liam would have finally shed his normally reserved behavior and Charlotte and Liam would have shared a remarkable evening together. However, as Liam collapsed into his bed, tore his shoes off and settled into a good night's rest, he had a different woman on his mind.

On the other side of the town, a certain professional woman, a woman always in control, and always on top of her game, sat at her kitchen table sipping a warm brandy from a brandy glass. She looked around the expansive kitchen, in a house entirely too big for just her to live in, and in the dim light of one lonely night light glowing on the counter top, Karen LeClaire tried as hard as she could to wipe her mind of this nagging loneliness. She had to admit to the fact that despite all of her success and all of her goals and ambitions, the one thing missing from her life right now was companionship. She tried very hard to tell herself that a man in her life right now would only cause complications and could cause her to stray from her immediate goals. After all, those dreams were just starry-eyed wanderings of roads in which she had previously been down before.

Now, those dreams were bitter memories. Deep within her mind, Karen knew that the loneliness was picking away at her. The memories of love gone wrong, as well as the events and tragedies of the past few months, were just too strong, too awful, and too painful to dwell upon for very long. This was going to be another sleepless night, unless she could somehow forget.

Deep in her mind, Karen knew that despite the influence of the warm brandy running through her veins, that forgetting was going to be a tough thing to do.

Chapter 4

Soirée Magique

Liam Murphy could handle his share of stout. However, too many double Scotch whiskies were out of the usual drinking realm of his normal intake of alcoholic adventures. Social drinking adventures or otherwise. In fact, other than his usual stops at O'Reilly's Safe Haven Pub, he had, until last night, no actual social life.

Once he shook a few vivid images of Karen LeClaire from his mind, then he slept like a rock. When morning arrived, Liam determined from the imprint upon the mattress that he did not even seem to move too much, from the spot where he first laid down in the bed. His socks and shoes were off, as well as his fancy button-up dress shirt, but when his eyes fully opened, he realized that he still had his dress pants on.

Oh well, he was sure the hotel could send them out for a pressing for him.

Liam rolled over; he flopped out of the bed and slowly stood up. He creaked and cracked a bit since middle-age was creeping up on him. He shuffled to the bathroom and determined he was not hung over; he was just a little hazy. Drinking high end, top-shelf Scotch, was worth it because if he drank too much of the cheap stuff, then he might be worshiping a porcelain god this morning.

A nice hot shower, a shave, and before he knew it, he was making his way down to the restaurant within the hotel for some breakfast. The weather was cold and clear, and Liam wanted to eat some breakfast and take advantage of the weather, to take some photos down by the lake.

To pass a bit of time at the breakfast table, Liam brought along his instruction booklet from the camera, as well as the tutorial photography book, but he found himself rather amused when he strategically hid the cover of the book from his server, while he sat and waited for his food to be prepared. Since he had gone along with this fallacy and "world famous," label this long—why shatter it now?

Besides, he was rather enjoying the attention.

Perhaps, the little tingling of newly found confidence he felt floating around in him was the result of the inspiration provided by O'Reilly and his apparently equally bombastic pal, Timothy MacQuaid.

Liam thought for a moment or two, how it was rather strange that the manager of the resort had not stopped by yet, or otherwise, sought him out to speak with him or introduce himself to Liam, especially after they had both shared such an engaging telephone conversation.

After breakfast, Liam found himself outside, along the shores of White Pine Lake. He was enjoying the wonderful weather, a cool breeze was in the air, but after a morning chill, the day was actually warming up rather nicely. The scenery was spectacular, the lake was breathtaking, the trees, while still stark in a late winter dormancy, had some bursting buds here and there on the few trees that had the courage to emerge just a little early.

Liam happily snapped roll after roll of film as he whiled away the morning. He felt as if he was slowly gaining increased knowledge of his complex camera, but when the film returned from the developing lab, he was sure that he would have some good shots, as well as some poor ones too!

Liam was sitting on a wooden bench, not unlike the benches you see in a city park. He was struggling with loading some film, when he heard footsteps echoing along the path, which lined the lake. Turning around to look in the direction of the noises, his heart fluttered when he saw that it was Karen LeClaire out for her morning run. She was dressed in a warm-up suit that fit her rather tightly, and Liam admired her amazingly shapely female figure in the suit, which accentuated her curves wonderfully. Liam quickly placed the instruction booklet as well as the photography book in his camera case so that Karen did not see them. He stood up, he turned and smiled, while Karen, when she saw Liam sitting on the bench, ran over, and she stopped in front of the bench.

She bent over slightly, in order to catch her breath and when she did recover, she spoke rather breathlessly between gasps of air, "Good morning! I hope that you are enjoying the scenery and capturing some good photos, Liam."

"Yes, yes, I think that I am. You are out for a run, eh? Yes, the lake is spectacular, the day is bright and clear and I am rather enjoying myself. I think that I have some good shots, although, you never can be too sure until you develop them."

While nodding, Karen pointed in the direction of the camera, which Liam had laid down on the bench, when he saw Karen approach. He had left the film half-loaded and the cover to the camera open.

"I am not too much of a camera buff, and you are the pro here, but I think you might have spoiled that roll of film, Liam. I do not think the film is any good after it hits the daylight."

Embarrassed, Liam stumbled and fumbled a bit while reaching for the camera, and to compound his ineptness with the camera, he could not quite figure out how to close the rear cover. Fearing the worse and knowing that his "world-famous professional" reputation was at stake; Liam ditched the entire mess into the camera bag, temporarily exposing not only the instruction booklet, but the tutorial book too!

He nervously and quickly gathered it all in while explaining, "Yes, well, it is a little frustrating. I just recently purchased this model, and it is so unlike all of my other cameras . . . it is a bit tricky to load the film."

Karen laughed and, while laughing, she walked closer to Liam.

With just a sly smile, Karen softly spoke, "I see, well, you will get the hang of it. I am quite sure. You seem to be quite brilliant and a quick study too."

Liam studied her in the bright morning daylight, her hair blowing gently in an early morning breeze, her brown eyes were clear and bright and her face and skin were flawless. She was glowing. She had to be the most gorgeous woman that he had ever laid his eyes upon in his entire lifetime.

"I trust that you slept well, Liam. The inn requires updating in many areas, it appears as if we are all stuck in the past, but the beds are all new and they should sleep very well."

Liam could hardly speak. Her beauty had this now rather consistent habit of stealing his voice and thoughts, but he mumbled, "Like a rock. I slept like a rock. I might say the amount of Scotch that I sucked down had a little influence on that fact too. You are quite correct though. The beds are wonderful. I usually do not drink that much, but last evening. . .."

Karen seemed as if she was wandering in her thoughts and in the conversation. She pointed back towards the building, while cutting Liam off in his confession, "Let me please ask you, Liam," Karen shifted her feet, and she leaned into Liam as she changed the subject from general small talk to a more serious subject, "do you think the facilities look that bad? Do they appear to be stuck in the past and rundown in your opinion? After all, you have an eye for detail. Being a photographer, subject matter is the most important thing for you to focus on in your profession."

The questioning caught Liam off guard a bit, yet it appealed to him, as he still rather fancied his previous aspirations in an architectural career.

"Well, the buildings and some of the grounds do require updates in certain places, the exterior requires some coats of paint, most of the trees and shrubs are mature and are well past their prime of being able to be pruned or shaped, however, I tell you Karen, the design and architecture are unbeatable. The appeal is something that I cannot quite put my finger upon, but it is magical. I feel as if I have transported myself to another place, and actually and honestly, to another time. It is remarkable. I love this place. My ideas would be to update areas, but retain the original design ideas, bring the facilities into modern times, refresh them, you know, but to keep the original flair and concept's intact."

Karen was clearly impressed, and she smiled widely while excitedly saying, "My goodness, Liam, you do have an eye for this type of thing! Perhaps, you missed your calling and architecture would have been a rather successful career for you to pursue. Those are the exact thoughts that I have been working with my architects on as they plan some renovations for me. They do not share my vision, and apparently, yours too, and they all want to go for a complete redesign. You are such an interesting man, Liam. The parallels between our thoughts are very exciting."

"Karen, I have to admit, I flirted with an architecture career when I was attending college, and well, sometimes, things change. For some reasons having to do with low funds and other matters, I just changed my mind and decided to do something else with my life."

She smiled again and melted his heart some more.

"You are still quite young. You should reconsider."

Liam moved quickly now, a sudden thought, an urge to not allow a special moment to escape.

"Please Karen, just a moment. Let me toss this ruined film, load a new roll and snap some pictures of you. Please, please, just a moment."

"Oh no, Liam. I am a mess. I have been out jogging."

Liam looked up, and for once in his life, he emerged from his shell, confident, clear and pointed in the right direction, "Karen, I do not think so. No way, in fact, you look gorgeous, beyond description. I cannot imagine that you could ever be anything but stunning and gorgeous."

She smiled and nodded while mumbling a slightly embarrassed, "Thank you."

He grabbed the camera, pulled the old roll out and even to his surprise, loaded a new roll of film as if he was an expert. He took the camera, waved her around a little to catch the proper light, focused the lens and snapped a number of pictures. The pressure was now on; Liam had to feign that he actually knew how to take a portrait shot.

In the viewfinder, she melted his heart.

Karen posed, and when he had shot the entire roll, he said, "Thank you, beautiful, wonderful pictures and a gorgeous subject."

Karen softly sauntered over to him.

She gently touched his arm and, in a voice full of softness yet edged with allure, she said, "Thank you, Liam. I must be back to my exercise. I would love to speak some more about your ideas for not only photography, but for architecture and a lot more too. Will I see you for dinner at the tavern later tonight?"

"Yes. Without a doubt. I would not miss it, or you, for the world."

"I will look forward to seeing you then, Liam. Good luck with the rest of your film."

She let go of his arm, smiled, waved, and gradually broke into a slow jog. Liam watched her until she disappeared from his view around the bend of the building where the walking path curled away from his sight.

Liam Murphy was now a new man.

The spring in his step was remarkable, his self-confidence overflowed; now, even he believed that he was indeed a "world-famous" photographer too. Karen LeClaire could make him believe that he could do anything.

She was beyond captivating.

After a few more photos, he packed his gear up and made his way back to his room. He did not capture, nor even see, any strange lights. The Will O' the Wisp proved to be elusive. There were no lights seen anywhere, except for the lamps over the walkways of the path to the tavern, which even in the light of the day glowed brightly. Other than the exterior lamps at the tavern, there were no lights or spooky encounters seen or experienced.

No ghosts.

No, Liam chalked it all up to very good marketing.

After washing up in the room, he enjoyed a light lunch in the hotel restaurant. Liam then spent the rest of the afternoon wandering the grounds, enjoying the great outdoors. His camera was a companion, but he found his mind was wandering so much, he was unable to focus upon any intense picture taking.

His mind had other thoughts at this point.

The truth be told was that he was as if he was an anxious child on Christmas Eve. He could not wait until dinnertime!

Liam showered, shaved again, and picked out his best dress slacks; a black pair with hard creases, and he matched it with a black button-up dress shirt that had subtle silver pinstripes. It was his favorite shirt and after carefully combing his hair, trimming up his beard and mustache, and double-checking his appearance, he made his way over towards the tavern. This time, his confidence overflowed, and he did not avoid the front desk where he knew Charlotte would be working.

Sure enough, as he strode confidently into the lobby, the young lady was there. Charlotte was working the front desk counter, and she immediately perked up. She had been waiting on a guest, and since timing seems to be everything in life, just when Liam strode by her, their business ended.

"Hello there, Liam. How are you tonight?" Charlotte asked with batting eyes and a seductive tone. She leaned forward on the counter a little, emphasizing her outstanding cleavage. "I was certainly hoping that you might come by last night, but I was disappointed." Liam stopped and smiled and Charlotte swooned, "You look, soooo nice tonight!" The young woman could not help herself.

You could dare to say that Mr. MacQuaid could interpret this for being inappropriate behavior for an employee towards a guest, but she did not seem to care.

"Oh yes. I am sorry that I did not stop and say good evening to you last night, Charlotte. I was rather tired, and it had been a long day and night. Thank you for the compliment. You too, look very nice tonight. I must be on my way, back over to the tavern for an appointment with, ah, roast turkey and stuffing."

"Thank you, but I think there is more than just your stomach calling and I guess that I do not look quite good enough," the disappointed Charlotte tugged at her shirt, in order to reveal just a bit more of her neckline in hopes of obtaining more of a rise from Liam. It was obvious that she was trying hard at tilting the odds in her favor.

One last comment from Charlotte as she tried her best to attract Liam into more of a conversation, "A certain Ms. LeClaire might be involved too! At least that is what I hear. I guess the competition is rough."

Liam smiled and waved. He did not want to carry on the

awkward conversation any longer; instead, he was going to leave it alone. His ego had grown enough, all these beautiful women vying for his attention! The former introverted loner was now a full-fledged Casanova.

The glow of the many oil lamps guided Liam on his way, and he made his way rather hastily up the walkway to The Oil Lamp Tavern.

In a repeat of the previous evening, Joanna was working at the hostess station, and she warmly greeted him. Liam looked quickly around the dining room. In his heart he hoped that Karen already was there and that she was waiting for him. His eyes carefully examined the large crowd packed into the tavern for this evening's dinner hours. He did not see her lovely face, or other exceptional parts, strolling around the dining room floor.

Liam thought, "Calm down, Liam, easy now. Do not blow this one."

Liam followed the gentle hand wave from the hostess, indicating for him to follow her across the dining room floor.

They conversed while they walked.

"I have your table right next to the fireplace all set, Mr. Murphy. We are quite busy this evening, but Ms. LeClaire told me to reserve this table for you. How are you tonight?"

"I am fine, Joanna. Thank you. You look lovely this evening, and yes, I had a great day!"

"Oh, thank you. You too, I mean you look marvelously handsome tonight too! I knew that you had a nice day, Mr. Murphy. I knew by the look on your face and the bounce in your step. I bet our wonderful scenery provided you with some wonderful photographic shots too."

"Oh, you bet, you have no idea."

Joanna smiled, placed the menu down in front of Liam's chair, and pointed at the oil lamp upon the table.

Joanna explained, "I apologize in advance, but this lamp

is rather temperamental. Honestly, it has been tricky all night. It keeps going out. I do not understand because Ms. LeClaire had our maintenance crew trim all the wicks today. She asked the crew to trim all the wicks, after this lamp, and the lamps along the front walkway started flickering the other day. I think it is the draft from the fireplace for this one, the lamps along the front walkway, well, I do not know. It is all very strange because they are usually so reliable."

Joanna leaned in closely and with a wry smile, she almost whispered to Liam, "Charlotte says it is because the old sea captain's ghost is fiddling with the lamps because Ms. LeClaire has found true love. I have to speak for some of us, as well as for myself, and say that this is rather bad news. Several young women around here have become rather smitten with a certain handsome photographer whose identity is all too clear, but I vow to keep under wraps."

She winked at Liam and walked away, once again swinging her hips in a vain attempt to advertise her potential availability to Liam. You cannot fault a lady for trying.

While fading away, across the tavern floor, Joanna gently broadcasted, "I will send Michael over right away."

Liam gathered some amusement at the thought of the particulars of the legend and the thought that he had somehow fulfilled it. Surely, the draft from the fireplace was the only explanation for the flickering and rather unreliable flame in the lamp upon the table.

It was indeed the only plausible explanation. Now, as far as the lamps out on the front walkway, well, who the hell knows?

Liam was holding his hand in the air, over the area of the lamp testing for drafts, when Michael came by and took his order. The order was clear and concise; a double Scotch, top-shelf, and he ordered the roast turkey.

"We will relight the lamp immediately if the flame dies out, Mr. Murphy. For some reason, it has been quite troublesome on this table and only this table, as of late," Michael faithfully reported as he scurried off with the order.

Funny, but Liam could not feel any drafts, but he kept testing for them by waving his hand in the air.

The meal and drinks were the same quality as the meal of the previous evening had been. The roast turkey, stuffing, mashed potatoes and other fare was memorable, and Liam enjoyed every morsel.

He did find himself wondering when, and if, Karen would make an appearance, and he continually scanned the dining room for her presence. She did say that she would see him later, and as he finished his meal, he had to admit that a slight pang of disappointment weighed in upon him. Perhaps she had another engagement that came up, or she was running behind her time in her plans.

A few minutes later, a gentle tap on his shoulder told him otherwise.

He turned around slowly. This time he did not jump through the ceiling and his eyes met the gaze of the stunning beauty of Karen LeClaire.

"This time, I snuck up on you and you did not seem quite the nervous cat on the hot roof that you were yesterday, Liam," she joked with a smile and a seductive wink.

Liam lowered his voice and softly replied, "I feel as if more than just the drink has mellowed me, and somehow, I anticipated your covert and clandestine arrival. Your chair waits for you!" Liam had left his old ways behind; this was the new and improved Liam Murphy, with his swagger restored and his green eyes aglow and sparkling. With a gentle push under the table, he placed his foot on the chair opposite his and slowly pushed the chair out from under the table. The invitation melted Karen's heart, and it proved to be a romantic and very seductive move on Liam's part.

Karen sauntered over to the table, and she, without any hesitation, sat upon the chair that Liam had gently pushed out for her.

"I cannot refuse an invitation like that one," she commented. As soon as Karen arrived, the oil lamp upon the table once again flickered and sputtered, and in an exact duplicate of the previous evening's events. The flame almost went out, but it recovered.

"That is so strange, we have switched these lamps out and trimmed the wicks, and still the draft from the fireplace overcomes those flames."

Liam did not comment, but instead directed his attention to Karen's gaze.

Karen changed the subject, "I think as the owner, I can decide to make an executive decision and take off from my work for the rest of the evening. I will join you in a Scotch or better yet, maybe, I will have some warm brandy. I will have Michael bring me one. Would you like to join me?"

"I think I will stick with the Scotch, not too sure about how brandy will affect me. It might make me howl at the moon after a few of these single malts."

"Oh my, I see, Liam. I will certainly keep that in mind. Now, about those ideas that you have, as far as the renovations to my property are concerned. I would really like to hear more of your thoughts on that."

The rest of the evening was magical. It was as if the two of them knew each other for years and years. The conversation flowed along so easily, they laughed together, and the conversation flowed so intuitively, instinctively. The connection between them was undeniable and before they knew it, the dining room had emptied out, and along with Liam and Karen, only Joanna, Michael, and a few kitchen staff members remained.

The night had passed them by very quickly.

"Well, I guess it is time to call it a night, Karen. I only have one more day here, and then early on Saturday morning, I have to ride back to New Jersey."

Karen carefully listened, yet she did not comment on his travel plans. The brandy might have been causing a bit of a haze for her now. She sat for a long time; she was obviously studying and admiring Liam's face in the glow of the oil lamp upon the table. She smiled and reached out for his hand. Liam grasped it tightly and for just a moment, he thought they would lean in for a kiss, but Karen did not move. Liam was growing increasingly bold, but not quite that bold.

"I really enjoyed meeting and chatting with you this evening, Liam. Your ideas for my renovations and observations of the grounds and facilities, I must admit, are remarkable. It has been my pleasure. I hope to see you again soon," Karen spoke softly while she let go of Liam's hand. She then stood up slowly, if not somewhat apprehensively, it was almost as if she was purposely keeping her distance, letting Liam know that she certainly was attracted to him, but not wanting to progress any further in her advances, or allow him to obtain a false impression of her ultimate intentions.

"It has been my great pleasure. Thank you, Karen, for sharing your time and the conversation. I do think that I will return for a visit in the near future. Because of the subject matter, I know, my pictures of you will be stunning. I will be sure to send you many printed copies. Thank you and goodnight. Perhaps, I will see you for dinner tomorrow."

"You are too kind, as well as quite a flattering and polite gentleman. Perhaps, you will see me. I usually do not work too late on Friday. Please stay in touch, Liam."

Karen stood up, walked closer to Liam's seat, and she gently touched his arm. She smiled, and she turned and walked away. Liam watched her walk away; he sat for a few moments, thinking. There were such mixed signals, too many drinks, and his thinking process slightly skewed. He did feel as if he was mishandling a perfect opportunity with a rare and precious woman, but for some reason, he felt that the time was not right to make a move. On one hand, with some deep thought, Liam felt as if he wanted to leap from his chair and to dash after her, grab her and kiss her right there in the center of the dining room, right in front of Joanna and Michael, and the remaining staff, but he just did not pick up the correct vibe. He felt as if he did so. Karen would not resist, but he also felt she was sending him signals that she enjoyed his company, but wanted to keep her distance for now.

On the other hand, perhaps it *was* the presence of the staff.

He watched Karen disappear; he caught out of the corner of his eye, the flames on the oil lamp upon the table slightly flicker once again, and then he watched while it gently recovered. Liam stood up, walked up to Joanna, and he graciously bid her good evening. From her body language, and slightly solemn facial expression, he sensed that even Joanna felt as if the entire evening ended in less than a romantic manner, and that it ended with a rather disappointing culmination. Joanna had obviously been eyeing the entire meeting between Karen and Liam very closely from her hostess post.

"Goodnight, Mr. Murphy. I hope to see you tomorrow."

"Goodnight. You will, yes, thank you, Joanna," was all Liam said as he walked by her and exited out into the cool night air. The bounce was still in his step; it was just greatly subdued from the previous evening's euphoria. Liam felt as if he had missed an opportunity to shelf his apprehension and move forward in his life with excitement, finally break the string of loneliness, and enjoy some romance.

In addition, Karen was exceptional.

In fact, she was beyond description, a rare and precious gem that he had found. He felt that because of his usual reserved tendencies that he let her slip right through his grasp.

Liam did not want to deal with a starry-eyed Charlotte. Therefore, he followed the same route as he did the previous night, and made his way into the inn through a side door and then to his room. He washed up, took his shoes off and he was just about to click on the television to check the late-night features, when he heard a gentle knock at the door. He hoped in his heart that it was not going to be some kind of awkward confrontation or meeting with Charlotte, as a quick glance at his watch told him that it was just about time for her shift to have ended.

He slowly made his way to the door, and at first, he was going to check the peephole to see who it was, but he decided to just go ahead and face Charlotte. He swung it open, and his heart stopped for just a fleeting moment when he saw that it was Karen LeClaire standing in the doorway!

"Oh, geez, Karen! Oh, hello!" Liam was not faring so well in hiding his surprise. He stumbled to control his shock and then corral his joy at the sight of the amazing Karen LeClaire standing at the door.

Karen leaned seductively against the doorframe. In her one hand, she held a bottle of brandy; in her other hand, she dangled two brandy glasses in the air. She looked beyond beautiful. Her smile melted Liam's heart into pieces, and he felt his entire body shake with the sight of her. Liam tried to speak, but Karen stopped him by leaning in and kissing him deeply. She gently pushed Liam backwards while their lips remained locked, and when they had both moved far enough into the room, she gently kicked the door closed behind her with her foot. The long kiss ended, and Karen set the brandy bottle down along with the two glasses on the wooden dresser inside the room.

She reached for Liam again and as they embraced, Karen whispered, "I think it is time for you to howl at the moon, Mr. Liam Murphy."

A long night of passion ensued. Never had Liam made love to a more beautiful woman and Karen never held a more skilled lover and handsome man. Years and years of pent-up lust, as well as years of loneliness, purged from both of their souls.

True love has a mysterious way of always finding the correct path and the right people. It may be right or it might be incredibly wrong, but when it finally arrives, it is impossible to deny.

As the long night of ardor dwindled and physical exhaustion from making love for hours on end finally took over, Karen whispered to Liam, "I have to tell you, you are the most amazing lover that I have ever had. Yet, despite my feelings, I cannot have a man in my life right now, no matter how much I have fallen in love with you. It would only complicate an already complicated situation. However, please know in your own heart, how much I have fallen in love with you. I have never been so comfortable with a man. It seems as if I have known you forever. You are very, very special, Liam. This type of behavior is not something that I have ever done before in my life . . . ever. When you did not make any move or romantic implications towards me after we finished dinner, I knew how special you were. Your respect for me is just one of the reasons that I knew that I have fallen deeply in love with you."

Karen rolled over on her back and seemed to be staring at the ceiling. Liam reached over, gently touched her arm, and then cupped her bare breasts and lovingly and slowly kissed each of them and then he kissed Karen's mouth, deeply, thoroughly and fully. It felt as no other kiss ever did before.

After the kiss, Karen explained, "This will be a tragedy of my own choice, Liam. You are a remarkable lover and handsome to perfection. Flawless. I must tell you that, we will only have this one moment in time to share, this one fabulous night. For now, this is all out of my control, but I will be gone in the morning."

Karen rolled back into his arms and she whispered once again into his ear. This time, she laced her whisper with a bit of a tinge of laughter.

"Confession time. I know that you are not really a professional photographer. I saw the how-to-do manual and the book on the bench."

Liam rolled his eyes and, in his defense, he tried to proclaim the truth one more time, "Karen, I can explain. I never said that I was. . .."

Once more, Liam could not tell the truth, even when he wanted to.

Karen cut him off, "Sorry to say, but the ways that you were fumbling with the film also gave your act away. Nevertheless, I do not care who you are, just hold me as if we will never part, because, damn, you can howl at the moon, Liam Murphy. I want you to make love to me all night, and this will forever be a Soirée Magique."

Therefore, it was exactly that in French, English, or any other language on Earth.

It was indeed a magical evening.

Chapter 5

A Long Trip Home

True to her word, Karen was gone when the daybreak arrived.

There was no note on the end table. No immediate indication that she had even been there.

Liam found himself awake, staring at the ceiling, wondering if this all had actually even happened. He had not heard her rise or leave. The combination of top-shelf Scotch and brandy, and remarkable lovemaking had made him not only howl at the moon, but sent him deeply into dreamland.

The release of years of bottled-up passion might have contributed too.

When he rolled over in bed, he thought that he caught a whiff of her perfume still lingering upon the pillow next to him. Or did he? Were his senses fooling him, or was his heart coaxing them? It had to be real.

What a night!

What a woman!

He had not imagined it; Karen had just taken him to a place in which he had never been to before. Looking around the room, he saw a half-filled brandy glass and the empty brandy bottle sitting upon the wooden dresser. Evidence that told him that this magical episode in his previously empty life was real.

"Hell, I wonder if that stuff did make me howl at the moon and I have to wonder where the other brandy glass went. Maybe, Karen took it with her as a memento. I swear that Karen left it there next to mine. Strange." Liam could not help but speak to the four walls. Walls do not usually answer, and these walls were no different.

They were ordinary walls.

Liam showered, shaved, and tried his best to become motivated for the day. The intention was to spend one last day out in the fresh air, taking photographs, enjoying the last hurrah of his holiday. He almost wished that it was raining outside, something to give him an excuse for the lack of motivation in which he felt. He had such mixed emotions at this point. There was elation at having shared the time of his life with the finest of all women and the elation, mixed with the cold, stark reality that she was painfully honest enough to tell him that it was only for that one special night.

Right now, the quote from the old sea captain in the legend seemed to be so poignant, "For the love of the finest woman of all women, it was all worth it!" He sat on the sofa in his hotel room, rubbed his forehead, sighed and mumbled, "It certainly was. Maybe marketing nonsense disguised as a spooky legend is not quite as stupid as what I thought it was."

He wandered down to the restaurant in the hotel, mindlessly ate a stack of pancakes, and then, rather joylessly, went for a stroll around the grounds. He walked with his hands in his pockets and his head down. It was mind numbing knowing and realizing that such a wonderful experience and what he felt to be true love had to end so abruptly, so definitive, so hard.

It was so special, so unique, and it seemed as if they had been lovers for hundreds of years. There had been absolutely no awkwardness, no fumbling, and no hesitations in their lovemaking.

It was all so intuitive and so natural.

Liam returned to his room and spent the rest of the day

sitting on the deck outside his hotel room, shooting random shots of the lake from the deck, but mostly just sitting and thinking. In the late afternoon, he did jump in his car, ride out to the main drag, and there, he found a wine, beer and spirits shop, where at first, Liam was going to buy a bottle of that same, special brandy, but he changed his mind and instead, bought a six-pack of stout. Liam thought, what in God's name are you thinking? Are you thinking that Karen would be lurking the aisles of this store, buying the same brandy!

No sense in reliving memories that you will never be able to duplicate.

He spent the rest of the day on the deck, randomly snapping photos in the late afternoon, while sucking down the stout, and when that all wore thin and he finally ran out of film, he crashed on the sofa in the suite.

Liam went to sleep, amongst shipwrecked eyes and in the comfort of a haze of the stout. He slept right through the dinner hours. He was content knowing that Karen would be true to her word and not be at the tavern tonight. He did not even give the potential of spending time with Charlotte another thought, because no other woman could ever compare.

Karen had no competition.

Besides, he was not hungry anyhow.

Liam slept the rest of the night away. A deep sleep, a content sleep, a sleep of which he had not enjoyed for many years.

He did not even recall dreaming.

He was up early the next morning; he eagerly packed, loaded his car with his luggage and camera gear, and for some unknown reason, he was very eager to return home. He could not understand his haste. He had until eleven o'clock to check out of the inn, but for some reason, he needed to leave and put this entire episode behind him. No matter how he twisted and turned the reasoning over in his mind, Liam could not really understand his propensity to leave the inn and to end his holiday so quickly. It was Saturday, and he was sure the traffic would be light while returning to New Jersey. Still, his focus remained on leaving as quickly as he could do so.

The lobby was quiet so early in the day. The fireplace was alive with a roaring fire; it was very warm and inviting. Liam met the front desk clerk, a short gentleman with white hair, a faint whisker of a beard and a reserved smile. James was his name, or something similar. At this point, details to Liam were of little importance.

James was very polite, and he thanked Liam as he settled the folio. James asked him all the correct and proper questions; it was all very professional and concise. No references to his "world famous" status, no silly questions. It was all very matter of fact, and before he knew it, Liam was strolling across the parking lot towards his vehicle. He gave one, last, quick glance at The Oil Lamp Tavern, and he could not help but notice that the walkway lamps were still being troublesome, and they refused to remain lit. In fact, right now, none of the exterior lamps remained illuminated.

Liam almost, for a brief moment or two, had an unexplained inclination to run up to the windows, peek in, and check the lamp upon his table, the table right next to the fireplace, but he resisted the urge.

It was time to leave.

Soon, Liam Murphy was dust in the wind; he became a faint memory, lost in the mix of hundreds, perhaps thousands, of other tourists who passed through the parking lot of this establishment.

His car taillights were just dim reminders to his spent joy, as he turned his car from the parking lot of The Centrebridge Resort and Inn on White Pine Lake, onto the main drag.

A short spin down the main road, a right turn, and then

a left, and he was on the interstate. It would be a long trip and ride home. Yet, in some wonderful roundabout way, it would give him time to think, time to contemplate all that had happened to him.

Was he a new man?

No, but was he a better man?

Oh, yes, for there was no finer woman than Karen LeClaire was, and he knew in his heart that she felt there was no finer man than a certain Liam Murphy was. Despite the intense sadness in his heart, in fact, to describe it better would be utter despair that it had ended almost as quickly as it had begun; he knew both of their lives were forever changed.

True love will do that to you.

Time, age, and distances mean nothing whenever you link two hearts together forever.

Still, it was a long trip home. Memories and ghosts have a strange way of following you, no matter how far away you flee in a vain effort to escape their grasp.

About two weeks or thereabouts after his trip up north, on a late Saturday afternoon, Liam Murphy had settled back into his normal loner lifestyle. It was now long after Saint Patrick's Day, and Liam Murphy had a bit of a thirst for a few pints of stout and time to kill a few hours. His intention was to bring his pal, Thomas O'Reilly up to speed on his recent adventures (he planned that he would wisely omit certain parts) and to enjoy a few pints.

A certain element of inner sadness and deep regrets followed Liam Murphy wherever he walked these days, but despite his baggage, he retained a certain bounce in his step. The lingering remembrances of the love and beauty of Karen LeClaire would do that to a man.

Liam strolled into O'Reilly's Safe Haven Irish Pub. Thomas O'Reilly spotted Liam right away, and his usual rousing manner of greeting him was somewhat subdued on this go around as Thomas softly spoke out, "How rya?

Been a few weeks or so there, Liam, old boy. How are ye keepin'? The usual?"

"Sure, sure, sure, thank you, Thomas. I am fine, a little preoccupied, but I am good. That trip up north really renewed me in many ways, but it also caused me some painful reflections." Liam took his usual seat at the bar as Thomas drew the cold stout into the glass.

Thomas glanced over as the glass filled and he asked, "The trip up north?"

Liam had settled into his bar stool now, and he watched Thomas fill the glass, top it off and carry it over to him.

"Yes, yes, to the resort . . . you know . . . when I went up to Centrebridge. That is where I was for a week or so. I took your advice and MacQuaid fixed me up. It was quite the time."

Upon hearing Liam's words, Thomas immediately reacted loudly and abruptly, "Here now, Murphy! Ye should not joke over such a terrible thing ya know. Never knew you to be a cold-hearted rogue or a stupid bastard. I never had nuthin' but respect for ye, but if you are going to be an arse . . . then go 'head and show ye bare arse!"

Liam was in shock, as he watched Thomas hold the glass of stout in his one hand and with his other hand, shake his finger angrily in the air at Liam while he shouted at him. The small groups of patrons in the pub all turned now and watched the scene unfold as the usual jovial Thomas O'Reilly had his ire up.

"Thomas. Hang on, man. I am very sorry, but I genuinely do not know why you are upset."

"Upset! Upset! You should not joke over such a terrible thing! What in Heaven's name, are ye talking 'bout, Liam? How could you have spoken to MacQuaid? When did ye speak to 'em, eh?"

"Why, a week or so after you gave me the sales brochure, Thomas. I called him on the number that you gave me and we chatted for quite a while. I made the reservation and spent a week at the resort and inn. He was a nice chap on the telephone, but I never did have the pleasure to meet him. But wow, let me tell you about the woman. . .."

"Impossible! That is impossible. Ye could not have spoken to MacQuaid or been at the resort in the last few weeks! Now, I already told ye to stop joking and being an arse. I guess you and I will have to tussle a bit today, Liam. You are young and strong, but O'Reilly can still knock your lights out! I will clean it up a bit now, and out of respect for the ladies, use the Irish version and not the Paterson version, but ye need to fleck off now, Liam!"

O'Reilly was even more red-faced than he usually was, a group of regulars gathered around the stool where Liam sat, in support of the old barkeeper, and even Mrs. O'Reilly charged out of the kitchen to see what the commotion was that had her husband so enraged.

O'Reilly filled the glass with stout; he walked a few steps closer to Liam, and then he placed the stout glass down on the bar. He seemed to be studying Liam, and he was still visibly upset while pondering his level of anger at the comments made by Liam. He then suddenly, in anger, knocked the glass of stout over with the back of his hand. The glass shattered, and the dark brew went flying in all directions.

Liam Murphy was still dumbfounded; he truly did not know what had caused Thomas O'Reilly to become so upset with him. He stood up and shook his head, while waving his hands in the air, to indicate how sorry he was to have upset his friend. Liam staggered a bit as he stood up. He looked around at all the patrons and then at Mrs. O'Reilly and then at Thomas.

He spoke quietly and apologetically, but truthfully, "I am sorry, very sorry. However, I do not know why I upset you so much. I just wanted to thank you for the trip and tell you about the great time that I had."

O'Reilly now changed his demeanor a bit more as he sensed some type of sincerity in Liam's voice and he felt as if some type of confusion abounded with Liam Murphy. He wiped the back of his hand with his bar rag while he absorbed a trickle of blood on it from the blow to the glass. Thomas slowly walked over to where Liam stood while carefully studying Liam's eyes.

Thomas O'Reilly had spent a lifetime studying people's eyes and something told him that this was an unusual situation, and Liam Murphy was not being an ass. In fact, it was quite the opposite.

Thomas asked, "Liam, old boy, rya feeling okay, laddie? Have ye been drinkin' before ye stopped in?"

Liam stood in shock, but he managed to shake his head to indicate that he had not.

"You say you spent a week at the resort and inn. When?"

Liam was still confused. He stood next to the stool. With a slight quiver in his voice, he answered, "Why, about two weeks ago. I left before the holiday, Thomas. I swear that I did. Spent a week there. I ate amazing dinners in the tavern. I met all kinds of wonderful people, and a woman, who I have fallen in love with. I swear on my dear mother's grave, Thomas. It is the truth."

Mrs. O'Reilly looked at her husband and she gently touched his arm to indicate that he should calm down and go to his friend's aid. They both felt as if something was seriously wrong with Liam Murphy. O'Reilly circled in; he came in close and gently motioned for Liam to sit on the barstool. Liam looked around, then he accepted his friend's invitation, and he slowly sat on the stool.

"Liam, old boy, I tell ye that ye could not have been there. Now, relax, think, man. Maybe ye have been on a long bender. Sit here and steady ye out a bit. Here, I will get ye a shot of good Irish whiskey. Settle ya nerves down, laddie. I am very sorry that I became so angry at ye, but

MacQuaid was a good friend to me."

O'Reilly reached for a bottle of Irish whiskey and quickly poured a shot glass full, and handed it to Liam. "Pour it down, Liam, and stop ye shaking."

Liam nodded his head, steadied his nerves, took the shot, and threw it quickly down his throat.

O'Reilly watched carefully while Liam swallowed the drink and seemed to relax just a little as Liam struggled to understand what was happening to him.

O'Reilly gently spoke, working hard to break the news and truth to his friend.

Thomas O'Reilly had resolved his anger and now realized compassion was in order as he quietly told him, just above a whisper, "C'mere 'till I tell ye, laddie. I have not seen ye to tell ye, and I figured that ye knew about it. Would've called you, but as I said, there was no way that I thought that you did not find out on your own and already knew 'bout it. Now for sure, I do not know what has happened to you, but the next day, after I gave you that brochure, the resort and inn, well, I have to tell ye that, it burned to the ground. Lock, stock, and barrel, Liam. Gone. Just a pile of smoking ashes left. The lobby fireplace caught the entire place on fire and MacQuaid, the man did not. . .." O'Reilly's voice choked off, and he fought back tears in his eyes as his wife steadied her husband with a gentle touch upon his arm. O'Reilly recovered and said, "Well, he was a hero."

"What? What? I do not think so! I cannot believe this! I tell you that I was there! I spoke to MacQuaid on the telephone. He joked about you always exaggerating!" Liam screamed aloud his testimony while he stood back up, his body shaking and trembling. O'Reilly motioned to one of the other patrons to grab Liam and hold him up for fear that Liam would topple over from shock.

"Liam! Liam! Listen to me, old man! You could not have spoken to MacQuaid! My friend, MacQuaid, well, he died in the fire. He went back in to save a young lassie who worked the front counter and he carried her out of the flames but the smoke got 'em! He died there. They tried, but they could not save him. MacQuaid died a hero. God rest his soul! He was the only casualty. Everyone else got out. Mrs. and I—we just returned a few days ago, from his funeral. All that is left of the building is a pile of rubble and smoking ashes. The old tavern next door, it remains, and that is all!"

Liam was now staggering in his stance, and two of the patrons held him up by his arms and forced him to lean upon the bar counter. Liam buried his head in his hands and he shook it slowly as he forced back tears.

"What the hell is happening? O'Reilly, please help me! Thomas! Help me! I swear to you, Thomas. I do not understand all of this!" Liam picked his head up as Thomas and Mrs. O'Reilly gently reached and held his hands.

"Relax, Liam. I will get ye another shot. I tell ye, laddie. I know what *ye think* happened. We believe ye, but it is impossible, Liam."

Liam remembered a conversation, his mind spinning as he recalled Charlotte at the front desk saying, "Someday, a brave and handsome man will rescue me and carry me away from all of this!"

Liam Murphy bowed his head down and he gently whispered, "Let me guess, the young lassie . . . the woman who MacQuaid saved . . . her name was Charlotte Walker. She is a pretty lassie, very cute, nice eyes, a wonderful smile, with short brown hair, very neatly kept. Beautiful figure."

Now, Thomas and Mrs. O'Reilly shared the same shock as Liam Murphy did, as the words in which Liam spoke resonated right to their very souls. They let go of Liam and staggered backwards. Mrs. O'Reilly gasped, crossed herself, and held her hand over her mouth as her husband put his arm around his wife.

Gathering himself, Thomas answered, "Yes, yes, yes, ye are right . . . it was Charlotte. Charlotte Walker. How in the name of dear Jesus did, ye know her name and what she looks like? Ye never were there or could have been there!"

The reaction of Mrs. and Mr. O'Reilly was more than Liam could stand. In shock, Liam turned away and ran through the pub as fast as he could without knocking over other patrons or tables and chairs.

"Liam! Liam! Come on back here, man! I am sorry that I became so upset! Liam, we will help ye!" Thomas O'Reilly shouted, but it was to no avail, as Liam Murphy fled in terror from the pub. He ran the entire distance back to his apartment, fumbled with the key in the door, opened it, and slammed the door behind him. Liam stood inside the door; his back leaned firmly on the inside of the door because it was all he could do to remain upright.

He stood there with his heart pounding, his body shaking in a mix of terror and confusion, sweat pouring from his forehead. He ran up the stairs to his bedroom, collapsed upon his bed, and stayed there while shaking and trying to comprehend what was happening to him. It was then that he remembered the photos! Yes, the photos! The proof would be in the photos. He had taken at least one hundred photographs, rolls and rolls of film. He dropped them off a week or so ago at the local lab for developing and they should be ready by now.

Liam jumped off the bed, scrambled over to his dresser, and tore open the top drawer. He searched madly for the claim tickets for the film and the telephone number of the developing lab. Finding the tickets and information, Liam reached for the telephone on the end table next to his bed and shakily dialed the telephone number. His hands were shaking so badly that he miss-dialed the number twice, and had to start over each time. Finally, he focused, and the number went through . . . two rings, and the clerk picked up the line.

"Hello, Quick Photo labs. This is, Andrew, speaking."

"Yes, Andrew, please, this is, Mr. Liam Murphy, calling. I want to check on numerous rolls of film that I dropped off a week or so ago. Can you please tell me if they are ready? I have the claim number."

"Oh yes, Mr. Murphy. I do not need the claim number. We were going to call you today, anyway. I am very sorry to say, but all of your film, well, it is exposed, but there are no images. I am sorry. Something must have gone wrong with your new camera. Perhaps. . .."

"Why, that is impossible! The camera is brand new! Top of the line! You need to double check the film! How can all of them be bad?" Liam screamed at the clerk over the phone, as his shaking and trembling now grew even worse.

"Mr. Murphy, we are sorry, but the store owner himself triple-checked all the rolls. He is an expert, having been at it for over thirty years. I am sorry but the rolls are all blank. Only one roll was spoiled by light exposure, the rest exposed, but without any images."

Liam's entire body quivered as he recalled the incident when he could not load the film correctly when Karen came by, and he spoiled the film.

This was more than he could take, and in shock, he mumbled a low and almost inaudible, "Thank you." He slowly set the receiver down into the cradle and collapsed onto the bed.

Liam Murphy had no idea what had happened to him. Right now, it was beyond his comprehension, but he knew what he had to do to set all of this straight in his mind.

He felt as if he might be going crazy, but first, he needed to confirm something. He jumped up and tore at a set of luggage that he had not yet unpacked from the trip. Inside were the clothes from his trip that he was going to bring to the dry cleaners this week. He had just not gotten around to doing so.

Thank goodness he had lingered on that errand. It could

be his salvation.

He tore at the clothes inside until he found it. He found the black button-up dress shirt that he selected to wear rather proudly on *the night*. Holding the shirt reverently in his hands, he brought it to his nose and took a deep breath of the material, right there, around the lapel, right where Karen LeClaire had placed her lovely head and neck.

Liam Murphy smiled as he caught the faint whiff and the distinct odor of her lingering perfume.

Unmistakable, unforgettable, an undeniable odor, memory, and he knew somehow, at least parts of this were real and he was not going crazy.

He mumbled, "For the love of the finest woman of all women, it was all worth it!"

Digging around in the same piece of luggage, Liam knew he had brought home some more evidence in his luggage that would help Liam to realize that he was not completely off his rocker. He needed to find the pamphlet that Charlotte gave to him, which told of the legend of the tavern, and the invoices and the receipts for his hotel stay, the six-pack of stout he bought and the receipts for his meals and drinks at, The Oil Lamp Tavern. Liam anxiously dug around in the bottom of the luggage, tossing the clothes back and forth and all about the room. Frantically, he realized that there was no additional evidence because all of it mysteriously disappeared.

Suddenly, his body and soul calmed as a soft and quiet awakening of understanding overtook Liam Murphy. Karen's love overwhelmed his heart and his soul. It all became clear to Liam . . . strange, unreal, but somehow clear. This was a love from beyond the ages, from beyond reasonable understanding, from a place that Liam now knew, embedded within both of their souls forever.

He could wait for the statements to arrive in the mail. However, why bother with that? He already knew they would not show any charges. He could check the mileage on his car's odometer, in order to prove he rode all of those miles. Why bother? He already knew what it would show. He knew that he was there. The evidence was in his heart, mind and soul, and he did not need pieces of paper and photographs to validate it.

Liam sat down on the floor of his bedroom and he sighed. It was now, all too, clear to him.

Mysterious, mystifying, yet crystal clear.

He had no explanation for all of these bizarre happenings, but the lingering odor of Karen's perfume called to him from beyond the ages. All Liam had to convince him that he was not completely crazy was the lingering scent of a mysterious perfume that drifted from a time and place far away, from where Liam or anyone else could ever understand or comprehend. How remarkable and profound that the perfume scent from his lover was his only evidence.

He knew her love was real. He might be crazy, but her love transcended the craziness. As difficult as this was right now for him to understand and to believe, somehow it became a reality. A blurred reality. His past now brought him to his reality.

In his mind, he knew the words of the legend in which he had read. He remembered them all, if not verbatim; he certainly could capture the general gist of them. On the other hand, did he know the words verbatim?

Liam stood up. He now sat on the edge of the bed in his room, his head still spinning, but when he recalled the words of the legend, certain parts and pieces of this madness almost made some type of sense.

Could it be that simple? The lamp upon the table would just not stay lit. What was going on with the lamps out on the walkway?

Life is so full of mysteries.

Liam thought aloud as he held his head in his hands, while he spoke, "Upon hearing of the loss of her beloved, the widow refused to accept that her husband had been lost at sea. The widow vowed to keep the lamps continually lit along the front walkway until he returned home. She also promised to keep the lamps upon the dining tables lit until his return. The legend tells us that the ghost of the old sea captain did return to the Oil Lamp Tavern and he continually searches the building and grounds for his lost love and his ghost chases away any prospective lovers and spurned lovers of his beloved wife. If an oil lamp accidentally extinguishes, the captain's ghost quickly relights the lamp to prevent any false loves from stealing his beloved's heart. The legend says that when his widow finally finds her long-lost love and they reunite, the captain's ghost will then extinguish one oil lamp on one special table where the two lovers now sit and reunite in love. The lamps upon the front walkway will no longer burn during the day at all. There will no longer be any need for them continually to light the way to the tavern's front door.

Fact or fiction or just a spooky legend, our proud tradition of the lighting of the oil lamps continues today at, The Oil Lamp Tavern."

Incredible, but why could he remember those words so vividly?

He sat on the edge of the bed, shivering, with his head in his hands and his heart searching for answers. The cold, stark reality of what he experienced ran through his mind. It all became clearer to him, as his body slowly stopped shivering, and his mind focused upon the past as well as the future events.

He now knew why and what he had to do.

This was finally the one true love in his life, and he was her true love too. They were two special lovers, who had been searching for one another longer than any timepiece could ever measure.

Liam frantically repacked his entire set of luggage.

Laundered or not, he grabbed his toiletries, his camera gear, all of it. He called his boss and left a message that he needed to take a few days off for a family emergency, and that he would call him at the beginning of next week to provide him with an update as to his status.

Somehow, when he hung up the telephone, he felt deep within his heart that he would never return to his position there. Yet, if you asked him, he could not tell you why he knew that.

He just knew somehow.

Yes, indeed, life is so full of mysteries.

Chapter 6

The Lamp's Final Flicker

Liam Murphy, after a restless night with only a few hours of broken sleep, drove nonstop through an off and on rainstorm, driving the entire distance to Centrebridge, Massachusetts. He did not stop to sleep, drink coffee or even to take a restroom break.

He only stopped to fill his car with fuel, and to check the oil and other fluid levels. Liam himself was surprised when the state border for Connecticut and Massachusetts loomed on the horizon as quickly as it did. It seemed to him as if he spanned the long distance so quickly, so easily and effortlessly. Before even Liam realized it, he was rolling down the ramp off the interstate. He was driving a short drive off the exit ramp, down a main road, a turn or two. Liam soon found himself turning next to the entrance sign for the resort and inn, as well as the road leading to the tavern, and slowly making his way down the long entrance road to the parking lot.

His hands trembled upon the steering wheel as he fixed his eyes on the horizon and prepared his very soul for the sight he was about to see. He knew it would be exactly as O'Reilly described since there was no other explanation for what drove him, what convinced him. It just had to play out this way.

It had to.

Liam decided to park his car on the outskirts of the parking lot. He shut the engine off, reached into the back seat for his camera and gear, and placed the camera on his lap in front of him. He pulled a roll of film out and expertly loaded it with a few quick moves. This was all so exact and very deliberate.

There was no longer any fumbling.

He placed the lanyard for the camera over his neck and let the camera sit upon his chest; he grabbed an extra roll of film and stuffed it in his vest pocket.

Liam jumped out of the driver's seat and slammed the door. When he lifted his eyes to gaze upon the decimation in front of him, he did so with a heavy heart. However, in his mind, he already had prepared to see exactly what he now saw in front of him. He forlornly watched as a team of heavy equipment bulldozers worked the rubble around, moving it systematically into piles that were loaded into the waiting dump trucks. All those piles of what used to be such a grandeur building, along with spent memories in front of him.

The lingering smell and pungent odor of smoke told a telltale story of the devastation and ferocity of the fire.

He stood there in the cold. There was moderate rain pelting down now. It was a cold rain, which shivered his bones even more than the trembling of his soul did. Liam Murphy stood there for a very, very long time, and then he crossed himself, said a prayer for MacQuaid, and turned his gaze upon the tavern standing about two hundred yards to his right.

His gaze confirmed what he already knew that he would see. Still, he was not sure how he knew this, but he knew that the walkway lamps, in front of the tavern, would not light. He knew they just could not stay lit; there was no way that they could.

You see, there was no longer any reason for their way finding services during the day.

All the rest of what he saw was exactly as he remembered it. The lake, the benches, the walking path where Karen ran, the trees, the landscape, all of it. Just the way he photographed it. He reached for his camera, unscrewed the cap on the front of the lens, and started to snap away. Liam shot one full roll of film, and right there, in the middle of the lot, he reloaded the extra roll while kneeling with the camera supported upon his leg.

Damn sure, he tried hard to convince himself; he was creeping closer to being a photographer now!

He captured it all, every shot. He was quite sure of it this time.

Liam walked quickly back to his car.

He placed his camera and gear on the passenger seat next to him, climbed in, and started the engine. He rolled out of the parking lot and hit the main road; he was sure that there was another hotel a short distance down the road. He thought he had caught sight of the sign for the hotel when he was here just a few weeks earlier.

And he *was* here, there was not a doubt in his mind, that he had been here and now, Liam Murphy had returned.

For the last time, he had returned.

Liam was correct; he found the hotel, said a short prayer that they had a room available, parked his car, and walked in. He was indeed in luck, and when the front desk clerk asked for how long he was going to stay, Liam did not know how to answer him.

"Let's go with a week. No, make it two weeks, and then I will let you know. I am on business. I am Liam Murphy, you know . . . the world-famous photographer."

The desk clerk, a tall man whose nametag proclaimed only "Billy," shrugged his shoulders and mumbled something to the tune of, "That he had never heard of you before, but if you say so."

"Say, Billy, is there a dry cleaner close by that would do a really rush job on a dress shirt for me?"

"How rushed is rushed, Mr. Murphy?"

"Pretty damn rushed. I need it for tonight."

"Yes, that is rushed. In fact, borderline bullshit dreamin' by a guy who just told me that he is world famous. Ha! Two dreams in a short amount of time. Sure, one mile or so down the road, this same side of the street here. The owner is a drinkin' buddy of mine. Dave's Country Cleaners. I will give him a ring and tell 'em to take care of ya."

"Thanks!" Liam said as he took the room key, signed the folio and told Billy, "I will be back to check out the room in a few. Right now, I have to drop this shirt off at your buddy's place."

Liam gave Billy a ten spot, ran out, and jumped in his car. He found the cleaners, parked, and ran into the front lobby.

He chuckled a bit when Dave took the shirt from him; he too caught the whiff of perfume on it and commented, "Oh boy. Perfume, eh? Don't want ya wife or the new girlfriend to smell it, eh? No wondah ya so rushed. Got to hide the evidence."

Liam smiled and stood taller while his heart filled with joy at the confirmation of what he already knew.

After some moments to compose his soul, Liam finally spoke, "Yes, something like that, Dave. Thank you for that. You have no idea what it means to me that you could smell that perfume. No idea."

Dave seemed to be a little puzzled at Liam's strange reaction to his observation of the perfume.

Dave shrugged his shoulders and instructed Liam, "Okay, well, whatever. Glorious scent, almost hate to wash it out, cuz it smells like a piece of Heaven. Well, I gotcha covered. Wait a few, maybe browse the wine, beer and spirits store next door and come back in an hour. I will do a damn good job for ya. Will remove all hints of her from ya shirt. I promise."

Liam took Dave's advice, and he strolled around the liquor store, quickly realizing that this was the same store he was in on the last day of his visit. He purchased the six-pack of stout in this store. It all looked the same, all of it. Even the clerk working the front register was the same person. For some reason, none of this bothered Liam; it was as if he now decided that this was exactly how this was all to work out.

Liam turned a corner of a store display; he was strolling a bit now, with his hands buried in his pockets. His heart stopped for just a moment, when he realized that this was the aisle where brandy was for sale, and there in front of one display, right there in front of him, in all of his shock and awe, he could not believe his eyes, but there was, Karen LeClaire!

She stood gazing at the selection of brandy bottles, picking up a few bottles, reading the labels and studying them. Liam staggered for just a moment or two, he even had to hold on to the edge of the store display at the end of the aisle in order to steady his stance, but armed with his new realization, he knew this too, was all part of the plan.

She was just as gorgeous now as she was a few weeks ago. In fact, even more so! She stole his breath, but not his spirit, dressed smartly in a black spring jacket, a jacket that fit her perfectly, her long black hair tumbling along the collar, and her fine, long neck, framed by the same gemstone necklace that she always wore.

This was almost too confounding and amazing for Liam to believe, but he knew how it needed to play out.

He mumbled to himself, while he garnered his nerves and shelved his introverted behavior forever more, "Shit, this déjà vu stuff is a real bitch."

"Might I be as bold as to recommend this one," Liam said as he reached for the only brandy that he felt actually existed in the world, the same brand Karen brought to his room on *the night of magic.* He picked the bottle off the shelf, handed it to Karen, who smiled as she studied his face.

'Oh my,' Karen thought, 'his eyes are the most

remarkable eyes that I have ever seen.'

She tried to recover, but this stranger was so handsome she found it hard to focus.

"Oh, yes, thank you. That was actually the brandy, in which I was leaning towards purchasing. I appreciate the recommendation. Do you enjoy it often? I am surprised to see it here. I hear that it is very difficult to find. Almost rare."

Liam smiled and his smile melted her heart.

"Not too often, too much of it mixed with a single malt Scotch and it all tends to make me howl at the moon."

Liam knew how to play this one. He smiled, winked, and strolled off, leaving Karen LeClaire alone in the aisle as she mumbled just loud enough for him to hear, "Oh my, I will certainly keep that in mind."

She watched him as he walked away and admired the view. Karen had a strong urge, a strange feeling that she knew this man. She swore she had seen him some place before.

Because of her thoughts, in an uncharacteristic move, she called out to him, "Do I know you?"

Liam continued walking. He never turned around, but he did coyly answer, "You might. See you at dinner tonight."

Liam picked up the shirt from Dave, threw him an extra few dollar bills, and returned to his room. He showered, shaved and dressed in the newly cleaned and pressed shirt. True to his word, Dave did a damn good job. Liam could not detect any lingering perfume upon the collar or anywhere else on the shirt. It was now a perfect fresh start.

He hoped that he could change that fact in the very near future.

He picked out a pair of casual dress slacks, well creased and a pair that fit him, in his opinion, rather nicely. He selected a different pair than he wore on that special night. Perhaps, he felt that he needed to change something, in order to force this all to make some type of sense.

Walking out of the hotel room, Liam was supremely confident; he knew exactly how this would play out. The drive to the tavern was short. He parked his car and made his way to the front entrance. The two previously extinguished oil lamps on the walkway burned bright and strong in the night. Of course, they would now. It was now dark, and the lamps needed to allow Liam to find his way to the front door one last time. The rain now had let up and Liam could see the moon working very hard to make an appearance through the holes in the clouds. The front entrance was just as he recalled it to be, the heavy oak door, the door handle, the lobby, the painting of the sea captain, all of it.

Funny, Liam thought, while he studied the portrait of the captain, "I only went to sea twice, and I got terribly seasick each time. How friggin' ironic is that. Guess that I spent too much time on the open seas in my past."

Turning into the dining room, he saw the fireplace roaring in the corner, the oil lamps glowing on all the tables, and of course, his table next to the fireplace was empty. Liam's eyes worked around the interior of the rest of the tavern, and it was all the same as it was before. The same white-haired barkeeper to his right. And of course, Joanna stood smiling in front of him at the hostess station. Joanna's appearance was the same, and she batted her eyes at the sight of the handsome Liam Murphy, as she immediately did her best at turning on her charm.

"Just one for dinner?"

"Yes, just one for now. Thank you, Joanna."

She stopped and looked at Liam. She tilted her head while she studied him for a few moments and she smiled, "Do I know you? Have you been here before? I usually remember all the handsome men with sparkling green eyes who come by, therefore, you would be unforgettable."

"Well, I have been here a time or two. Might not have

been recently, but a time or two in the past. You might say that I have finally returned. Say, ah, Joanna, can I sit there at that table right to the side of the fireplace?"

Liam pointed to his table.

"Of course, please follow me."

"Is Michael working tonight?"

"Yes, sir, he is. Would you prefer Michael to be your server?"

"Please, yes, hey, Joanna please, just call me, Liam. Liam Murphy. I am a photographer. I am not yet world famous. Actually, and honestly, I am not famous at all, but I am working on it."

Michael walked over and introduced himself, thanked him for requesting his services, feigned that he knew him from a previous time, and took his order. Liam was not going to alter fate, be it either from the future or in the past.

He studied the oil lamp upon the table glowing brightly, powerfully, setting the night and his table aglow with a basking allure of comfort. He knew what was going to happen and that fate would alter the lamp's glow forever by the end of tonight.

Liam placed exactly the same order that he did on the first night when he ate and drank here at the tavern. Yankee pot roast, top-shelf double Scotches, and all of it tasted exactly as it did before.

Marvelous.

In reality, our lives are actually just a brief moment in time. Our past is simply a shadow of memories within another passage of time. Oftentimes, it is difficult to determine exactly where one life starts and another life ends. The line between reality and the past is merely a blur. When two long lost lovers unite across the ages, then fate has finally fulfilled their mutual destinies. Somewhere, perhaps, in Heaven, even the angels rejoice at the reunion of their love.

It is all part of an unavoidable plan.

Michael returned with another drink and he set it upon the table, right next to the oil lamp. The time was now near and Liam slowly sipped the drink. He watched and waited.

While lifting his eyes over his glass was when he saw her.

She was standing next to the bar at the far end of the dining hall.

Lean, tall, with a flawless face and long black hair. She was speaking to two patrons. A couple who was sitting at the bar and Liam imagined that she knew them. She was laughing, and she seemed so confident. In fact, she was radiant. She was wearing the same tight black dress as she did on the night when he first saw her. A dress which flattered and enhanced her amazing figure. The dress was professional, yet dynamic, with the remarkable gemstone necklace still hanging around her neck. It was too far and too dim for Liam to make it out, but Liam knew that it was the same necklace.

Liam laughed and whispered, "For the love of the finest woman of all women, it was all worth it! Imagine how glorious this all is for the both of us to wait for all of this time. . .."

Liam sat back in his chair, studying her from afar; he prepared himself for her voice to appear from behind him and vowed not to jump out of his chair this time around.

Liam raised his hand to wave Michael over and ask for his tab, when, sure enough, her soft voice appeared from behind him. Liam remained steady because this time; he had an advantage since he knew it was coming. He turned and faced her, then slowly rose out of his chair to greet her.

Karen stood there, posing, radiant, glowing as she gently spoke, "If you are one thing, Mr. Murphy, you are true to your word. Joanna told me your name. Please forgive my interruption. I guess that you knew I would be here tonight? You did come to the tavern tonight, and you did see me at dinner. You are true to your word as well as a person who picks out a very fine brandy. A brandy, I might add that strangely enough, my own liquor suppliers do not carry, forcing me to prowl the local stores. I just sampled a snifter, and it is marvelous. Even the name of the brandy is perfect. I speak French. Therefore, I find the brandy's name, Soirée Magique, quite enchanting and well-chosen."

Liam smiled, and Karen swooned.

He spoke in a lower voice, seductive in its calculated delivery, "Interruption forgiven and welcomed too, and yes, I was counting on you being here tonight. Glad to be of assistance on the brandy, and yes, it is a magical evening. I can guarantee that to be a fact."

Karen tried hard to find the correct words in order to frame her visit with a business purpose, "I see. A guarantee of magic. Interesting. How was your meal tonight, Mr. Murphy? By the way, I am the owner of the tavern. Sadly, I own what is left of the former resort and inn too." With the mention of the fire, Karen briefly lifted her eyes to gaze out the windows of the tavern in the direction of what was left of the resort.

Recovering from the reality, Karen spoke again, "I guess that you saw the remnants of tragedy, but please know that I never give up. Ever. We are rebuilding the resort. Onward and upward. Tragedy will not keep us down for long." Karen's eyes wandered from looking out the windows, to return to staring at Liam Murphy.

"I just wanted to stop by and thank you for the brandy suggestion and to make sure that you enjoyed your meal. Please, excuse my misstep. My mind wandered in mid-sentence. I should have mentioned and introduced myself before this. Hello, my name is, Karen LeClaire."

Karen extended her hand, and Liam reached for it. He gently grasped her hand, and he immediately felt her warmth and the softness of her touch.

This was the final piece of the puzzle. It was the moment of which many years had come and had gone, years that were waiting for this very moment to occur.

Magical, electric, passionate and finally, their love reunited. Liam felt the connection, as did Karen. The energy shifted between them and it vibrated all the way to their souls.

Liam held her tightly as he saw her swoon a bit, her dizziness readily apparent as the energy of the connection consumed her spirit. Liam reached out, and he gently steadied Karen; he led her over to the other chair opposite his and pulled the chair out from the table. He motioned for her to sit at the table.

"Your chair waits for you," he said once again. He smiled at her reaction, and Karen immediately took him up on his offer.

"Oh my, I am so sorry. I apologize. My goodness. Perhaps, I will sit for just a minute here. Yes, thank you, Mr. Murphy. I only had one brandy. Maybe, it went to my head a bit."

Liam knew what was coming next, so he sat back down in his chair, reached across the table, and he grabbed Karen's hands. For some reason, a reason, in which she did not fully understand, she instinctively and without any hesitation took Liam's hands. She felt strange holding this relative stranger's hands, yet it was so comfortable, as if she had held his hands so many times before.

"Do you feel better?"

She nodded that she did feel better while still staring into his eyes.

"I will stay away from the brandy. Brandy mixed with these single malts, makes me howl at the moon. Therefore, I do apologize in advance, for my abhorrent and eccentric behavior, while under the influence of the devil's brew."

Karen let go of his hands, and now she smiled and laughed, while explaining, "I do recall you telling me that fact this afternoon. As far as your prediction of your potential behavior, I am afraid that is copyrighted material,

Mr. Murphy. However, please, no apologies are required in advance, for whatever you might decide to do. I assure you that over our many years here, we have seen much worse behavior than yours is right now. Since I needed to sit down, then I am the one who needs to be aware of my behavior."

It was all just a rerun to Liam.

He was amazed at how it all unfolded so perfectly.

Liam said, "Sorry, I assure you that I will remain under control and not infringe upon any copyrights. I had read the story of the tavern legend a little while ago and I guess the story seemed as if it fit, well, never mind."

He could now see the fabulous necklace around her neck, dangling from a chain, a sapphire framed in gold and silver, with some diamonds running around the perimeter of the gemstone. Stunning, and a fitting tribute to her spectacular beauty. In the glow of the lamp upon the table, she astounded him.

"I must say Mr. Murphy. . .."

"Liam. Please just call me, Liam, and if I may call you, Karen." Liam cut her off, and his assertiveness once again struck a chord with her.

She smiled and said, "Then, Liam, it is. And yes, Karen, is fine too. Please do call me, Karen. I must tell you that you have caused quite a stir amongst my female staff here at the tavern, particularly with my hostess, Joanna. Something about a photographer and fantastic green eyes."

"Well, not really a photographer, so to speak. I am right now, a dabbler in photography. I think to call me a photographer is quite a stretch. I am working on my skills. Since it is too difficult for me to see my own eyes, it might be best that I do not even comment on that observation. However, I do want to tell you about a vision that I have for rebuilding your resort and inn. I might be a fledgling photographer, but I will tell you, I have an amazing eye for detail. Keep it retro, Karen. Rebuild it all within the same manner of which the original architects designed it so many years ago. Go ahead and modernize it where you need to, but please, you must keep the original flair, concept and design. It is the only way to go. Do not pay any attention to what the architects are telling you. I would love to share my ideas with you!"

Karen studied his eyes in the glow of the lamp upon the table. This was an amazing looking man, and she became captivated by what he just said, as well as his stunning and heart stopping appearance.

"Really? I would love to hear more. I have been telling my architects the exact same thing! How did you know the direction that they are pushing me all the time? The conceptual sketches are without flair, without the original concepts. Your observation is remarkable. The place had such character."

Karen paused in her comments and she carefully studied Liam. It was obvious that his appearance captivated her, and Karen focused upon the glow of his remarkable eyes within the flame of the lamp upon the table.

After her short pause, and a nervous but a quick smile, Karen continued, "I must tell you, Liam. Well, I swear I have met you before, somewhere, someplace. I mean before this afternoon at the store, with the brandy."

The usually, always in control, Karen LeClaire was now fumbling; her immediate attraction to Liam caused her a stir in her soul. She changed her voice to contain an element of allure, a quiet tone, while she told Liam, "Your appearance, and I do not mean to embarrass you, but your eyes seem to have garnered quite a bit of attention. Not only with Joanna, but I must confess that they are now with me, too. I have to say, I know that I have stared into your eyes before."

While he pondered his next move, they both noticed the flame in the oil lamp upon the table flicker, it sputtered, and for a second or two, it seemed as if the flame would extinguish.

"Oh my, the flames cannot go out! It is our tradition. For some reason, ever since that heinous fire, the lamps in the front of the tavern have given us such trouble as of late. We cannot seem to keep them lit during the day. Now, this one is sputtering too," Karen said as she prepared to jump into action, positioning herself to either relight the lamp or replace it with extra ones that lined the windowsill behind her. Liam grabbed her hands tightly and pulled her gently, but forcibly, back to her chair at the table. He knew that it was now time. Time had finally run out and their love had finally arrived at its final destination.

He leaned in and held her hands while he whispered to her, "Please don't bother, Karen. It will go out in a second, anyway. He will never allow it to burn any longer. He knows who I am, and in your heart, you do, too. I must tell you that despite all of your efforts, it will never burn again. Not ever. The flame has flickered for the final time. Please, it is not the draft from the fireplace, or a wick that requires trimming either. Furthermore, the lamps that have given you such trouble out on the walkway, will only burn at night from now on. It has nothing to do with the winds coming across the now empty property. No, it has nothing to do with what the maintenance man told you about his theory that since the resort and hotel are now gone, the winds are not blocked by the building and that is what keeps blowing the flames out. It is something much more than that . . . so much more."

Karen tried to relax as Liam pulled her back down; she slowly sank into her chair, while she held his hands tightly, still locking onto his eyes. She was now clearly bewildered, confused, and puzzled by what Liam had just told her.

She thought, what the hell is happening? Who is this man? They both watched as the flame sputtered a little, and then, just as Liam predicted, the flame went out.

Karen leaned in with her heart pounding in her chest now. She was confused for a moment or two, but while she gripped his hands tighter and tighter, she now knew that she would never let go of his hands and stop admiring his eyes. Ever. While she studied Liam's eyes, it all became much clearer to her. She finally understood. Her soul could no longer keep it a secret from her heart.

She whispered, "My goodness, my heart is pounding right out of my chest. My goodness, tell me, Liam Murphy, is this all real? Are you really the man whom I have searched for all this time? The man that I have sought in my heart for so long?"

"It is real, Karen. It is all real, and I am that man. Please understand, my love, that reality and the past are more of a blur than we can ever understand. True love is never lost. You have stared into these eyes many times before, and you will forever more. Now, and you always will until the end of all time. All we have in front of us will be endless love. Starting with tonight. Soirée Magique."

Karen shook her head in disbelief as she gently whispered to him, "I do know you. You are home, or perhaps you have been here the entire time, in my heart, in my life, and I just could not see you until now. It does not matter because now I know that you are the one and all this time, all of these people, I included, always thought it was just some ghosts and a silly legend."

While they kissed, the smoke from the extinguished wick of the lamp upon the table, funneled out of the glass chimney, it chased up into the air. The smoke swirled around and around, until it disappeared forever more.

THE END

Epilogue

About two years or thereabouts removed from that very strange afternoon when Liam Murphy fled O'Reilly's Safe Haven Irish Pub in terror, Thomas O'Reilly sat at a table in his Irish pub. He was sorting through and opening the daily mail when a large envelope caught his eye. He picked it up and he studied the return address.

Speaking aloud, he read it, "The Centrebridge Resort and Inn on White Pine Lake in Centrebridge, Massachusetts. Okay . . . I wonder what the hell this is all about," he said as he tore the envelope open and removed the contents. He pulled out a full color sales brochure, a brochure laden with wonderful photographs, detailing in awesome and vivid color, the newly rebuilt and fully restored resort and inn. Thomas studied each page of the brochure and he admired the quality of the promotional photographs.

There was a handwritten letter inside too, and Thomas pulled his reading glasses out of his shirt pocket to allow him to focus in on what the letter said,

"Dear Thomas,

I guess you had to wonder where I disappeared to after that strange afternoon. I have to tell you the entire story, but I would much prefer to tell you in person. Needless to say, it is a bit difficult to relate. After we share a few hundred nips of our favorite Irish whiskey together, then I think it will become just a bit easier to understand. Not much, but a little easier. Regardless, inside this letter are personal invitations for you and the wife to come up to the resort, visit and spend time with my newlywed wife, Karen, and with me. Our grand reopening is in three weeks, and we would be thrilled to have you as our special guests. Please study the invitations, my dear old friend. The invitations are for a free stay. Very soon, I hope to hear from you with a positive response. We can sample that whiskey, I can tell you my strange tale, and you can meet my gorgeous and amazing wife. Most of all, we can bask in the mutual joy of our lives, and my wife and I will share in the pleasure of your company, along with the company of the lovely Mrs. O'Reilly. I also will explain that true love always prevails and sometimes, what you think is real is just a vision of who you really are, both now and in the past.

All the Best,

Your old friend,

Mr. Liam Murphy"

Thomas smiled; he pulled his reading glasses off his head and set the letter aside. He then picked up the sales brochure again and studied it carefully. On the final page was a picture of Liam standing in front of the resort and entrance to the inn, with his arm around a gorgeous woman with long black hair. She was perfect, and her beauty was beyond description. His mind seemed to have recalled meeting her at the funeral for MacQuaid. O'Reilly would never forget such a gorgeous woman. Karen, yes, the owner of the resort! Amazing.

Thomas focused in on some fine print on the bottom of the last page of the brochure; he put his glasses back on and carefully studied it. There, in small letters at the bottom of the brochure.

He read the words aloud, "All photographs by Mr. Liam Murphy."

Thomas laughed so hard and so loudly that Mrs. O'Reilly came running out of the kitchen to see what had caused her husband such joy. She spotted Thomas laughing and waving the brochure in the air while shouting, "Well, I will be a son-of-a-bitch! Now and in the past, eh? What in the hell could've happened? A few hundred nips of whiskey, eh? Easier to understand? I doubt it but, good for ye! More than the power of the world to ye. She is gorgeous. Love is grand. Ye can bet that Mrs. O'Reilly and I will be vistin' ye. Liam, ye got my admiration. What a glorious tale. In the end, I guess ye finally figured out *all* those bloody buttons to push, eh?"

Afterword from the Author

I seldom feel as if a book or story, in which I have composed, warrants an afterword, but in this case, I felt that I had to share some events, which I experienced shortly after completion of the initial draft for, *The Lamp upon the Table.*

Never one to underestimate the strange, unusual and eccentric adventures of my own life; I usually manage to take it all in a casual stride when strange things happen to me. It is a part of my life, in which I have grown to accept.

For the most part, I had parts and pieces of the nucleus of this storyline floating around in my head for quite a bit of time, but a business trip to Massachusetts finally provided the full inspiration for me to write this story. The trip turned out rather well and much to my surprise, I found one of my days ended earlier than expected. As a result, I had some very rare free time to explore the town where the hotel was located, as well as the grounds and property of the hotel and adjacent resort.

My visit was during late autumn, the ghosts were swirling in my mind and within the spent leaves that were dancing in the air on cold New England evenings, and it all served me rather well to provide inspiration.

The actual setting was very much the same as depicted in this story, with a historic tavern building near the hotel, a captivating setting and other aspects mentioned within the story's setting. A tavern dating from a bygone century, steeped in local legends and folklore, and fully equipped with oil lamps sitting upon every table, a fireplace, and oil lamps mounted on the walls outside to illuminate the walkways. The hotel was an older facility, and it held the key basis for the story's turning point, which was a roaring fireplace in the hotel's lobby. Directly adjacent to the hotel is a scenic lake and other historic buildings, all contained within a very quaint New England town and setting.

As is my usual practice on my trips, I carried along with me my wide assortment of cameras and photographic equipment, and made use of the unexpected free time and opportunity to take quite a few photographs during my stay.

When I arrived home, the inspiration of my venture led me to write the initial draft outline of this storyline. It took me a day or so to compose, and with that out of the way and out of my mind, I finally found some leisure time to check out the photographs that I took. When I did so, then I received quite a surprise.

Despite following my usual careful and deliberate practices in extracting digital photographs from my cameras, I managed somehow to have nothing but blank SD cards. No doubt, I found it very strange that the many photographs that I took with my own cameras during the business trip to Massachusetts all mysteriously disappeared from the SD cards of my cameras. Without any actual reason, they all vanished shortly after I finished the majority of the outlines for the story lines of the draft of this novelette.

Disappointed, the next day, I took the camera's SD card to a specialist in restoration and recovery of corrupted or mistakenly deleted files.

Even with the best software, and his expert skills, he could only restore one picture. Remarkably, the one picture that he could restore was a photograph of an oil lamp sitting on the table in the resort's tavern.

He was amazed and shook his head while telling me, "I

just have to say that I have never seen a set of JPEG or RAW files disappear like these files have."

After my spine stopped tingling, I thought that perhaps it *was* just a strange coincidence. It might be, but perhaps, the line between reality and the past is more of a blur than even this humbled author ever realized that it was!

The Epilogue

In the early evening of a Friday in early February, Charlotte Walker smoothly slipped into a bar stool and weakly smiled at the bartender. Charlotte had decided to end what was a very long week, with a simple dinner and a few glasses of wine at a local watering hole. The bartender waved to Charlotte, knew ahead of time what type of wine to pour, and when he had poured a glass, he carried it over and set it in front of Charlotte. The bartender, whose name was Charlie, had worked here forever. He was an older man, very kind and a lot of fun too.

"Here you go, darling. Menu too?"

"Yes, please. I will order dinner in just a bit. Want to settle in first."

The bartender nodded and handed Charlotte a menu, while saying, "If you don't mind me commenting, you look a little down in the dumps. Long week? You, okay?" Charlotte took her first sip of wine, and then she gently set the glass down.

She nodded, weakly smiled again and explained, "I am okay, Charlie. Just a very long week. I need a new job, something more exciting. I love to interact with people. Data entry, while sitting at a desk all day, typing mindlessly away, is not working for me. Plus, I ended it with Dave the other night. That was not working out either. I am too needy and I need a hero in my life. Someone who is not lazy, a man to sweep me away and save me from this madness. Someday, a brave and handsome man will rescue me and carry me away from all of this!"

Charlie nodded, picked up his bar rag and wiped the top of the bar while telling Charlotte, "Oh, sorry. Well, you are still very young, very beautiful and it will work out for you. Maybe look for a career in hospitality, ya know, where ya meet many folks . . . sorta as I do. With your good looks and personality, you will knock it out of the park."

"You are too sweet, thank you, Charlie."

He nodded his head, leaned in with a wink, and slyly told Charlotte, "Not sure that I qualify for the hero's role, but I would marry ya in a bloomin' second . . . say, I am sorry, I might have said too much. Anyway, I will be back for your order. You relax and let that wine work some magic."

Charlotte chuckled and mumbled as Charlie walked away, "I will keep that in mind."

From a table a few feet away, a tall, lanky man watched the gorgeous young woman and studied her for quite a few minutes. He waited to make sure that no one was joining her, noticed that she did not wear a wedding ring or engagement band, and pondered his next move. My goodness, she was very pretty with a great figure, too. Just his luck too, because the bar stools on each side of her were empty. Since she seemed to be alone, he figured in his mind that he might as well take a chance and see if she would like some company. He picked up his beer, waved to his server that he was moving to the bar, and slowly made his way over to the empty bar stool next to the young woman.

He picked a bar stool on the right side of the young woman, placed his beer on the bar top and when Charlotte Walker looked up at him, he asked, "Might I ask ye without being a bit too forward to ye? Is this seat empty? Were you expectin' sum company? If it is empty, do ye mind if I occupy it?"

Charlotte smiled widely and answered, "Oh, please do. It is empty. I am alone."

Immediately, his wonderful Irish accent captivated her, not to mention the flicker in his amazingly dark eyes. He settled in, smiled and slid onto the bar stool while working up the courage to introduce himself . . . no doubt, she was gorgeous.

"Thank ye. Good evening, I am Timothy MacQuaid. Just arrived in town from Boston late today. Originally, as ye might be able to tell from my accent, I am from Ireland. County Monaghan. Now, I might add, I am a very long way from me old home. However, as things work out, I am lucky enough to be starting a new job tomorrow. It is my dream job as the general manager at the beautiful resort and hotel complex over in Centrebridge."

ABOUT THE AUTHOR

If you ask Paul John Hausleben, he will tell you that he is not an author, he is just a storyteller. His mission is to continue to write and tell stories to warm your heart, make you laugh, and sometimes make you cry, just a little. Most of all, he deals in memories, and helps you to remember the good times of your own life, and the special people who touched you along the way. Paul was born and raised in Paterson, and then nearby Haledon, New Jersey, and began writing at an early age. He revisited a writing career later in his life, and he now is the author of a number of novels, compilations, short stories and audio and video works. Most of his work touches upon nostalgic remembrances of simpler times, and tells the stories of heartfelt, humorous, and special human relationships. Other than writing, among many careers both paid and unpaid, he is a former semi-professional hockey goaltender, a music fan and music reviewer, an avid sports fan, photographer and a former military and current amateur radio operator. He now resides in Somewhere, U.S.A., but his heart always remains along Belmont Avenue in good old Paterson, and Haledon, New Jersey.

Other Work by Mr. Paul John Hausleben

The Time Bomb in The Cupboard and Other Adventures of Harry and Paul

The Night Always Comes, Another story from the Adventures of Harry and Paul

Reunion, A sequel to the Night Always Comes and Another story from the Adventures of Harry and Paul

The Miracle Tree, Another story from the Adventures of Harry and Paul

The Chronicles of Henson

Heaven's Gain
The Final Adventure of Harry and Paul

Geyer Street Gardens
Beneath the Mask of a Hockey Goaltender
Another story from the Adventures of Harry and Paul

Where the River Bends and Curls

And a few others too!

You may write to the author at ctte27@gmail.com

Published by God Bless the Keg Publishing
Somewhere, U.S.A.

You may write to the publisher at
Godblessthekegpublishing@gmail.com

"Life's simple pleasures are so often the best ones!"

www.ingramcontent.com/pod-product-compliance
Lightning Source LLC
LaVergne TN
LVHW091043080826
845145LV00002B/605

* 9 7 8 0 9 9 0 6 9 7 9 8 5 *